CITY
HEAT

A That's Entertainment Novel

By Christine Harvey

That's Entertainment Series
Take Two
In Concert
Tasty Dish
City Heat
And Action
Rising Stars: a Prequel Novella
Sweet Tidings (novella)

CITY
HEAT

A That's Entertainment Novel

Christine Harvey

MVP
Meadow View Press

Published in the United States by Meadow View Press

Copyright © 2021 by Christine Harvey

ISBN: 979-8-9852182-0-6

Meadow View Press
www.meadowviewpress.com

ACKNOWLEDGMENTS

Writing each book is its own unique experience, and while I love all of the characters in *City Heat*, this one was a challenge, beginning to end. You might not be reading it right now if not for the support (and patience!) of my writing partners. Cary Sparks and Tracy Tandy: you are the absolute best!

Thanks to Kath D., for all of the years of fun writing together, and who was there when I came up with the character of Denny Linstead. Who knew he had a twin!

To sign up for my mailing list and get a free novella, go to:

www.christineharvey.net

CHAPTER ONE

March, 2018

Kristen Clausen lay in bed in that hazy stage between sleep and waking. She smiled, pressing her face into the pillow. Tomorrow she'd be dancing at the club as an extra in a TV show. She didn't have any lines, but she could still add to her mental resume: yoga instructor, dancer, house cleaner, waitress, and now actress.

And she would be making more money in one day than all of her jobs combined. It would be nice not to stress about rent for once. She curled into herself, stretched with a happy sigh while wriggling her toes, and wondered what her life would be like if she hadn't left Illinois for San Francisco. She might be spending less money there, but she wouldn't have her sister nearby, her tribe of people, or—

"*Mama!*"

Kristen's eyes flew open to see two-year-old Daisy standing next to the bed, Fuzzy Bunny clutched to the front of her pajamas. Daisy grinned and held her arms out, Fuzzy Bunny now dangling from one hand. "Snuggas!" she announced.

Kristen lifted her daughter into the bed, curled around her warm little body like an apostrophe and covered them both with the comforter. She swept tangled strawberry blonde curls from Daisy's forehead. "Snuggles are the best," she said.

Daisy pressed her bottom to Kristen's stomach and started sucking her thumb. "Best," she agreed, although it came out sounding like "Bsshh."

Kristen did a quick check and said, "Did you already go pee?"

Daisy sang around her thumb, "Pee-ee."

"What a good job." As independent as her mother, Daisy had recently insisted on using the toilet and they'd had great success with potty training. Most days. "Remember you're coming to Mommy's yoga class this morning?" Kristen asked her now. "And playing with Star later?"

Star owned a floral shop and often watched Daisy on Kristen's busier days.

Daisy nodded emphatically, eyes on the linen curtains as they shifted in the breeze flowing through the tall bedroom window, thumb still firmly in her mouth. Her eyes drifted slowly shut, but her rosebud mouth continued its sucking motion and Kristen heard small snuffles and snorts as Daisy fell back asleep.

Kristen kissed the top of Daisy's warm head, and began to slide backward out of the full-sized mattress, the biggest one that fit in her and Daisy's tiny room. Good thing San Francisco had so many outdoor activities available, because their living space would only get more cramped as Daisy grew. Kristen was reaching back with one foot, searching for the floor with her toes when Daisy jerked upright and said, "*No!* Mama bed."

"Time to get up, baby. Lots to do today."

Daisy sat in the center of the bed, the sheet and comforter wound around her, and scrunched her face at Kristen. "Sleep, Mama," she said in a puzzled voice, as if she couldn't understand why Kristen would want to be anywhere else but right there with her.

"Nope. Mama needs to pee, too, and get you fed and get us to the yoga studio."

Daisy's expectant expression disappeared and she fell face forward on the bed and started to scream as if Kristen had just poked her with a branding iron.

The bedroom door opened, and her roommate Indica, in a Giants jersey sleep shirt, her hair rumpled around her face, shoved a bright blue mug at Kristen. "It's a good thing I love you both."

Over Daisy's continued, if muffled, wails, Kristen said, "Sorry. Thin walls, right?" She inhaled the scent of white tea before taking a sip.

Indica nodded and said around a yawn, "Thin walls."

Kristen and Indica had recently shared a flat on Russian Hill but their landlady had taken advantage of rising house prices and sold the building. Their new landlord increased their rent and was not interested or amused when Kristen and Indica asked if he would be open to barter, say, yoga classes? They realized later he'd translated that as sexual favors. That house had had well-insulated walls. Their current place in the Castro, while in a sweet, candy-coated building with wonderful landlords, did indeed have thin walls.

"Sorry again," Kristen said, her voice raised. She looked at her daughter, who was now shouting "*No no no!*" into the bedclothes, and stepped into the hall, gesturing for Indica to follow her. "I was thinking of taking her to early morning yoga with me, but not if she's starting off with a bad attitude. The sitter there already has her hands full with the clients' kids."

"She's two, honey. She's full of bad attitude. And the center gives you babysitting for free. That's unheard of."

Kristen sighed, leaning against the wall. "I used to think I had enough energy for me *and* a child. Maybe even three or four."

Holding an "I'm Not Weird, I'm Limited Edition" mug up to her face, Indica did her own lean on the opposite wall. "Be careful what you put out into the universe; it'll challenge the shit out of you."

Kristen laughed, remembering something similar she'd told another friend a year or so ago, after that friend declared to the world that she would no longer run from conflict. Two or three difficult situations had immediately popped up for her. "Heard and noted. What's your day like?"

"I'm opening today and I'm interviewing for a new manager." Indica owned a bookstore café a few blocks away; her mother had made a fortune in tech stocks in the '90s and generously shared it with Indy. This meant she could afford to run an unprofitable business for now, but she wanted it to be successful. "Fingers crossed this one will be capable, so you won't have to fill in so much, and I can take that marketing course. You still want me to get Daisy later and bring her to Star's?"

"Yes, please. Star will drop her back to me late afternoon if you can come get us at the end of the day?" Being a single mom and sharing a car often involved convoluted scheduling.

"It's a date." Indica pushed off the wall and kissed Kristen on the cheek before heading into the kitchen.

Kristen turned back to the bedroom to deal with her unruly

daughter, thinking that Indica's kiss was the closest thing to sex she was going to have until Daisy was at least eighteen.

KRISTEN SCOOPED UP DIAPER BAG AND CHILD, locked the door with one hand, and bounded down the front steps. She almost crashed into Indica who stood near her purple Prius, chatting with one of their landlords. Kim grinned, his dark brown cheeks rounding from his smile. He and his husband August were Jack Sprat and his spouse, and Kristen and Daisy adored them both.

"Sorry, sorry," Kristen said. She bounced Daisy up and down on one hip. "She had a moment over the f-i-s-h not saying good morning to her."

"Tragic," Kim said in his British East Indian accent. He sighed through his nose and tugged lightly on one of Daisy's curls. "You have my condolences, darling girl."

Daisy fell against Kristen's shoulder and nodded her head up and down as if in agreement over the gravity of the situation.

"I'd best let you go," Kim said. "Indica tells me you're off to teach the fine art of relaxation and introduce the rewards of yoga to actors from the show you're starring in—"

"I'll just be dancing in the club as a background extra," Kristen said.

"—while Indica is setting out to caffeinate the world, hire the most responsible manager ever, and conduct grand experiments in scented bath items with your lovely floral shop friend." Kim beamed at them as if they were his children.

Indica tilted her head, brushing her wavy brown hair over her shoulder. "Well, we're making soap..."

"I'll let you go," Kim repeated, "but we did want you to know that we're having some work done on the house soon." He and August lived in the downstairs half of the Victorian while Kristen, Indica, Daisy, and two fish had the upstairs. "We'll get extra insulation between the floors and walls, so you won't hear the dogs barking. But we'll miss out on Miss Daisy's spectacular morning greetings."

"You two are the best." Kristen meant it. Not only did her landlords put up with their bedlam, but they agreed to a large discount on rent in exchange for cleaning their unit and watching their dogs while they were out of town.

"There will be plenty of construction chaos in the meantime. You may wish to hold the praise until the job is complete."

"Are you kidding?" said Indica. "We'll have hot construction guys to ogle. I can't complain about that."

"Well we did request the extra attractive workers."

"Ugh." Kristen made shooing motions toward the car, ignoring the look Indica and Kim exchanged. "Time to saddle up, partners."

"May I join you?" Kim asked. "I'd love to hear more about this television show and your acting debut. Along with, I'm hoping, a discourse on that 'ugh' comment, which is quite unlike you."

Indica opened the passenger door for him. "I can't run you back, though."

"No worries." He patted his belly. "I could use the walk."

Kristen settled Daisy in her car seat, then the adults popped into the car. The studio was only three blocks away, but walking a toddler for that stretch took double or triple the usual time.

As Indica headed down 18th Street, Kim asked if they could watch the dogs for a few days the following week. "Another business trip," he sighed. "Tedious."

At Indica's nod, Kristen said, "Of course we'll watch them."

"Grand." Kim stuck his head between the front seats and swiveled it back and forth. "So do tell about this acting gig."

"You know I dance at Club Nuance a couple nights a week, right?" She danced on a platform, usually on '80s nights, and she loved the freedom it gave her, those few hours during her shift. "Well, this scouting crew came in for some new show. They said it was like an updated *Streets of San Francisco*. They wanted to film there and they hired me and another dancer to be in the background."

Kim leaned back with a happy sigh. "Grand," he repeated.

Kristen bounced in her seat. "It sounds like so much fun."

"It's ironic that you don't watch TV yourself," Indica said. "But," she added to Kim, "they're paying her an insane amount of money to do what she does anyway."

"That, too." Kristen peeked over her shoulder at Daisy, who sat quietly chatting with Fuzzy Bunny. Knowing she wouldn't be able to avoid explaining her "ugh" comment, she turned to Kim just as he opened his mouth. "Do you believe in destiny? That things are predestined? That there's that one perfect person for us?"

"August believes in making your own destiny. And that it's cruel to stay alone if something happens to your mate. But, then, he doesn't believe in God."

"And you?" she prompted.

"Oh, I believe in God." He winked at her, then looked out the window. "And love at first sight, sparkly vampires, destiny..."

"But that we *should* be with someone?" She watched his rounded profile, the way a dimple winked in and out as he spoke.

Indica double parked in front of the yoga studio, waving at a driver who honked and sped around them. "What are you asking here?"

"And why have we just gotten to the good part?" Kim asked.

"I'm kind of done with looking for the perfect man. Or even a semi-perfect one. I'm not even sure about soul mates, anymore." She sighed.

"But..." Indica protested. "Your list..."

At one time in her life, Kristen had told anyone who listened about her list of "signs" to help them recognize their soul mate. But now? "I've been wrong before." Kristen turned away from Indica and Kim's shocked looks to open her door and back out of the car. "With certain exceptions, men just seem to be trouble."

"You...are you sure?"

Kristen nodded. "I don't need a man to be complete." She smiled down at her daughter, then at her friends. "I have my people; you're my family. You're Daisy's family." She had desperately wanted a dad for Daisy at first, but her thinking had evolved. Now she felt they didn't need a man as long as they had each other and their chosen family.

"What about Peter?" Kim asked. "The yoga god."

"Paul," she corrected, unclipping Daisy's car seat belt.

"Of course. Wrong apostle."

Kristen set the diaper bag and Daisy down on the sidewalk, but held onto Daisy's hand; she'd become a runner recently. Kristen shrugged in response to Kim's question about Paul, even though it made her chest tight. "I found out he's married." She bent to look through the open back door and Kim leaned in her direction while Indica strained against her seatbelt.

The three of them looked at each other and shuddered in unison. Even though Kristen didn't know it when she was seeing him, Daisy's father had been married, too.

"I also think I'm ready to tell everyone about Daisy's dad, the whole story. No more secrets."

CHAPTER TWO

Danny Linstead sprinted up the grassy slope at Alamo Square Park, his muscles finally loosening after running this stretch multiple times in twenty minutes. Sweat rolled down his back despite the brisk San Francisco air that cooled his face and bare arms. His ankle turned in a small divot but he ignored it, pushing hard against the ground with his other foot to close the distance between himself and his imaginary quarry. His breath, steady but still loud in his ears, fell away as he charged uphill, focused only on his goal. Then other distractions retreated: honking horns, the line of television crew arrayed parallel to his chase, remorse, guilt, sorrow. Arms pumping, thighs working, he squinted into the distance and increased his pace. It would happen this time.

As he neared the end of his run, his ankle complained. He continued the punishing pace. He deserved the pain, every bit of it, but it hadn't taken him down yet. And it wouldn't today. Ten feet until the top of the hill and the stationary camera. Nine, eight, seven…

To one side, an assistant cameraman lifted his arm, raising an orange flag on a pole to indicate the direction Danny should go. One end of the flag flapped in the breeze but the AC's extended arm remained rigid.

Danny charged straight at the camera; his character, Seth, knew the quarry was close. His squint hardened into determination. The AC's arm jerked, a reminder of his assigned path. Danny gave a minute shake of the head; he knew what he was doing. Six, five…four feet away now, still at top speed. Three feet and the AC squawked, breaking the rules. Danny slowed only long enough to shift his body lower before he dived directly between the camera and the AC, rolling as he hit the ground. His shoulder hit too hard, but the rest of it would look great on screen.

"Cut!" the director called into the quiet that had descended. "Print that!"

Cheers broke out from the fans lined up behind the street barricades and Danny pumped a fist in the air.

The AC held a hand out, the flag abandoned on the ground behind him. "Hell, man, that was close. I almost pissed my pants."

Danny stood and clapped him on the shoulder. "Needed to get the shot, Steve. And we got it."

They grinned at each other and Steve jogged away as the first assistant director called out, "That's a wrap. Moving across the park for scene twenty-three."

Sweat dripped in his eyes and Danny whipped off his blue t-shirt to wipe at his face. His ankle throbbed, but he ignored it. The crew moved into action around him, and now the director, Gary, approached from behind a bank of computers, hands in the pockets of well-pressed chinos. He lowered his headphones to his neck, shaking his head but smiling.

"Beautiful," he called. "Brilliant. Next time no drop-and-roll without a stunt bag."

Their continuity supervisor Samantha, her blonde hair tucked back in a smooth ponytail, stood next to Gary. She cradled a binder in one arm and had also dropped her headphones. "How's your ankle?"

Danny slung the shirt over one shoulder. "Fine. Great."

Samantha's eyes narrowed at his response and she opened her mouth, but a production assistant appeared next to Danny with water bottles and a towel. He took them with thanks and drank the entire bottle. He exchanged the empty for another, flipped the towel around his shoulders, and took his cell phone from the PA. A quick check: three texts from his agent, one from his manager, nothing else. He sighed and slipped it in his pocket. He actually needed to ask Samantha to read lines with him, but wasn't ready to risk another question about his ankle. It was fine, he was fine. He always was. Some people just needed more convincing about that than others.

After all, it was Samantha's job to pay attention to details.

By the time he'd finished the second bottle, Gary and Samantha were surrounded by the first AD, director of photography, cameraman, and production designer. Keesha, the first AD, caught his eye as he was turning away, and pointed at him with a "stay" gesture. He wiped at the sweat on his chest with the towel and obeyed, relieved at the eventual success of this scene, but apprehensive about the long speeches in the next. He took a step to the side, already needing to expend more restless energy.

Keesha, her dark, toned legs in their usual spandex bike shorts, pulled a walkie from her utility belt and spoke into it. "I've got eyes on Danny," she told the person on the other end. Her eyes stayed on him until she'd reached his side, as if he'd scamper away otherwise. "Lady Boss needs to talk to you," she told Danny. "She's on her way."

Danny took a couple steps downhill. "Where's she coming from? I can meet her."

Keesha held her palm out to him in a "stop" command. "On her way. She's not far."

He popped one heel up and down on the short grass, then cocked a thumb behind him. "Okay if I talk to them while I wait?" A few fans remained, even though the the scene had ended and the usual crew ant-farm activity had taken over.

She gave him a raised eyebrow. "Want a fresh shirt first?"

He waved away that idea; he was still hot from the run.

"After you," she said, and followed him to the barriers set up near the top of the wide park stairs.

The fans called out to him as he approached. "Danny!" "We love you, Danny, you were great!" "Can we get a selfie?" "Warhawk!"

He paused in his stroll, but continued with a smile on his face. He'd rarely heard that one over the years, but it was showing up more frequently lately. Warhawk was one of his favorite characters. Too bad the film had tanked.

His phone buzzed twice as he reached the barriers and he itched to check it, but instead answered questions, posed for group photos with the fans, hugged them against his bare chest, and gratefully accepted the Sharpie Keesha offered when they asked for autographs. He wiped at his still warm face with one end of the towel and a short girl with a ponytail sprouting from the top of her head said, "Omigod, can I have that towel?"

With a shrug, he handed it to her, but stopped when she said, "Signed?" He had her spin around so he could spread it on her shoulder, and ran the Sharpie over it.

"Oh lord, it smells like you," she said when he handed it over.

"I promise I don't always smell like that."

"You should," she said, and wandered away with the towel to her face.

The t-shirt he'd slung over his shoulder earlier went to a muscular guy and after signing it, Danny held it up against the guy's broad chest. "Not gonna fit, bro."

The guy smiled and accepted the shirt, holding it tight in one hand. "Who says I'm gonna wear it bro," he said with a grin.

Danny saluted him and turned to the last person, a woman about his age—late twenties—with blue hair, liner accentuating round brown eyes, and cleavage to get lost in. He looked her in the eye.

"What are you filming?" she asked.

"A TV pilot. It's called *City Heat*." *And my life is depending on it getting picked up*, he thought, but kept that to himself.

"Is your brother visiting?"

"Ah. Not right now." His phone buzzed. Although, who knew? His twin, Denny, could show up any place, any time, even though they hadn't spoken for the last eight months. "He your favorite brother?"

"Is there going to be a *Warhawk* sequel?" she asked as if she hadn't heard his question.

"No plans for one." The original film, based on a graphic novel anti-hero, had floundered in the theaters, but gained a cult following over the years. "I hear there's an online petition—"

"You should come home with me," she said, thrusting her breasts over the barrier.

"All righty then," Keesha said. "Mr. Linstead needs to get going."

"It's all right," Danny told both of them with a smile. He'd heard far more colorful propositions in the past. "How about an autograph instead."

At her request, he signed the top of her breasts while his phone buzzed multiple times. He waved goodbye with one hand and slid the phone out of his pocket with the other as Liz, the producer, and Olivia, the costume designer, neared them. Agent again, his publicist, roommate, and—

His heart jolted. Lorelei. He saw only "*good news!*" before Keesha cleared her throat. He jammed the phone back in his pocket.

With her long legs, Olivia outpaced Liz, one hand held out to Danny. "I need your shirt."

He lifted his arms and turned in a circle. "Gave it away. All for a good cause," he added as she huffed at him.

"You want to come to dinner?" she asked. "Bunch of us are going to this new place in North Beach."

"Sure. Text me the address."

She patted his bare pec. "You need to stop giving away shirts." As she strode back down the hill, sleek ponytail swaying across her back, she called out, "They're gonna start taking them out of your pay. They're sure not taking it from mine."

Liz charge-walked up in wedge heels and a tight skirt. She rested her hands on her thighs for a second, panting. When she straightened, she said, "Why are we filming on a hill?" Before either Danny or Keesha could attempt an answer, she glared at Danny's chest. "You're naked. Maybe that's why I can't breathe." She pressed a hand to her own chest. "Or maybe I gave up cigarettes too late. I should start up again." She looked at Keesha. "You don't have any cigarettes, do you?"

"No way, lady producer," Keesha said. "You said to kick your ass if you asked for one."

"Fine." Liz flapped a hand and addressed Keesha. "Did you tell him about the yoga thing?"

"Above my pay grade." Keesha zipped up her windbreaker as the breeze brought a wave of fog their way. She held up her walkie talkie. "Things to do. See you on the other side."

Danny's phone announced more notifications and Liz eyed his front pants pocket before raising her gaze to his chest and then his face. "You need to get that?"

He shook his head, but slipped the phone out and handed it to a passing PA. "Can you put this in my trailer, please?" He crossed his arms over his chest, his skin cooling rapidly now. "What can I do for you?"

"Yoga. Tonight. We're in San Francisco, it's supposed to be good for us, so everyone's going to a class this week. I'll send an Uber."

As Danny passed Samantha on the way to his trailer, she handed him a sheaf of blue script changes. "For the next scene," she called out.

More lines to learn. He gripped the pages tight in one hand. Keep moving forward, he told himself. Just keep moving.

CHAPTER THREE

With some time to herself before her next class, Kristen decided to work on an advanced pose. She started out in *Tadasana*, a deceptively simple standing pose that centered and balanced. She crouched, then twisted to the side and put her palms on the floor. Through a series of precise movements, she ended up balanced on her hands, with one leg straight back and the other crossed underneath it at an angle, both parallel to the floor.

Someone made a noise nearby.

Kristen raised her eyes and saw a very beautiful, very tense man in the doorway. Upraised shoulders, clenched jaw, chest out as if holding his breath, and feet set wide. Ready for battle. And had he just crossed himself?

Kristen took in all of these stress indicators, as well as his lean frame in shorts and a clinging t-shirt and wavy black hair, but focused on his eyes. Sharp. Blue. Unwavering.

She held her pose, but something wobbled inside her. "Well, that was fast."

"Sorry?"

"I'm pretty sure the universe sent you in response to my challenge."

"How are you—?" He pointed at her legs, but was interrupted.

"What's the hold up?" A woman in a long purple tank top and wide-legged capris elbowed the man aside and charged into the room. "Whoa," she said when she caught sight of Kristen.

Kristen focused her breathing, pulled her legs in so they were bent, balanced on one elbow, straightened, and stood to greet her students. "Pose Dedicated to the Sage Koundinya I," she told the wide-eyed woman with a slight bow. "We can start with that one, if you'd like."

When the woman's mouth went into a little "O," Kristen strode forward, hand outstretched. "Sorry, just kidding. Are you Liz? Thanks for bringing new people to Priya Yoga Center." She gestured for the others that had gathered behind Liz to come inside. "Welcome, everyone. Please take off your shoes, grab a mat, give yourself plenty of room, and get comfortable."

The others wandered in to settle on benches at the back, but the tense man roamed around the room's edges, those sharp eyes taking in props, folded blankets, mats, and the high windows along the back wall. A line of muscle split into a Y-shape at the back of his calf, accentuated with each step, and she noticed a slight hesitation in setting one foot down. A minor injury?

"You don't have to stay if it's not right for you," she told him.

He turned from the back wall and strode to stand in front of her. "What did you mean earlier? About some sort of challenge?"

"The universe has a sense of humor." Her chest tightened as she said it and she had to force a breath out. "Why are you here?"

He lifted his chin toward the rest of the group. "Job requirement."

"But you don't really want to be." In response to one uplifted shoulder, she nodded. "What's your name?"

"Danny."

"I'm Kristen. I'm not going to tell you to give it a chance, or to trust me, or that yoga sex is *the best sex* you could ever have, even though it is, and actually that's the one that usually convinces people to stay. It takes hours of practice to get there." She said it with a smile, but she could tell from the look on his face he was still processing the "yoga sex" comment. "In the meantime, I can help with that foot."

He didn't blink or look away. "What foot?"

"The one that's bothering you. On the right."

"Ankle," he said. "And it's fine."

"Ankles represent flexibility. If it's hurt, it could slow you down from moving forward or accepting change."

She immediately recognized the expression on his face: a polite, silent rebuff combined with wondering if every northern Californian believed in crazy woo-woo. It amused her, mostly because she was from Illinois. She wondered where he was from.

"I appreciate it," he said, "but it's fine."

He was clearly resistant; she wouldn't push it. She turned to the rest of the group. "I only have two rules for my classes," she said as she wandered the room's perimeter, noting the class watching her as she walked. She in turn began her study of their potential strengths and vulnerabilities; she'd continue to evaluate them throughout the class. "One is that if it hurts, stop. Yoga isn't always easy, but it should never hurt. I can help you adjust a pose if it's difficult for you and we also have props like blocks and straps."

At the back of the room, she turned and paused, catching each person's eye before she continued. "Rule Two is: no phones." She picked up a large box with a lid and waved it back and forth. "Please put them on mute and set them in the box until the end of class."

She held the box open and waited, noting those who made a face at her rule, the ones who hesitated but nodded, and any who came forward and immediately dropped a phone inside. She thanked each one. Danny had hesitated, no nod, and was close to the end of the line.

She thanked him, studying his hand as he set the phone into the box. He caught her eye, still unsmiling, but definitely curious. He stayed there, as if waiting for something, and she leaned around him to instruct the group to stand in the center of their mats, facing forward.

"What did you mean?" he asked. "About—"

"I'm happy to answer any questions about yoga sex after class," she told him, even as she remembered telling Indica and Kim earlier that she was done with men. *But look at him!* she argued to them in her head. *He's gorgeous.* And the universe clearly sent him as a personal challenge. She liked a good challenge.

Smiling at his surprised expression, Kristen peered around him again at Liz, who clutched her phone in her hand.

"I produce a television show," Liz said.

"I know. I'm going to be dancing at the club during your filming tomorrow. And my sister's in production, too." As she spoke, she felt Danny's gaze on her, not lascivious, but definitely assessing.

"Really? What's her name?"

"Victoria Clausen. Or Victoria Clausen Tyler." Kristen shrugged, reminding herself to breathe again. The room felt smaller, warmer with him in it. "She's still trying to figure out if she wants to hyphenate."

Liz's eyes went big again. "I *know* her."

"You do?"

"Well, I did. She was roommates with my best friend a few years ago. In L.A. I haven't seen her in ages."

"Who's your best friend?"

"Samantha Jamison-Gallagher." Liz's turn to shrug. "She hyphenated."

Kristen grinned at her. "I love the universe." She caught Danny's eye after she said it. "Other times it confuses me." She turned back to Liz. "We'll have to reunite everyone. She travels a lot with her husband, but she's in town right now." She raised the box. "You still need to put the phone away."

Liz now clutched the phone to her chest. "Something important—"

"Never comes up," Kristen interrupted in a gentle tone, "in all of the years I've been teaching."

Liz leaned over to peer in the box, then settled her phone in one corner, away from the pile of others.

Kristen thanked her, covered the box, and slid it under a bench before striding to the front of the class. She enjoyed teaching yoga at any level, but she especially loved that moment when beginning students first grasped both how challenging and rewarding yoga could be. When they realized that simply focusing on breathing could shift a blockage inside them. And the amazing capabilities of their bodies.

She moved them through a series of poses, starting with the grounding Mountain Pose. They did Downward Facing Dog, Plank, Triangle, and Warrior 1 and 2. If any of them wanted to take another class, she'd include other levels then, like minor backbends and balancing poses.

While she walked around the class during Downward Dog, Kristen noticed that Danny kept shifting his feet side to side, his heels raised very high up from the floor. Tight hamstrings, she noted, which took time and practice to loosen up, but a simple hip adjustment could help for now. She'd tried not to stare since doing so nudged against her personal ethics, but he moved like a cat, lithe, prowling. He clearly understood his body well, even as it telegraphed his discomfort at slowing down. It was her calling to help students get quiet and breathe into the poses, and into their lives. But he wasn't ready for that yet.

Kristen helped a few other students adjust their poses, aware of Danny's own observance, before she moved to his side. "With a slight alteration, that could be more comfortable." Her hands hovered near his hips and she caught his eye when he tilted his head to look at her. "May I?"

She noticed his hesitation before he nodded and looked ahead again. With a practiced move, she grasped his hips and eased them back until his body relaxed into the pose and his heels drifted closer to the floor.

She moved on, but her fingers still tingled at his sharp inhalation and shudder. She completed the class, lying on her back during *Savasana*, Corpse Pose, and breathing into her belly to calm her heart. Her touch and his response had been brief, but his body had been almost hot, and her heart still beat fast at the thought of his jolting hips.

Sighing, she watched him wander to the side of the room to replace his mat and tie his shoes. He had the dazed look of a student that experienced a shift during the class—success in a challenging pose, profound relaxation, maybe even the solution to a worrying problem. But Danny's gaze didn't remain inward; it kept shifting toward her, then sliding away when their eyes met. He wandered out with some others, not speaking, and Kristen wondered if she'd see him again during filming. Had she just imagined their connection, having gone too long in her single motherhood without the touch of a man? Or was the universe really messing with her because of her recent declaration?

Probably the latter.

Students thanked her on their way out, and Liz came by, phone in hand, to express her appreciation.

"I'm from New York and I make fun of California a lot, but that was awesome."

"I'm glad you enjoyed it. You and your crew are welcome back any time."

Liz left, already texting, and the happy release of another

successful class washed over Kristen. She went to the daycare room and swept up Daisy.

"Know what time it is, baby?" Kristen swayed back and forth, releasing her hair from its long braid. "Dance time!"

Daisy let out her version of a cheer, which sounded like a tiny owl hoot, while Kristen thanked the babysitter. "I'll clean up my room, then see you tomorrow." Hers had been the last class of the evening; it was closing time and they could celebrate and clean at the same time.

She set Daisy down and pushed Play on an ancient boombox in one corner. "Walking on Sunshine" blared out, and she and Daisy twisted and bopped while Kristen folded blankets, rearranged blocks, and stacked mats. Daisy stood in the middle of the room, sometimes stamping her feet out of rhythm, or else standing with feet firmly planted while her upper body rocked side to side, chubby fists closed but swinging wildly.

The song changed to Sade's "Your Love is King," and Kristen closed her eyes to sway and move her hips, arms winding around her in time with the elegant music.

Above the music, she heard a throat clear, and her eyes popped open to see Danny in the doorway. Her entire body flushed hot.

"Oh, hi," was all she could think to say. She lowered the volume, but Daisy continued to stamp her feet. Kristen pointed to her. "My daughter, Daisy." Daisy looked up at her name and grinned, then spun in a circle.

"Hey." Danny cleared his throat again, then gestured inside the room. "I forgot my phone."

"Sure." Kristen walked with him across the room, each of them glancing at the other along the way. She lifted his phone out of the box and handed it to him.

He slid it into his pocket without taking his eyes from hers. "You like to dance?"

"I love it. I dance a few nights a week at Club Nuance. What about you?"

He nodded. "I'm actually—"

Indica careened into the room, apologizing before she even got through the doorway. "Sorry, sorry, I had to deal with a cranky customer at the café and there was an accident down the street, blocking all lanes, and—"

Daisy screeched, "Inca!" and threw herself at Indica, who lifted her up, then stared at Danny. "Oh. Oh, hey, you're—"

"Danny Linstead," he said quickly. "Nice to meet you."

"Indica," she said. "What are you…how…?"

Danny's phone pinged. "My car's here," he told Kristen. "Thanks. For the class." He nodded at Indica, smiled at Daisy, and jogged from the room.

Indica let out a breath. "What the *what?*" she asked Kristen.

"I know. He's handsome, right?" Kristen pulled her bag out from under the bench and slung it over her shoulder. She should probably make an appointment to get her IUD checked. The universe might have its own plans, but a little precaution on her end wouldn't hurt.

"Do you know who that was?" Indica's naturally tan cheeks had gone pink.

"I think he's an actor. Why?"

Indica jiggled Daisy up and down, as she'd started to complain about the inattention. "I appreciate that you don't watch TV, but…" She took a breath and pointed toward the door. "He's an actor, model, athlete, singer. He does it all. And he's engaged to the biggest reality star in the world."

CHAPTER FOUR

Danny trudged up the stairs to his third floor condo and collapsed face first on the couch. He'd been up since 4:00 AM, a long day filming, that crazy yoga class, dinner with some of the crew, then for a run around the neighborhood. Yoga had been too slow. Breathe through it? What? He'd breathed through his run afterward, that's for sure. His skin still tingled where that yoga instructor had grabbed his hips. No other body parts had come in contact, but he'd burned hot at her touch, even as his body relaxed into the pose. Then, coming back for his phone, to catch her dancing, her unbound hair caressing her bare shoulders and face. God, but she was mesmerizing. He rolled onto his back with a groan and kicked off his shoes. His head pounded from the long run and he got hard thinking about her swaying to Sade.

Or maybe it had been her "yoga sex" comment.

It had been way too long since a woman's touch electrified him, and this woman...this quirky Valkyrie—Kristen—with that big crazy hair, and her curvy hips that would fit perfectly in his cupped hands. He hadn't left his phone there on purpose for an excuse to go back and talk to her, but part of him wondered how in-depth her answers might be to his "yoga sex" questions. But she had a daughter, and then her friend came in, and the friend obviously knew who he was...and he really didn't have time or energy for any of it.

Did he?

With another groan, he slid off the couch to the area rug and pumped out fifty push-ups in rapid succession. There was a gym down the street, but he didn't need a full workout right now, just a distraction from Kristen so he could focus on tomorrow's script. He had another early call, and a hard enough time with his lines these days without obsessing over a woman's touch.

Once Danny built up a good sweat and was breathing heavily, he stripped off his clothes and jumped in the shower. Hard exercise had kept him in shape, but also focused. Dressed in loose sweatpants and nothing else, he dug among the papers on the crowded coffee table and freed the script pages for the next couple days. He didn't have many lines tomorrow, so he wasn't worried about those, but he wanted to get ahead as much as possible. Lying on the couch, he ran through the scene of his character, Seth, and his partner Louie interrogating a witness. Seth is playing "good cop" here. Danny set the pages down and reviewed the first speech in his head.

"C'mon, man, you tell us what you know and this ends. It's all over, no more pressure, no more questions…" He had about three more sentences to go when they drifted away like the San Francisco fog. The harder he tried to pull them out of the air, the more they blurred. He'd been acting his entire life, never a problem with lines, but lately…

He jumped up and paced. Picked up the pages and went through the speech again. He got the first one down, and almost had the second one, was moments away from finishing it when the front door opened and his roommate, Glen, showed up with one of the production assistants, Chloe.

The words disappeared again.

Chloe waved and Glen said, "Hey, man. Just passing through." He sidestepped to the open kitchen and nearby refrigerator.

Chloe said, "I've been meaning to say how much you look like your brother. I love his show."

Danny nodded. "I get that a lot."

Glen grabbed a couple beers, and wrapped an arm around Chloe, tucking her tiny frame against his burly side. "Hey, we shouldn't bug him. Star of the show and all that, got lines to learn."

Danny held up the script pages as proof, suppressing a frown.

"We headeth to the bedchamber. Continue anon," Glen announced to Danny, and leaned into Chloe, both of them giggling.

"Doesn't make any sense, man," Danny said lightly. "Just try to keep it down, okay? Early call tomorrow."

Chloe's face went pink. "Oh, we're not—"

Glen looked down at her. "But you said—"

"He doesn't need to *know* we are," she whisper-hissed back at him.

"Too late." Danny waved them away. "Go. Anon."

They disappeared down the short hall and Danny shook out his arms and shoulders before looking at the script pages again. He resumed his pacing. Second speech, here we go.

Music started up in Glen's bedroom. Cardi B, "I Like It." Small space, San Francisco rents, broke actor. He couldn't make it here without a roommate. Glen was a good, easy-going guy, but he brought a different woman home every other night, mostly one of the crew. It was manageable at first, but as moans crept past Cardi B's rap, Danny realized they needed more ground rules. He sent a text to Glen: *Roommate talk soon.*

He wasn't expecting a response, so he took a deep breath to refocus.

His phone buzzed. He was mentally preparing to reply to Glen's text with "dude, don't interrupt your time with a woman by checking your texts" when he saw it was from Keesha, reminding him of tomorrow's early call. He sent her a thumbs up, then stared at the phone, remembering Lorelei's earlier message.

"Good news! Your mom is moving in with us!"

She meant it to be reassuring, a kindness, but it only added another weight to his burden. Bad enough he could only get news about his family from his brother's girlfriend, but if Ma was moving from New York to Florida to live with Lorelei and Denny, that meant the last of her money had run out. Lorelei and her sisters starred in *"The Fabulous LaMontaines,"* a reality show that followed her celebrity family and highlighted their dramas. His mother liked the money, but she didn't want to be on camera. They might be able to work around her, considering Lorelei and Den lived in a mansion in a family compound in Naples, Florida, but that was beside the point.

The point was that eight months earlier, Danny had lost all of the family's money to a bad investor. Seven and a half months ago, his stepfather Vince died from a stroke. Then he'd had a knock-down, drag-out with his brother, which ended with Den shouting at him, "You know what, man? I trusted you, but I never trusted that guy. So I kept a little back. That's right. And I gave it all to Ma, so she could cover the hospital bills and pay for his funeral."

Living in New York at the time, Danny had to borrow money from his agent for the subway ride to visit Art in the hospital and his mother at her house in Queens. Lorelei and Denny had flown up in a private jet from Florida. He and Den had knocked each other to the grass at the funeral home, of all shameful things. His mother told him to leave. He hadn't heard from either of them since, despite his multiple attempts to apologize. He heard about Den from entertainment news and his mother from Lorelei. When he'd asked her if his brother knew she was in contact with Danny, all she'd said was, "He knows."

He didn't give up after that, but he did retreat. He and Den had been in the industry since they were babies. He'd planned to retire by now, maybe try something new, but instead he kept working, setting aside the majority of his earnings to pay everyone back. And he prayed this pilot got picked up so he wouldn't have to do another toothpaste or deodorant commercial. But, he'd do it if he had to.

A long, drawn-out female moan rose from Glen's bedroom, followed by Glen's encouraging bass. "Yeah, baby, go baby, yeah, yeah, that's it…ohhh…yeahhh."

A grunt, and then quiet. Even Cardi B had been silenced.

"Wait," came Chloe's voice. "Did you *finish*?"

Danny rubbed at his forehead. From what he'd heard before, that was actually a pretty long stretch for Glen.

He looked at his phone. It had been awhile since he'd sent one of many unanswered texts to his brother.

Should he try again?

He switched his gaze to the script pages. He really needed to learn these damn lines. He kept forgetting what he should say after Louie, his partner on the show, asked if they should just cuff the guy or kill him. Danny repeated, "Nah, just chuck him in the bay," a few times, but blanked on the next line.

"Screw it."

He typed out a quick, "hey, what's up?" to his brother then put the phone face down on the coffee table.

He re-read the script pages over and over, trying to force the words into his brain, but as he paced the small living room, the majority of his attention focused on the silent phone.

When it buzzed, he lunged for it.

CHAPTER FIVE

Purple paisley go-go boots in one hand, Kristen headed down the alley behind Club Nuance. Keesha had said to wear her usual dancing gear, so along with snacks, phone, incense, and her lucky rock, her large shoulder bag contained a glittery purple halter top and gold boy shorts. She'd change at the club, but for now she wore sandals, yellow leggings, and a black dress printed with over-sized daisies. She and Daisy liked to point at the flowers on the dress and laugh together, while Kristen assured her daughter that *she* was the prettiest Daisy of all.

Kristen waved at the guys at the computer store on one side and the motorcycle place on the other, noting that the production had taken over the rest of the alley. Panel trucks and large pieces of equipment lined either side. People rushed around, carrying clipboards, ladders, sheets of plywood, large white screens, and tall lights, one of which looked like it had a black umbrella over it. Everyone seemed to have either tool belts, walkie talkies, or headphones. Or all three.

She stopped at the opening to the parking lot directly across the alley from the club's back door. Rows of trailers had been lined up with precision in the lot. A food truck at the entrance displayed a variety of grab-and-go snacks and a few crew members hung out drinking coffee and eating. Beyond them toward the back, two people stood outside a trailer, one unmoving, the other pacing. Kristen walked through the gate toward them as if pulled by an invisible string.

Danny Linstead clutched some green papers in his hands, and a tall blonde woman followed his movements with her eyes, a sympathetic look on her face.

"Do you want to go over it again?" she asked.

"I had both of them memorized last night," Danny was saying. He was in profile to Kristen, still with that lithe, feral look that stirred her senses. His ankle seemed better, but there was still a slight hitch in his stride. "These changes don't really fit Seth."

"I know," the woman said. "Just the messenger here. I actually heard—" She broke off when she saw Kristen. "Can I help you?"

"Hello," Kristen called out, eyes on Danny as he turned. His expression lightened, then shuttered, all within seconds. "Sorry to bother you. I'm checking in as an extra. I'm Kristen Clausen."

The woman's head tilted slightly at that, even as she reached for a walkie talkie on her belt. "I'll get someone to help you." She asked for Keesha and clicked off. "Samantha Jamison-Gallagher," she said, holding out her hand. "Welcome to the set of *City Heat*. You…" She seemed about to say more, but stopped.

"Samantha…" Kristen remembered her conversation yesterday with Liz. "Your producer, Liz, said you were my sister's roommate years ago."

Samantha's eyes widened in surprise and a soft smile appeared. "Your sister? What's her name?"

"Victoria Clausen. Tyler." Kristen shrugged. "She's figuring out if she wants to hyphenate."

Samantha's face lit up and she made a little sound of happy surprise. She turned to Danny, as if wanting to share her excitement, then back to Kristen. "She was my roommate in L.A. a million years ago, when I was acting. We—" She stopped, fingers to her mouth. "I mean, I haven't seen her in ages, how is she?"

Kristen caught both the hesitation and the confused look Danny gave Samantha.

"She's really good," Kristen said. "Married, living here, but she and her husband travel to Nashville a lot. He's in a band. She never talks about her actress days," she added. "I'd love to hear some of those fascinating stories…"

At that, Samantha's face turned pale and then rapidly pink. She reached for a big bag at her feet and hefted it to her shoulder. "Here's Keesha. She'll help you from this point on."

She hustled away and Kristen looked at Danny. His brow had crinkled in puzzlement, so she assumed something was off, but couldn't tell from that short interaction. "I always figured Victoria got up to something when she was in L.A., but I could never pry it out of her."

"So she's an actress turned producer?"

Kristen nodded, but before she could say more, Keesha and two other women reached them. Keesha wore walking shoes, black cycling shorts, and a bright green windbreaker, and introduced herself with a firm handshake. She then introduced the young woman in a ball cap as Camryn, the second assistant director. Kristen already knew the other woman: a tall, big-haired fellow dancer in boy shorts, a sequined halter top, and knee-high spike-heeled boots.

"Nicole!" Kristen cried, and gave her a hug.

At six-one, Nicole was already an inch taller than Kristen, but her boots added even more to her height. Nicole had once described herself as a more pronounced, dark-side version of Kristen—extreme hourglass figure, darker hair, full lips, and a gorgeous Roman nose.

"You look amazing as always," Kristen told her.

"And that's even without the movie magic hair and makeup." She gestured to Keesha and Camryn. "They're gonna take us to the trailer." Then she looked at Danny. "I can't decide which is hotter, you or your brother."

"Well, we're twins," he said with a grin. "So…"

"Maybe I need to see the two of you together," Nicole replied with a toss of her hair.

"Okay, then," Keesha interrupted. "Time to let the actor get to his lines." She started herding them away.

"You know, mindfulness practices can help with that," Kristen said over her shoulder as she pointed to the green pages in his hand. "Meditation, guided imagery, belly breathing. Yoga," she added with a smile before turning to follow Keesha to one of the trailers near the entrance of the lot.

Keesha led them up the creaking stairs and into the long, narrow space. The far end was curtained off, and a counter ran along one side with mirrors and two chairs. "Erica, Trudy, this is Kristen and Nicole, club dancers." She turned and was about to say something else, when she put a hand to her ear. Kristen noticed a small Bluetooth device looped over it. "Well, shit," Keesha said. "Yeah.

Yeah. Okay. We'll just do what we can. Keep him distracted. I'll tell hair and makeup," she added before ending the call.

Erica and Trudy stood next to each other, arms crossed, eyes narrowed. "He's on set today?"

Keesha nodded. "I gotta go let the others know. Tell Olivia, Rashika and Samantha if you see them, okay?"

She gave Kristen and Nicole a tight smile and edged past them. "I'll leave you in Camryn's capable hands," she said. "She'll take you through the rest of the day. If she's not available, come to me. Ask anyone with a walkie." She indicated the one attached to a belt at her hip. "They'll track me down. Don't forget to let the others know," she repeated to Trudy and Erica before trotting down the steps.

"Not that Samantha has anything to worry about," Trudy grumbled as she shook out a cloth and patted one of the chairs. "Have a seat," she told Nicole. She asked Kristen if she was already in her dancing outfit.

"I brought it with me."

Trudy pointed to the curtained off area at the back. "Go ahead and change and we'll get you fixed up."

Camryn said, "I'm going to grab a quick coffee while you change, and I'll be right back." She jogged down the steps.

"So who's on set?" Kristen asked.

Trudy leaned over to close the door behind Camryn. "The EP."

"EP?"

"Executive Producer," Erica clarified. "Perry Jenkins created the show, it's kind of his baby. And he's...." She lowered her voice, as if they might be overheard. "Particular."

"Creepy is what he is," Trudy said. "Whenever he comes on set, he hangs over us, watching everything. Really close."

"Why don't you tell him to back off?" Kristen asked.

"We like our jobs too much," Erica said.

Kristen and Nicole exchanged a look. Both strong, capable women, they also danced in skimpy costumes for money, and often had to deal with their share of creepy men. Bouncers protected them, and they watched out for each other, but they constantly straddled the line between entertaining club-goers and fending them off. Because they not only liked their jobs, they needed them.

"Hear you," Nicole said with a nod.

"So why is Samantha safe?" Kristen asked, thinking of the blonde woman who had been talking to Danny.

Trudy made a huffing noise. "Well, she's married to Evan Gallagher."

"The actor?" Nicole asked.

"The hot actor," Trudy replied. "And I mean that on more than one level. He's hot to look at and he's hot property right now. Jenkins would give his left nut to get Evan Gallagher in one of his movies, so he's not going to risk it by messing with his wife."

Camryn arrived with her coffee, and the women went quiet while Kristen stepped behind the curtain and slipped into her dance outfit. When she came back out and sat in the chair, Erica said, "You two are pretty hot property yourselves. Be careful out there."

Before Kristen could reply, the trailer door opened again and everyone turned. A large man in a black suit and white shirt grabbed the door jamb and stepped inside. Kristen could hear Keesha calling to him from outside.

"Mr. Jenkins, a minute."

Erica and Trudy quickly tossed fabric capes across the front of Kristen and Nicole, covering their skimpy outfits. Jenkins glared at Camryn until she dropped her gaze, but she didn't move otherwise.

"Hey, Mr. Jenkins." Trudy addressed him, but kept her focus on Nicole's hair while she brushed it out. "I think we're already at capacity here and we've got some other people waiting on us."

Jenkins stood watching them all, the fingers of one hand stroking the lapel of his suit jacket over and over. "Who are these two?"

"Just club extras," Erica told him.

"I don't like them," he said.

Kristen watched Nicole shift one shoulder so her cape slithered down her breasts to her lap, revealing a lot of cleavage in her sequined top. Kristen hissed at her in warning just as Keesha pounded up the steps.

"Mr. Jenkins, could I have a minute of your time?" she asked from the doorway.

He waved her away without taking his eyes from Nicole's breasts. "This one can stay. I don't like that one." He pointed at Kristen, the cape still over her shoulders. She clutched at it from underneath to keep it in place.

Jenkins finally looked at Keesha. "Get rid of her."

CHAPTER SIX

Danny had been pacing outside his trailer, jamming the lines into his head, when he saw Jenkins heave himself up the steps of the hair and makeup trailer.

"Shit." He dropped the pages and jogged over.

Keesha stood in the doorway and Danny saw Jenkins's bulk on the other side. When Danny put a hand on her shoulder, Keesha started, but stepped aside.

"How's it going, Mr. Jenkins," Danny called in a cheerful voice. He peeked around the door frame. "Good morning, ladies." His vocal chords strained as he worked to maintain an upbeat tone.

Jenkins turned to him. He stopped caressing his jacket lapel to clap Danny on the shoulder. "PJ, my boy," he boomed in the small space. "Call me PJ. How's my money-maker?"

Just as Danny would never call the man PJ, he hoped no one would ever refer to him as "money-maker" again. "Fine, sir. It's going well."

Jenkins gestured with one of his fat hands at the women in the makeup chairs. Kristen was covered up, but Nicole revealed a lot of skin. Not that that should matter. "You seen this one dance?" Jenkins said. "The redhead."

"Yes, sir…" The other day at the yoga studio he'd wanted nothing more than to pull her close and dance with her. But he'd plunge down a cliff before doing something like that without her permission—or treat her in any way like this meathead was. "Hey, I think Keesha's wanted on set," he added, gesturing behind him for Keesha to get out of harm's way. Behind her, he saw Jenkins's two usual goons, shoulder to shoulder.

Keesha glanced at them, turned back to Danny, and crossed her arms over her chest.

He nodded at her and returned to the tableau inside the trailer. He was about to invite Jenkins outside when Kristen rose from her chair, holding the drape in front of her.

"He's seen me dance. But you haven't." She said it in a straightforward, almost flat tone, no seduction in her voice. "Give me a chance and I'll show you."

To Danny it felt like everyone in the vicinity held their breath, waiting for Jenkins's response. Then the producer's phone rang. He pulled it out of his jacket pocket, said, "She stays for now," then barked, "What!" into the phone.

Danny and Keesha bounded down the steps and Jenkins barreled past them, stomping toward the limo as the goons followed. A shudder ran through Keesha before she jumped back up the steps. "Whenever you're ready, ladies, Camryn and I will walk you to the set."

Danny watched them go, four women capable of kicking ass and taking names, but he still waited until they all went inside while Jenkins stomped around his car, yelling at the person on the other end of the phone.

Danny rushed through his wardrobe change, then hair and makeup, everyone around him subdued. They all usually chatted and joked together, and even he couldn't summon the energy to distract them. This was their fifth day filming, but it was Jenkins's third disruption, and only the first Danny had witnessed. He'd heard rumors of the producer's despicable misbehavior, but now that he'd seen it for himself, he didn't know whether to quit or deck the guy. Either way, he'd be out of a desperately needed job.

For now, he needed to get inside the club and be sure Kristen and Nicole were okay.

He jogged from the trailer across the narrow alley to the back door, nodding at Glen on the way. He strode through the low-ceilinged hallway, his dress shoes ringing on the bare flooring, dodging crew members with cameras, rigging, and lighting in the narrow space. He leapt down the stairs to the underground club area, ending up near the front entrance, a long, exposed-brick corridor that separated a karaoke bar from the main dance floor. The cast and crew filled all the small rooms, including extras behind the bar, electricians on ladders in the corners, and props crew rearranging items on tables. Danny headed straight for the dance floor. The bar ran along one side, a large gilt-framed mirror above it, and across the room stood two raised dance platforms with widely spaced metal bars.

Danny's gaze riveted on Kristen, standing in front of one of the cages. A Valkyrie in glittery purple top and gold shorts, her red-gold hair flowing around her face and shoulders. He hated that Kristen would be in a cage, but she looked magnificent. He scanned the room again. No Jenkins.

Danny leaned against the wall next to the door, out of the way of the crew, his heart finally slowing as he watched Keesha and Camryn direct the extras dressed as club patrons. One of Keesha's multiple tasks was to manage any extras on set, but she often left that to the very capable Camryn. With Jenkins on premises, they were watching out for each other.

"Club dancers," Keesha said, "meet platform dancers." They all nodded to each other. "While the crew finishes setting up, we're going to do a quick run-through to see how everything looks. We'll be playing music in the background so the actors' lines can be picked up by the mics. When I say 'action,' pretend it's the usual loud DJ mix and that the overhead lights are flashing. Ignore the crew members and just pretend you're in the club on a Saturday night, doing what you do. Dance, drinks in hand, flirt, yell in each other's ears. But don't really yell. Pretend. And when you hear 'cut,' whether it's from me or the director, you stop and pay attention to the next set of directions."

She looked around at the group. "Any questions?" No one moved. "Groovy." She gestured toward the platform. "Ladies, you're up."

Kristen and Nicole exchanged grins, slipped through the opening at the back of each platform, leapt up to their spots, then stood waiting for the music.

Keesha twirled a hand in the air and The JoBoxer's "Just Got Lucky" started up in the background. "And dance, everybody!" Keesha said.

Everyone started to move, but Kristen kept his full attention. In that bikini top, boy shorts, and purple go-go boots, Kristen thrust out her breasts with each "ooh!" in the song and Danny felt the impact as if she'd pushed them right against his body.

Danny straightened from the wall, drawn by her irresistible force. He swayed in rhythm with the song's catchy beat and Kristen's seductive yet playful gyrations. Flipping her hair from her face, she finally caught his eye and smiled at him. He smiled back, lifting his arm to mirror one of her movements. She kicked a foot out and he did the same. She swayed her hips in his direction and Danny followed suit. Her smile turned into a grin, and she rotated on the balls of her feet, lowering herself to a crouch, her hips still swiveling back and forth. Danny tried to copy her pose and movements, but almost fell on his ass and had to straighten up.

Glen dragged a ladder in front of Danny, breaking his line of sight with Kristen and when the view cleared, he saw Keesha backing up from the dancers. She edged into the space next to him, nodding in time to the music, watched for a few more beats, then called out, "Cut!"

The music stopped, the dancers paused, but it took Kristen longer to come out of her dance reverie. Danny found it hard to take a breath as Kristen looked at him again, her red hair curving over one eye as she grasped the bars in both hands.

Not a Valkyrie, he thought. Barbarella.

"Nice," Keesha said, and for a second he thought he'd spoken out loud.

"What?"

"The dancers," she said. "They did a nice job." She pushed away from the wall and looked at him over her shoulder, one eyebrow raised. "So did you."

Danny hadn't been dancing in years. And he'd never spontaneously danced across a crowded room from an extra. While Keesha addressed the extras, his attention returned to Kristen. Hands still on the bars, she watched him.

She shouldn't be in a cage, he thought, and had taken a step toward her when a bellowing voice stopped him.

"I love the smell of an active set in the morning."

Half closing his eyes in dismay, Danny pasted on a smile and turned around to greet—and hopefully distract—Jenkins. The two goons flanked him, their eyes hooded.

"Mr. Jenkins," Danny began, digging in his mind for a neutral conversational subject.

"PJ, my boy," the producer boomed, clapping Danny on the back. "How's my production going?" He jerked a thumb over his shoulder at the director Gary and his producing partner Liz. "These two give me nothing, but you'll tell it to me straight, right, boy?"

Danny's nostrils flared.

Jenkins simpered, "They won awards for their little movie," then held his hands up and flapped his fingers. "So the studios love them. Give them a TV show, they say, they're money-makers. But all they can tell me is, 'all good, all fine, we're on time, we're on budget.'"

He snorted, his head swiveling around the room, and Danny knew the exact moment Jenkins's gaze stopped at Kristen, even before he said, "What have we here? They're in cages?"

"Just extras." Danny gestured toward the main group, who had gone silent, standing in a clump.

"Not those." Jenkins dismissed them with a wave of the hand even as he stared at Kristen. "That one."

Danny's hand curled into a fist, but Jenkins missed it because he marched across the room to the cage, his bodyguards trailing. Gary put a hand on Danny's arm and shook his head even as Liz nodded at the fist and whisper-hissed, "I wish you could."

Danny, Gary, and Liz followed Jenkins, but Danny edged around all of them and reached Kristen first. He swiveled to face the producer, arms crossed over his chest, before turning to look at Kristen. Even though she stood on a platform with bars around her, she looked more confident and in control than the rest of them. She stood straight, made eye contact with Jenkins, and smiled.

"Hello," she said with great cheer. "I'm having the best time. My sister said filming could be slow, but I'd love to start dancing again."

"I'd love to see that, too, sweetheart," Jenkins told her.

Danny made a noise in the back of his throat.

"Stop puffing up, money-maker, and move out of the way. I want to see this one."

A short time earlier, Jenkins had declared Kristen out. Now he was laser-focused on her. Danny itched to slam a fist in Jenkins's flabby, fatuous face, but he couldn't lose this job. It was *his* money-maker, and he needed to replace his family's nest egg. He risked another glance over his shoulder at Kristen. She smiled at him. Did she realize how precarious this situation was?

"She's just a dancer," Danny said, hating having to say it. "No big deal."

"They look like a pretty big deal to me," Jenkins said. He held his hands in front of his chest, miming breasts. "Pretty expensive, too."

"That's it," Danny said, done with this bull.

He took a step toward Jenkins, fist raised, but Jenkins moved back as if he'd practiced it, and his goons took his place, flanking Danny. Jenkins slipped around until he stood at the bars of Kristen's platform.

"I know you," she said, shaking a finger at him. "You like to shake things up, but the universe always finds a way to balance."

"I like you, sweetheart," he told her. "I want to see more of you."

"When the casting people called, I told them no nude scenes. Or private parties, if that's what you're thinking."

Jenkins laughed. "I wasn't thinking that before. I am now. I'm talking about the show. I want you in more of this episode." He pointed at Gary and Liz. "Make it happen."

Gary's mouth dropped open. "What?"

"Do I need to prance around while I say it?" Jenkins pointed at Kristen now. "Get her in the show. A speaking part. An audition tomorrow, on film, wearing that." He flipped a hand up and down, indicating Kristen's dance outfit. "And I'll be there."

"No," Danny said. He pushed against the goon in front of him, but the guy pushed back. Then he opened his coat just enough for Danny to see the shoulder holster. What the hell?

Kristen reached through the bars and grabbed Jenkins's jacket sleeve. "I'll do it," she said. "If someone from the set will help coach me. I've never acted before."

Jenkins grunted, then turned to Gary. "Why's everyone standing around with their heads up their asses? You have a scene to shoot." He mock-punched one of the goons. "Check my schedule. I need to be at that audition. You!" he said to a nearby PA. "Get me a chair. I want to watch. But I want lunch first. Where's catering?"

CHAPTER SEVEN

Once the bully left the room, Kristen released the breath she'd been holding. She'd dealt with overbearing men like that before, but never ones with bodyguards. Or guns. Keesha announced a break for the extras and huddled in a corner with Gary and Liz. The crew continued bustling around while Camryn herded the dancers toward the back rooms. Nicole jumped down from her platform and went with them.

Kristen caught all this in her peripheral vision, mostly because she couldn't stop looking at Danny, who still stood in front of the platform, face raised up to her. His ice blue eyes turned a warmer shade as he and Kristen continued watching each other.

"You okay?" he finally asked.

Without thinking about it, she wiggled her fingers through the bars and Danny took hold of her hand.

"Most people don't understand it, but I sometimes have more power inside the cage than out." She squeezed his warm fingers, then let go. She popped around the back and stepped down so she could see Danny face to face, nothing between them. "Thanks for defending me."

He shook his head, his lips pressed in a grim line. She could tell his pride hurt that he hadn't been able to defuse the situation while she had. She believed he'd done his best, considering the circumstances.

"That guy had a gun," she said. "I saw it."

"And that guy's boss still has more power than him." He rocked back on his heels as if ready to take off.

"He's just a big bully."

"I'll get you out of that audition." Now he took a couple steps away.

"I don't want you to."

His head jerked back as if she'd smacked him. "You *want* to do it?"

"Yes." She held up a hand to stop his response. "Not for him. I deal with men like him all the time. I want to go for me. And my daughter. But I need a coach to get me through the audition. Will you help me find someone from the cast?"

She wanted to ask him to do it, but he was engaged. To the lovely Lorelei. Indica had shown her a picture of them, Danny's arm around a tiny woman with long, curling blonde hair, his face in profile as he looked adoringly at her. Just yesterday Kristen had announced out loud: *no men.* They just brought complications. The moment Danny Linstead walked in her yoga studio, she knew she wanted more of him. She couldn't deny her curiosity, the heat between them. The more time she spent around him, the more those feelings intensified. She wouldn't do that to him, to Lorelei, to Daisy, or to herself.

His eyes softened at her question before the blue turned sharp again. "You shouldn't do it."

"It's not up to you." She crossed her arms over her chest and looked around the room. "What happens now?"

Danny looked like he wanted to say more, to be an overprotective male and insist she bow out. She was ready to blast him not only for his sexist attitude but for making assumptions about his place in her life when he said, "We wait. They need to find a way to get you in the show."

Kristen's heart thumped hard once. "Wow. It's probably naïve, but I thought they'd just have me say 'wanna dance?' to you or something and just keep filming. You mean everything is paused because of me?"

"Because of Jenkins's antics, but yeah."

She took a few steps around the room, looking at the exposed brick walls, the glossy bar, the crew now hanging out and chatting with each other or checking their phones. Keesha, Gary, and Liz had disappeared. No lights flashed, no music played.

"This isn't right." She shook her head. Everyone's jobs halted, because of one ridiculous man's pronouncement.

"They'd all agree with you," he told her. "But they won't blame you. Look, you can wait in my trailer, if you want. I'll go take a run or something. It could be all day."

"My sister told me to expect delays, but nothing like this. I need to call her. And my babysitter."

Keesha trotted up and addressed Kristen. "Are you open to being filmed coming out of the cage, taking Danny's hand, and leading him through a side door?"

"That was fast," Danny commented.

"First option that came up with our head writer," Keesha told him. "Nothing in stone yet." She turned back to Kristen. "You don't have to do this if it's not right for you."

Kristen glanced at the nearly empty room. Most of the crew had wandered out. "What will happen if I don't?"

Keesha took a deep breath. "We'll figure it out. We always do. I'd never put anyone in that position, actor, crew, or extra." But still, she waited, and it was clear that a lot depended on Kristen's response and that Keesha needed it soon.

"Of course I'll do it," she said.

"Great." She handed Kristen a piece of paper. "This is your new pay."

Kristen couldn't help a gasp. "This is just for me to add some time to my day and say a few things?"

Keesha nodded. "Consider it combat pay. We'll get you a new contract and let you know when the script's been updated. You're welcome to review the contract with a lawyer first. But we can fit that change in today while we have access to the club."

"You only have the club for today?"

Keesha's shoulders went up. "Technically until 8 AM tomorrow morning, but yeah."

"I need to call a couple people."

"She'll be in my trailer if you need her," Danny told Keesha. "I might go for a run."

"Keep your phone on you," Keesha said, "in case anything changes." She thanked Kristen and jogged away.

"You don't have to give up your trailer for me," Kristen told Danny when they were alone in the room. "Why are you doing all of this?"

"I like you," he said, and seemed surprised by the admission.

Same here, she wanted to tell him. So much so that she wanted to push him up against the bar, cover him in cherry sauce, and lick him all over. Instead, she let out a breath and said, "I can hang out with the other extras. I'm going outside to make my calls."

"I'll walk with you."

Kristen snagged her bag on the way and once in the alley, opened up her trusty flip phone. She understood the necessity of cells, but she didn't like them or their potential health consequences, so she always put the other person on speaker. She would have used the earbuds Victoria kept giving her, but they usually disappeared after Daisy turned them into some important accessory for Fuzzy Bunny. Kristen moved away from the clumps of people waiting for the latest updates. She put in a quick call to today's babysitter—Indica's mom—who reassured her that Daisy could stay as long as Kristen needed. Kristen knew Nella would adopt the both of them if she could. Then Kristen called her sister.

"Hey, how's the filming going?" Victoria asked.

"Fun. Weird. This nasty producer wants me in the show more."

"What? Who's the nasty producer?"

Someone stepped in front of her and she gasped, jerking her head up from where she'd been watching the phone, as if she could see Victoria on it.

In a low voice, Danny said, "You might not want to have this conversation where everyone can hear it." He tilted his chin and looked behind him. Kristen followed his gaze and saw the bodyguards, hands clasped in front of them, dark sunglasses on, standing next to an over-sized limo that blocked one end of the alley.

"Oh."

"Kristen," Victoria's voice called, "what's going on?"

"You can talk to her in my trailer if you want privacy," Danny said.

Kristen agreed, and told Victoria to hang on a second. Danny led her up the steps and once she was inside, he said, "I'll be right out here."

Kristen thanked him, and sat at a small banquette, placing the phone on the table. The space was small, but tidy, with no personal items anywhere.

"Where are you?" Victoria's voice sounded insistent. "Should I be there?"

"I'm in Danny Linstead's trailer on the set, and no. Everything's fine."

"So what's going on? Who's this nasty producer?"

"PJ something? Jenkins something?"

Victoria swore. A lot. "I'm coming to get you. I didn't know he was part of this production. You need to get out of his sphere, right this second."

Kristen heard shuffling in the background and waved her hands at the phone. "No no no. You don't need to come rescue me. It's fine. He wants me to have more of a part on the show, and they want to film some more things today, but they only have the club for a short time. So there's a delay and I don't know how long it's going to take. I wanted you to know about the timing since you asked me to check in."

A pause, then, "I don't like this scenario."

Kristen named the amount of money they were going to pay her.

"Not worth it if there's any trouble."

"I agree, but I feel good about this overall. It's like the universe is trying to tell me something. Even if it's just to help out with rent."

"The universe won't protect you from a predator."

"Disagree, because I can protect myself, but go on."

"I don't like you being involved in a PJ production. He's the worst kind of slime. There's been too much talk about him over the years, and it's starting to come out in the open now."

"Which means he's on his way down. And I witnessed some of that slime, but I'm really okay. The crew is watching out for me, and Danny's acting like my personal bodyguard."

"Wait. That just clicked. You said his name earlier. Danny Linstead? The model-slash-actor?"

"I don't know about the model part, even though he has the looks for it, but yes. He's on the show. He stood up for me and he let me use his trailer so I could have this call in private."

"And now that you're done, you need to leave his trailer."

"He's not going to hurt me."

"*Kristen.*"

"Thank you for taking care of me, big sister, but I'm fine. Besides, he's engaged. Indica told me."

"Really? I hadn't heard about that. I thought he was a workaholic." Before her marriage, Victoria had been a reality TV producer. She now spent her time managing Tyler Landry, her husband's country western band, but television still consumed her. "Either way," Victoria continued. "Engaged, married. That hasn't stopped men before."

"I'm wearing my go-go boots."

"The paisley ones with the pointy toes?"

Kristen nodded as if Victoria could see her. "Those."

"Make sure he sees how sharp they are when you leave. And call me when you're done filming. No matter the time."

When Kristen hung up, she looked around the space again. It was warm in here, quiet. No one demanding gummy worms, asking for help with a pose, or could she come in that morning and clean a house after a big party. She loved her life, she wouldn't trade her daughter, yoga classes, or her side hustles for anything, but sometimes…sometimes a little quiet alone time was a great and glorious thing. She snuggled into the corner of the banquette and closed her eyes. Just for a few minutes.

CHAPTER EIGHT

Danny eased open the trailer door and looked inside. He'd heard Kristen hang up, then go quiet. He'd actually heard the entire conversation through the open window, and even though he kept telling himself to move out of earshot, he couldn't quite do it. But her extended silence worried him.

She'd propped her head on her forearms and her phone lay on the table. Her hair floated around her shoulders and over the bare skin of her arms and thighs. Her strawberry blonde lashes rested against her cheeks.

Danny eased a blanket from a cupboard and draped it across her back. He wished he could scoop her up and set her in the small bed in back, tucking the blanket around her. She smiled in her sleep as if she could hear his thoughts. He should go. The production could be on hold for hours. She had a child, she probably never got enough sleep. Just leave her to rest, and go.

But he stood entranced, protector and lust-filled idiot warring with each other.

He shuffled a step back and she blinked.

"I'm not engaged," was all he could think to say as those blue eyes lasered directly at him.

Without lifting her head, she said, "You're not?"

"No. That's my twin brother."

She straightened, grabbing the blanket as it slid from her shoulders. "You have a twin? How fun is that?"

He didn't know how to answer that. He also found it hard to shift gears from the fantasies rolling around in his head a few seconds ago to her steady clear-eyed gaze. "It has been," he said. "Mostly."

"Are you identical?"

He nodded.

"What's his name?"

"Denny. He's engaged to Lorelei LaMontaine."

"Indica had it wrong," she said with a grin.

"Who had what wrong?"

"My roommate thought you were engaged. She thought you were Denny."

"Yeah, that happens a lot."

"Wait." Kristen glanced around. "Was I that loud? Did you hear my whole conversation? And did I actually fall asleep? Did you put this blanket around me?"

"Yes to the last two. You weren't out very long." He ran a hand through his hair and ducked his head. He really wished he'd just gone for a run and let her be. "Sorry. I had left the window open earlier. But I didn't want to leave you alone."

"Everyone's being so protective today."

His gaze slid from her eyes to her purple bikini top, glitter-enhanced torso, metallic gold boy shorts, and down her legs to her boots. She watched his examination and kicked one foot up, tilting it back and forth so he could see the sharp boot tip.

He grinned. "Even before that, I figured you could take care of yourself."

"My sister hasn't grasped that yet. She's used to taking care of other people." She twisted her boot one last time, then started to edge out from the banquette. "Thanks for letting me use your trailer."

He stayed in the narrow aisle, blocking her way. "You should stay. I'll go. Finish your nap. I'll close the window."

"Would you be the one?"

He stared down at her. "Excuse me?"

"To be my acting coach. Well, my audition coach."

"I don't think that's a good idea..."

She managed to shift out of the booth and rise directly in front of him, practically sliding the front of her body up his as she went. The blanket slithered to the floor. Their thighs touched. Her face was inches from his, her body radiating heat. All of the oxygen disappeared from the trailer.

"I gotta go," he said. He dashed out the door and down the steps, running out the alley and down the block before remembering he still wore his outfit from that day's filming. He stopped, and fell back against a building, his heart pounding and thighs shaking as if he'd run for hours. He ran his hands over his face and through his hair, letting out a groan.

What the hell had just happened?

She got to him, that's what. And he'd scampered away like a little boy.

He trotted back to the trailer, but she was gone. He looked around the alley. No Kristen. No Jenkins, either. He jogged to Jenkins's limo parked by the club's back door. The driver sat with the door open, smoking. He smirked at Danny, but Danny ignored it.

"Mr. Jenkins inside?" he asked.

"Stretching his legs." The guy gestured with his cigarette down the end of the alley Danny had just come from. It was empty. Danny couldn't imagine tubby Jenkins taking any exercise, but that didn't matter right now. "What about one of the dancers. Long red hair, boots. You see her?"

"Nope."

Danny tapped the top of the limo and took off in the other direction. Of course the guy would say that, whether he'd seen Kristen or not. He jogged to that end of the alley, head swiveling. No one. Which was crazy because there were always people on a set. You couldn't get away from them, even in your own trailer. He suspected everyone had scattered to avoid Jenkins, and his desperation increased. He edged around a dumpster and stopped, heart pounding, when he heard a woman's voice nearby. It rose in emotion, but it wasn't Kristen's. He already knew the timbre of her voice; it was lower, even when keyed up.

"It's not right," the woman said. "It doesn't make sense."

"Producing doesn't always make sense," a male voice replied, and Danny's body tensed. Jenkins. A nearby building was being remodeled and a chain link fence surrounded it. A small gap between the fencing led to an alley created by some stacked plywood and drywall, and the voices seemed to be coming from there. "Linstead's doing crap work. He doesn't improve, he goes."

A hard ball formed in Danny's gut. What the hell?

During the long silence while he waited for the woman's reply, sweat beaded on his scalp and slid between his shoulder blades. Someone had finally noticed, and of all people, it was that asshole.

"Mr. Jenkins, with all due respect—"

"Forget the speech, sweetheart. People only respect my power, not me."

"We've already put a lot of money into Danny." It was Liz, the line producer. "And this pilot. A lot of time and marketing and promotion. His fans want to see him in this role."

"This pilot lives or dies by me and my money, Mendenhall. Not the fans. If I pull out, it disintegrates. Poof. I tracked the time he wasted with his flubbed lines. Just yesterday afternoon, he cost us a lot of money."

No, you waste of a human. *You* cost us a lot of money by changing the script.

Still, he wasn't totally wrong. Danny had choked multiple times yesterday. He'd been too distracted, and that needed to stop. Especially if he might lose this job. He'd known it was backed by PJ Productions, which always got a lot of funding, but the amount of money had blinded him.

He leaned against the dumpster, heart pounding. He'd thought getting this role was the answer to all of his problems. He could return most of his family's lost money, and he could add to his savings. Now that he'd seen the true cost, was it worth it?

He shook his head. No. It wasn't. He was about to charge into that alley and quit, tell Jenkins all the places he could shove his money, when the click of heels behind him caught his attention. Before he could move, Kristen walked by, wrapped in a long sweater, head down. Construction debris stacked by the dumpster kept him partially hidden, but if she turned, lifted her head, she'd see him.

She'd asked if he'd be her audition coach. He'd turned her down. If he quit now…

He couldn't do that to her.

With a last look up the alley, he pushed away from the dumpster, calling after Kristen.

She jerked to a stop, and swiveled with impressive speed on those heels. Her large blue eyes opened wide. "Where did you come from?"

"Just taking a walk," he said. "Listen." He glanced over his shoulder, but didn't see or hear anything near the construction. He gestured toward the parking lot, away from Liz and the demon producer. "Will you walk with me?"

She nodded, and they turned back. She wrapped the sweater around herself, and kept her arms around her waist. Danny shoved his hands in his pockets, still processing everything he'd heard. He couldn't keep going with this job, but he didn't want to leave her alone. He needed to find a way to stay until her part was done.

"Listen," he repeated. Out of the corner of his eye, he saw her head turn toward him, but he stared at the pavement as they sauntered back. "I'd like to help you. With the audition." Then he remembered what she'd said earlier in the day when she first showed up. "If you'd...if you'd help me with..." He closed his eyes briefly against the thought. "With some relaxation techniques."

CHAPTER NINE

As she nibbled a tofu vegetarian roll later that evening, Kristen still felt Danny Linstead's thumbs brushing against her hip bones. She'd spontaneously hugged him when he offered to help, the sweater she'd borrowed falling open. As she did so, his hands came out of his pockets and grasped her hips; his thumbs grazed the bare skin of her belly.

She shivered now, and focused her attention on enjoyment of food and friends. She sat next to her roommate Indica and across from Gail and Star in a booth under the multicolored neon "Dragon Dim Sum" sign. The four of them met here every week after she danced. Indica would talk about her latest diversion—currently it was homemade bath items—Star updated them on the flower shop she and Indica owned, and Gail often shared a selection of her latest novel in progress.

Gail tucked her spiked hair behind her ears and swiped at her tablet, continuing her reading. "Sophia straightened, her eyes daring Antonio to challenge her. 'Listen, I'm not your secretary,' Sophia told him. 'You don't pay me enough for that. But I'll do the French maid thing.'"

Star sat wide-eyed, while Indica shook her head, smiling indulgently. Across the room, another group of late-night diners laughed and sang happy birthday to a beaming friend. Kristen wondered if Danny Linstead could sing. She took a deep breath through her nose, and let it out for a count of eleven. She would be

45

seeing him tomorrow at her audition and could ask him then. Tonight was for her friends.

"What happens next?" asked Star in a breathless voice. Even though her ratfink boyfriend left her after they moved to San Francisco, she still believed in romance.

"That's all I've got so far, but she does do the French maid thing," Gail said with a shrug. "I think I'll have her go over his privates with a little feather duster." She waved her chopsticks around to illustrate.

"Eww." Star wrinkled her nose. "That's not a good visual."

"That was one of my more tame ideas." Gail reached for a shrimp dumpling. She bit into it, made loud "mmms" as she chewed, then added, "It'll have to be a one-use feather duster, though, right?"

Kristen and Indica laughed.

Star pressed her palms over her ears and whimpered, "Visual, visual."

"I don't know how you come up with these stories, G-Dog." Indica set down her pork bun and brushed back one of the tendrils of thick brown hair that framed her face. "Or how you have the patience to write a whole book."

"Some of us can focus and the rest of us like to flit from thing to thing." Gail clicked her chopsticks over the table at Indica. "Either way, it's fun. Oh, shit." She dabbed at a drip on her "Catch Flights Not Feelings" t-shirt. "And speaking of fun..." She looked at Kristen. "I can't believe we've been here this long and haven't heard what it's like to be a movie star."

"Television," Kristen corrected.

"Whatever. Spill the good stuff."

"It was fun," Kristen said. "So much happened. They did my hair and makeup, I got to dance for hours, this nasty producer showed up and harassed everyone, but he also wants me to be in the show more. I'm actually doing an *audition* tomorrow."

"Whoa," Indica said. "You packed a lot into one day."

Kristen grabbed her arm. "I didn't get a chance to tell you. That guy at my yoga class isn't the guy you think he is. He's not his twin brother, so he's not engaged."

Gail blinked. "Do you have low blood sugar or something? Is this a movie, or a soap opera? You're not making sense."

But Indica understood. "He has a twin brother?" Her eyes went wide. "Omigod, the twin brother! They were on some show together forever ago, but one of them dropped out of sight and I completely forgot about him." She turned to Gail and Star. "Denny Linstead from *The Fabulous Lamontaines*—he's engaged to Lorelei Lamontaine—has a brother and the brother was at Kristen's yoga class yesterday."

"Danny." Kristen couldn't help smiling when she said his name.

"Well, that's not confusing," said Gail.

"Is he handsome?" Star asked.

At the same time, Kristen and Indica said, "*Very.*" They looked at each other and laughed.

"I saw him," Indica explained. "At yoga."

Kristen nodded. "His producer brought a bunch of people from the show to the yoga center."

"Wait." Gail clicked her chopsticks again. "The nasty producer brought people to your yoga class?"

Star's eyes went wide. "This *is* like a soap opera."

"Television has multiple producers," Kristen said. She'd asked Camryn a few questions during down time. "The nasty one is the executive producer. He's not on set all the time. Liz, the one who brought people to yoga, is a line producer. She oversees the production on a daily basis like budgeting, rentals, and the schedule."

"Look at you," Gail said. "Hitting the big time and talking the lingo. So what else are you going to be doing?"

"As far as I know, I'm still going to be me, a go-go dancer. I guess Danny and I are going to have some history, but I don't know how much." Kristen cut into her rolled rice noodles and tofu. Saying Danny's name left her breathless, and she needed a moment. "There's going to be some kind of ruckus, and Danny runs through the club, and I help him. They added that to today's scene, and we already filmed it. That's why I was later than usual tonight. Filming takes forever. Anyway, he's helping me with the audition tomorrow." Flashing back to his thumbs brushing against her hip bones, she took a large bite of the luxurious roll, her eyes drifting shut as the seasonings rolled across her tongue. "Mmm."

"Whoa." Gail held up a hand. "That was like a sex sound."

It took a moment for Kristen to come out of her reverie. "I can't stop thinking about Danny," she admitted. "I hugged him when he said he'd help me with the audition. I was wearing my dance outfit—

you've seen it—and we kind of bumped into each other at first and his thumbs brushed my hips and…" She sighed. "*Three years*, you guys. It's been almost three years."

"Oh, man." Gail slumped with an elbow on the table.

"I almost exploded right there. But he's…" Kristen stopped, not sure how to explain.

"He's what?" asked Star.

"I don't know. He's…he scares me a little. Not in a creepy way, but in a skittish colt way. Like—"

Indica gasped and put a hand to her mouth, pointing at Kristen with her free hand. "It's your list," she breathed through her fingers, then dropped her arm. "Your soul mates list."

"But that's…" Kristen shook her head. "It couldn't be. I just met him."

Gail chuckled. "It's so good when the teacher becomes the student. So what's the list again?"

Star answered for her. "One is instant attraction. Two, you're always aware of the other person, like a kind of homing beacon. Then an intense need to be with them, even if you don't know them well. And four." She looked away from Kristen. "Fear…"

Gail leaned over and pretended to release something from her hand. "Boom," she said. "Mic drop."

"Wow, I know you guys love me, but I didn't realize you paid such close attention." Kristen shook her head. "I told you, though…I don't know if it's true anymore. Or if I even need a man."

"Well, the universe definitely called you out on that one," Indica said. "Test it it out when you see him tomorrow."

"Yeah." Gail shrugged. "What's the worst that could happen? Um, I don't know. You could have some *sex*. After *three years*. It's more action than I've been getting lately."

Indica raised her hand. "Same here."

"What about Cort?" Kristen asked. Cort was her brother-in-law's best friend.

"Our off-and-on is officially off." Indica swiped at a tendril of hair in her eyes, shoving it behind her ear. She and Cort had dated after their mutual friend Teresa had broken things off with him. "He wants to start sowing his wild oats again, and I'm welcome to join him if I want. I don't."

"Cort's pretty hot, though," Gail said. "I'd share him."

Star sighed, her eyes gone soft. "He's very dreamy."

Indica leaned over the table to pat Star's arm. "Oh, honey."

Star looked at her. "What?"

Kristen loved each of these women for different reasons, but Star touched her the most. Star adored Daisy, even when the two-year-old pitched a fit over nothing and screamed bloody murder in the middle of the street. After Star's boyfriend left, she partnered with Indica to start a successful flower shop. Kristen knew about the steel core behind her brown doe eyes, but strength didn't guarantee freedom from pain, and Star saw the world of romance with rose-colored glasses.

"Do you have a thing for Cort?" Indica asked her now.

Star chewed her lower lip and rearranged the napkin in her lap. "I just said he was dreamy," she repeated, her face gone rose-petal pink.

Her voice gentle, Indica said, "He's a dog, you know. He's kind of a woman eater." She clapped a hand over her mouth. "Oh God, you know what I mean."

"So you *did* sleep with him," Gail said, one side of her mouth turned up in a little smile.

Indica took a long sip of tea before answering. "Actually, I didn't. I think I might be..." Indica paused and stared down at her plate. "Well, looking for something serious. I *am* going to be thirty soon, you know. It's so freaking depressing. Which is why I'm so glad I finally found a decent manager for the café, so I can take that marketing class in Sacramento. Star and I really want to take our merchandising to the next level." She and Star sold a lot of homemade items like soaps, candles, and shampoo. "There's another class coming up in the next six weeks or so, so the place will be all yours," she told Kristen. "But Mom will still babysit."

Kristen squeezed her arm. She was so grateful for all the help she got with Daisy.

"So why didn't you sleep with Cort?" Gail asked.

"I figured, if he could get all serious for Teresa, he had it in him to be committed to someone, and if that was me, then I thought we should actually get to know each other. Then he had to go and announce that he wanted to date other people, sow his wild oats some more and all that." She smacked a palm to her forehead. "Ugh. I should've slept with him when I had the chance. That body of his is obscene. Does he live in the gym or something?" she asked Kristen.

"He has weights in the Barn." Cort owned an old garage

converted into a downstairs music studio with two flats upstairs. Cort lived in one and his best friend Luke lived in the other with Kristen's sister, Victoria. Cort and Luke fronted the successful country western band Tyler Landry. "And he plays football at Fort Scott Field in the Presidio."

"Shirts and skins?" Gail asked.

"No," said Kristen, "but the shirts often come off at the end when they're cooling down." She smiled, remembering one day in particular when she'd seen Luke strip off his shirt and douse himself with a bottle of water. She wasn't interested in him, but she'd enjoyed the view. Now that she thought about it, Cort had flirted with her that day, too. He was a sweet guy, but she didn't think he was right for Star, who continued to look moony-eyed as they talked.

Gail pointed at Kristen. "You need to let us know when the next game happens. I'll bring out my cheerleader costume."

"Ha!" Indica pointed back at Gail. "You, in a cheerleader costume. That'll be the day."

"You don't know all of my sordid past," Gail said with a grin.

"That will be next week's highlight," Kristen said. "For now, I need to get back to Nella."

"You know mom would keep Daisy all night if you let her," said Indica, flagging down the waiter.

"I know, but I don't want to take advantage." And she missed her baby. She'd talked to Daisy on the phone a couple of times throughout the day, but her old-fashioned flip phone didn't have video, so they couldn't see each other.

"Hey," Indica said, pulling out her wallet, "it keeps some of the pressure off me to present her with a grandchild. But she really does love watching her. I'll pass on the football, though. I don't need to see Cort flirting with other women."

"There are a lot of other men there, too," Kristen told her. "Even some straight single ones."

Indica took a second to think about it. "Yeah, well...okay. Maybe. We'll see."

As they divvied up the bill, Star said, "I might want to go to a game." Before anyone could respond, she added quickly, "And I want to learn more about your acting experience. And this brother. Danny Linstead."

So did Kristen.

CHAPTER TEN

That producer had wanted Kristen to wear her dance club outfit to the audition, but she showed up in black leggings and a top that swirled with psychedelic colors. She might not be an outright rebel, but no man was going to tell her what to wear.

She stared up at the beige warehouse and checked the address Keesha had given her. Located in a light industrial park, the building had three bay doors and an attached office space with tall narrow windows that looked out at the PG&E transformers across the way. Certainly not glamorous.

She walked into the warehouse and was greeted by Keesha, who wore black bike shorts and sneakers, a cycling jersey and windbreaker, and held a small camera. A Bluetooth phone hung on one ear. The large space was crammed with boxes, tools, lumber, household items like phones and floor lamps, rolling garment racks, three brown sedans and one fake SFPD patrol car. A few people with clipboards wandered around, muttering to each other and rummaging through boxes.

Keesha gestured her into the office connected to the storage area. At the threshold, Kristen said, "My sister told me she called you." Victoria had reassured her the night before that the production was a good one, despite Jenkins's involvement. Kristen hadn't been worried, but she knew it reassured her older sister to have checked up on things.

Keesha nodded. "I have one of those older sisters, too," she said in an amiable tone, walking into the office and setting the camera on a tripod. "Wouldn't do us much good to harass anyone in our production, certain people not withstanding." She leaned forward to adjust the camera and looked up at Kristen from that position. "I don't swear much, but that shit doesn't fly with me. Had my share of it, and won't put up with it now. Gary and Liz don't, either, and that's one of the reasons I stick with them. They're quirky, but I can deal with that." She straightened and gestured Kristen inside. "We're working on that one fly in the ointment. And today's good news is he had to go out of town so he's not coming today. You're safe here."

Kristen let out a whoosh of breath. She would have managed Jenkins if she had to, but she hadn't realized she'd been holding so much tension in her body at the thought.

"I *told* Victoria you had a good vibe. With badass undertones."

Keesha grinned, and rested her elbows lightly on top of the camera. "You're quirky, too. I like it."

Kristen looked around the tiny space, just as crammed as the warehouse, only with two desks, chairs, paperwork, and smaller items like Polaroid cameras, carousels of colored pens, white boards, and overstuffed binders. "Where's Danny?"

"To the point, too. Even better. He's stuck on set, but he asked me to help you out." Keesha straightened, studying Kristen. "Honey, your face just fell like someone just stole Christmas."

"I'm disappointed that Danny's not here." Before Keesha could respond, she added, "But I'm ready to go. So how do we practice without him?"

Keesha handed her a few printed pages. "You read lines for DANCER. You'll probably get a name at some point. I read lines for SETH and anyone else who speaks. Pretend I'm a sexy plain clothes cop you just dragged out of the club."

"Not hard. You're gorgeous."

Keesha grinned. "If I was white, I'd be blushing."

Kristen smiled back. She could tell Keesha was too self possessed to embarrass easy. "Do I read and look at the camera, try to memorize the lines, look at you, or what?"

"Whatever's most comfortable. The camera will capture what we need and you and I can look at it after one read-through. I'll let you know when we do a final shoot. I'll read Seth's first line, and you do whatever feels natural."

Kristen nodded, glancing at the pages. She didn't have a lot of lines, and most of them were short, one or two sentences. The majority of the text described action outside the club. She stood and set the pages on top of the stool, wondering what real actors did to get into character. She'd be feeling it more if she was in the club itself.

Swaying her hips, Kristen said, "I wish I could actually do some dancing first. It would get me in the mood. And of course it would be better with music. A little Beyoncé or something."

"It'd interfere with our reading, but do what you need to to get in character."

"I can make my own music anyway." Kristen smoothed her hands up her thighs, across her belly, along the sides of her breasts and through her hair, hips swaying to the soundtrack in her mind. Keesha, the camera, and the tiny office's contents remained, but Kristen only saw the club, felt the press of other bodies moving in the same rhythm, absorbed the heat and lust rising and enveloping them all in a communal dance. Her eyes closed and her body took over, as it always did when she moved to music.

She spun in a slow circle, arms over her head, hips thrusting toward an unseen man who leaned toward her, a sheen of sweat at his open collar, dark hair falling over one eye, his scent seeping into her pores. He moved closer, lips forming words she couldn't hear, so he was forced to press them to her ear, to say—

"Holy Mary Mother of God."

Kristen startled back to the real world, her eyes flying open, to find herself facing the office door and Danny Linstead crossing himself.

From behind her, Keesha said, "Indeed."

"Are you real?" Danny asked Kristen, then shook his head as if trying to clear it.

"One hundred percent," she answered. "Including my boobs."

Danny nodded, still watching her. "I have no words right now."

Keesha stepped in front of Kristen and handed the pages to Danny. "Well, since you're here," she said, "let me give you some," and moved back to the camera.

He lifted his hand and accepted the pages without taking his eyes from Kristen.

Kristen stared back at Danny. He wore dark jeans and boots, and a dress shirt open at the collar. Danny Linstead looked better each time she saw him. Taller, more muscled, eyes set deeper, with an intense gaze. He looked flushed and her own skin heated in response.

"Let's go, then," Keesha said. "Keesha has things to do."

Danny finally stepped into the room. "Keesha," he said, smiling at Kristen, "you don't usually talk about yourself in the third person."

Keesha snorted. "Things are a little upside down right now. We already talked about doing a quick run-through."

"Great. You ready?" Danny asked Kristen.

"Magic words," Kristen told him. If he knew just *how* ready, it might catapult him out of the room. But any man unable to handle her intensity wasn't right for her, and Danny Linstead was right for her no matter her fear. Little bubbles of lust tingling through her middle confirmed that. She opened her mouth to add, *you have no idea how ready.*

"Camera's still rolling," Keesha informed them.

Danny shifted immediately from grinning to serious. "I'm glad to see you," he told Kristen. Those sharp blue eyes remained warm as he watched her.

"I could live in your eyes for days," she told him.

He raised an eyebrow at her. "That's not the line."

"What?"

"My line is 'I'm glad to see you,' and yours is 'what fresh hell is this'."

She turned more fully toward him. "Why would I say that?"

Danny lifted the papers clutched in his hands. "It's in the script. They decided to give us a little back story, remember? We were involved once, things went sour, so when I come into the club to escape the bad guys, there's some tension between us."

"But why would things go sour?"

"They didn't tell us that. But it helps if you open yourself up emotionally when you read the lines, that you believe them."

Keesha made a sound in the back of her throat. "It would also help if Kristen's back wasn't to the camera."

Danny took Kristen's script pages and set them on a nearby table with his own. Resting his hands on Kristen's upper arms, he tilted his head toward her, watching intently as if waiting for her response. No zing this time, but her shoulders lowered and she came back to herself. "I forgot we were acting," she whispered at him.

"That's the best kind," he told her gently. "But we should follow the script here. Things get a little chaotic otherwise."

"Heard that," Keesha said.

Hands still on Kristen's arms, Danny guided her so they both stood sideways to the camera, but still faced each other. He handed the script pages to Kristen and waited until she nodded at him.

"I'm glad to see you," he said with his own small nod of encouragement.

"What fresh hell is this?" she said, trying to sound like an angry ex-girlfriend and knowing she failed. The only time that had happened was when Daisy's father left her, and she'd never had the chance to express herself to him. Or find out why he'd done such a despicable thing.

"I need your help." Danny looked over his shoulder. *He* sounded wretched and desperate. "What's the best way out of this alley?"

Kristen glanced at the text. "I got you out of the club, isn't that enough?"

"Those guys won't stop."

"What's it worth to you?"

Danny stepped closer. "Get me away from here alive and I'll tell you."

Kristen tilted her head toward his, falling into his eyes again. "This better be good. You owe me a lot."

"And, *cut*," Keesha said dramatically. "That looked pretty good to me. You want to see it?"

Kristen shook her head. "I know I'm not a good actress and that pushy producer just wanted you all to do this so he could throw his weight around. And see me in my dancing outfit again. Do you think it'll make a difference if I do it again?"

"Truth?" Keesha asked.

"Always."

"You'd be on the show regardless."

Kristen's shoulders lowered. "Then I'd rather not do it again until the actual filming."

"Good enough." Keesha turned off the camera and detached it from the tripod. "Thanks for the entertaining afternoon."

"Thanks for your time, I know how busy you are. Sorry I got so distracted."

Keesha hefted the camera. "He's handsome. I get it."

"It's more than that," Kristen told her, watching Danny. He

looked both bemused and amused. She dug in her bag and pulled out a card, handing it to Keesha. "My way of thanking you."

"Just doing my job." She read the card. "Good for one yoga class. I was there the other day. Enjoyed it."

"I'm glad. The schedule's on the center's website. The first class is always free." She gestured at the card. "That's for a second class."

"Thanks." Keesha lifted a bag to her shoulder.

"You need any help with that?" Danny asked.

Keesha shook her head. "I got it. You're going to need all your strength for that one." She winked at Kristen and walked out.

CHAPTER ELEVEN

Danny stood staring at Kristen in the middle of the crowded office, unable to banish the image of her dancing in front of the camera.

"Keesha's perceptive," Kristen told him. "I am a handful. But I'm worth it."

He shifted, still watching her. "I don't know what to make of you." He'd thought she was brave yesterday, but she also seemed vulnerable, especially when he saw her walking alone down the alley.

"What do your instincts tell you?"

"That I got on set at five-thirty and haven't eaten since six." To underscore this, his stomach growled. It was true, but he didn't know how to really answer her question. His instincts seemed upside-down right now and part of him wanted to take her face in his hands and kiss her senseless, to lose himself in her and just forget everything else. Another part told him to run, far and fast.

"So where should we go to lunch?" she asked.

"I—"

She touched his arm. "I forgot that you're not used to me yet. That's okay. I'm not a steep learning curve. Pretty much what you see is what you get." She tucked her hand in the crook of his elbow and steered him out of the office, grabbing a small knapsack along the way. "There's a great café up the street and around the corner. We can work on some relaxation techniques while we're there."

Right. Relaxation. Learning his lines. That's why he was really here. Even if Danny quit, PJ would not ruin the work he'd put it into it in the meantime. Or would he? Outside, a mix of clouds and fog moved across the sky, and the breeze pushed long tendrils of Kristen's hair across her face. Danny smoothed them back behind her ear with his free hand.

She smiled at him. "It's a never-ending battle, but I appreciate the effort." When she turned her face away, the breeze caught more hair from the back, dancing it around her shoulders.

"It's beautiful," he told her as they stopped at a red light. "When it moves like that. The way the light catches it and shows off the different shades." He watched the strands still tossing in the wind. "Red. Gold. Amber."

The light changed and they moved across the street, her arm still in his. She held tight, but didn't cling, more in tandem with him than guiding or clutching. And Kristen Clausen was a tall, curvy girl. She could probably kick his ass if she wanted to, at the very least put a good dent in him, and lead him around without a problem.

Instead, they moved together, and he liked walking so close with this cheerful, funny, quirky woman. It warmed him inside. It felt...comfortable.

His gut clenched, and he stumbled on the sidewalk, then stopped altogether. Kristen guided him under the awning of a hardware store and away from a group of businessmen heading inside a restaurant.

She peered at his face. He probably looked a whiter shade of pale, and no wonder. He couldn't be *comfortable*. Danny Linstead didn't have time for comfortable. He needed action, movement, keep running so the devil won't catch up.

"What happened?" she asked.

Not "what's wrong?" or "are you okay?" but "what happened?" Like she wanted to hear everything, and wouldn't accept some surface answer like "I'm fine" or "Nothing." But what the hell *had* happened? He'd stepped into some comfortable shoes, that's what.

And liked it.

Kristen no longer held his arm, but her fingertips rested near his elbow, as if ready to respond to any need. A light rain pattered down, but the people around them continued on their way in that unfussy style he'd noticed about San Franciscans. Standing under the green awning, he stared at Kristen Clausen's face as she waited patiently for his response, round blue eyes open and inviting. He mentally ran through a few responses, but there really was only one answer.

"You," he finally said. "You happened."

The concerned frown that clouded her face now cleared and her bright smile took over. "So I unsettled you?"

He nodded. No use lying to her at this point, and he didn't want to.

"That's the nicest thing anyone's said to me in a long time." She pointed next door to a grouping of tables set under yellow umbrellas. "The café is right there. Let's get some food in you and see if I can unsettle you some more."

After sharing an appetizer of samosas, Danny's confidence reasserted itself. Kristen had insisted they sit outside, that she liked the cool weather because she usually ran hot, and they leaned close to each other over the small metal table. Kristen asked him what his life was like in sixth grade. Except for a short time in high school, he and his brother had been tutored on set. But he did have a crush on his on-set tutor, and one day he snuck a handmade card on her desk in the small office they used as a classroom. He'd copied lyrics from the punk poet John Cooper Clark, called "I Wanna Be Yours," but didn't sign his name.

He didn't remember all of it, but it had something to do with wanting to be a vacuum cleaner so he could breathe in her dust.

"What was her reaction when she opened it?" Kristin asked.

"She used it as an example of excessive metaphor usage, and my brother never let me forget about it."

She leaned closer to him, chin resting in her palm. "What did you do?"

"Stopped having a crush on Ms. Rodenbeck and trying to be what I'm not."

Kristen laughed and stood up. She lifted the sole of one foot to the inside of the other thigh, then pressed her palms together and raised them over her head. It wasn't half as entrancing as what she'd been doing when he walked into the warehouse office earlier, but he still couldn't stop staring at her.

"What are you doing?" he asked.

"Don't be embarrassed, it's San Francisco."

He lounged back in his chair, completely recovered from his earlier stumble. "I don't embarrass easy. My brother tried to embarrass me every chance he got. It gets old."

She glanced down at him. "I guess that makes being an actor

easier. Speaking of which, is filming always that repetitive, but slow at the same time?"

"It's definitely a lot of 'hurry up and wait.' So what's with the interpretive dance?"

"*Vrksasana*. Tree pose. I need to get centered. My daughter is throwing me off balance."

"Where is she?"

"With her aunt and uncle. Where she's always a dream child." Kristen set her foot down. "My brother-in-law really wants a child, so my sister agrees to babysit so he'll see what it's really like to have children. And Daisy might be a screaming mess up until we get to their door, then she becomes a poster child for perfect behavior." She tilted her head. "You asked about help with relaxation techniques. For acting?"

He straightened with a nod. "Remembering lines."

She slid into her chair, then set her chin in her hand and propped an elbow on the table. "Well, there's yoga, but I have a feeling that class was a one-time thing for you."

"No, it was—" He started to defend himself, but wondered why. The relaxation had lasted about five minutes, replaced by a current up his spine from when she'd touched him. It still tingled when she was around.

She straightened. "I know it's not for everyone. We just need to find the right thing for you. It's best to set up an ongoing practice so you're separating stressful moments from your thoughts. Reducing the negative thoughts helps decrease the stress, which lessens the impact on your body."

"And how long will that take?"

He liked her laugh, a light trill followed by an earthy chuckle. "Years. But you need results yesterday, right?"

She had him there. "More like the day before yesterday."

She looked at his feet, and he watched her gaze move up his legs to his midsection, his chest, do a quick left-right on his arms, focus on his shoulders, then linger on his face. Her eyes unsettled him; their round shape suggested innocence, but she observed and absorbed everything.

He wanted to shift under her gaze, to ask, "What?" to break the tension between them, but made himself wait. And Danny Linstead rarely waited.

She reached a hand toward his arm, but didn't touch him. "You can stop holding your breath."

He didn't realize he had been, and let it out in a rush.

"That's what will help you," she told him. "Belly breathing."

He repeated the term and she nodded. "Watch a baby sleeping." She patted her stomach. "They breathe deep into their bellies. Adults usually stress-breathe, shallow breaths in their chest that barely expand their lungs." He tried not to watch her fingers tapping at her breasts. "In its simplest form, belly breathing is just a shorter breath into your belly and a longer breath out. Doing that a few times in a row short circuits your fight or flight and lets relaxation take over. Here."

She scooted her chair closer so they sat side by side. "Imagine a balloon in your stomach and when you breathe in, try to fill the balloon. I'll do it with you."

She pressed one hand to her stomach and the other against his and he jolted up when her palm landed on his abs, his metal chair screeching against the concrete. When he came back to himself, her hand still pressed his shirt to his abdomen and she watched him, unblinking.

"That happens a lot," she said.

"What?" He knew what she meant, but he needed a moment.

"Sparks. When we touch."

His focus narrowed down to her wide eyes and warm palm, rising and falling in time with his breathing. The sparks had gone off and he expected the effect to dissipate, but it didn't.

"You caught me off guard," he told her. It was lust, he told himself. Simple lust for a beautiful woman, that's all.

"Not at the yoga class." She let out a quiet breath, then said, "Breathe in through your nose, until you feel the balloon fill up..." Her fingers pressed in to his belly for a moment before she removed her hand, gesturing for him to put his own hand there. "Might be hard, since it's so...very...flat. But hold the breath for two beats, then breathe out again while the balloon 'deflates.' A longer breath out than in. Hold that for two beats, then repeat it five or six times."

He did it a couple times, noticing his stomach rise and fall, then looked at Kristen. "When should I feel something?"

"You might want to try it a few times throughout the day. The response might be subtle at first. Once you get a feel for it, you won't have to put your hand on your stomach. You can do it any old place, kind of like kegels."

The waiter dropped off Danny's steak sandwich and Kristen's bagel and cup of soup; she turned her bright light on him and thanked him. Danny wasn't convinced the breathing thing would work. He felt more hyper than usual, and half sat up from his chair. Could he do a set of push ups here? Like she'd said, it was San Francisco, and Kristen herself had just done some yoga pose without anyone blinking over it.

Kristen broke off a piece of toasted bagel and ate it, closing her eyes as she chewed and let out a satisfied, "Mmm." She sighed, opened her eyes, and gave him a serene smile. "Now you know my secret."

"What's that?" he asked, settling back down, but shifting in his seat.

"Vegan cream cheese makes me ecstatic."

He stopped shifting. "Vegan."

"Cream cheese." She nodded. "Are you a meat eater?"

He lifted his sandwich. "Well, yeah."

"That's okay. Some of my favorite people are meat eaters."

She took another bite, and Danny watched her go through the same ritual, make the same noises. He had to stop himself from shoving the metal chair back and running down the block. Damn.

Kristen's ringing phone wrenched away an array of images of him bringing out that same pleasure response in her, no food necessary.

Kristen dug in her bag and pulled out a classic flip phone. She opened it and said, "Hi!" in a bright voice, but held it a few inches from her face.

"You said you were going to call me," a woman's voice barked from the speaker. It sounded familiar.

"But I'm fine."

"*I* didn't know that."

"Don't we have a psychic thing?" Kristen broke off another piece of bagel and popped a small piece in her mouth, as if some woman yelling at her on the phone happened every day. She smiled at Danny.

"We are sisters. Not twins. And you know I don't believe in the psychic thing."

"There's some solid research showing that psychic phenomena is—"

"*Kristen,*" the voice demanded. "You could have been in a ditch somewhere."

"You said the production was fine, nothing to worry about."

Danny looked up from his sandwich, no longer pretending not to listen.

"How's Daisy?" Kristen asked.

"Fine. Asleep. Luke is mooning over her."

"He'd moon even more over his own."

So this was the sister again, the one whose husband wanted a kid, but she wasn't sure. Damn. He already knew so much about Kristen and her life.

Danny heard the sister's sigh from across the table. "So you're okay?" she asked. "How did it go?"

"It was great fun. They filmed it, and now I'm having a lovely lunch at one of my favorite spots with a really handsome man."

Danny waved at the phone.

"Danny says hi."

"Oh my God, are you holding your phone away from your head like you always do so you won't get cancer, and so *everyone* can hear what I'm saying? Where are the ear buds I got you?"

"Daisy keeps hiding them."

"Well, handsome man," the voice demanded, "be good to my sister, or I'll kick your ass."

Kristen looked at Danny. "She means it."

He nodded. "I believe it."

Into the phone, Kristen said, "I'm fine. Danny is a perfect gentleman, and I'll be back by the time we agreed on. Long before Luke starts growing his own uterus so he can have a baby."

"*Kri—*"

"Love you, going into a tunnel!" She clicked the phone shut and dropped it in her bag. "My sister, Victoria," she explained to Danny.

"I gathered."

"She's older than me, and protective since our mom died, and thinks I can't take care of myself." She shook her head. "That's not true. She knows I can, but it's ingrained in her to make sure I'm okay."

"I'm sorry about your mother."

"Thanks. I was two, so I don't really remember her, but Victoria told me stories. She was seven, so she remembers much more. And I wouldn't change her caring about me for anything. I just have to give her a hard time about it every once in awhile." She took another bite of bagel, closing her eyes in ecstasy, and when they popped open again, she asked, "Are your parents alive? Any other siblings? Where do they all live?"

"My ma's alive, living in Florida, but…" He'd been about to tell her about his stepdad Vince and how his mom was moving in with his brother. Too much too soon. What was it about this woman? "It was just me and Denny growing up. He's in New York or LA or London. Not exactly sure right now. Maybe Florida."

Kristen leaned forward in her chair, palms flat on the table in front of her and her eyes wide. "There are so many exciting things about those five sentences I don't know where to start. Your mom's alive, but you didn't mention a father. And you called her 'ma.' Is that a Florida thing? And I forgot about the *twin* part. So do you two have the psychic thing, like I was teasing Victoria about? I do actually believe in that, but not for me and her. We are so, so very different. And *where* does your brother live? I mean, why don't you know—"

Danny half stood in his chair, holding up one hand. "Whoa, whoa. One thing at a time."

In fact, all of her questions slammed into him and reminded him that they'd just met the other day and really didn't know each other. And that he had no clue where Denny was right now because his own brother wasn't speaking to him. Her questions bumped up against that "comfortable" thing he'd experienced earlier, rotating in a whirlwind over him and in his head.

"Actually." He pulled his own phone out of his pocket and looked at it. "It's getting kind of late. I have to be back on the set for a night shoot. Can I walk you back to your car or something?"

"But—"

Danny set more than enough bills under his plate for the food and tip, and stood. "This has been great. Thanks for the relaxation breathing thing." He gestured around. "Your car, or…?"

Kristen stood, too, her bag hanging from one hand. "I took a bus, I'll take one back. But I don't understand. I thought we were getting along."

"Yeah, sweetheart, we were." He flinched at his own words; he'd used similar ones before, when breaking up with someone. Call them "sweetheart" and they're less inclined to kick you in the nuts as you walk them to the door. "I just need to get back. Sure you don't need a ride anywhere?"

She shook her head and he strode away, knowing he should kick *himself* in the nuts.

CHAPTER TWELVE

The next day at the Muni bus stop, Daisy scowled at everything, including her mother. She stood chin down, lower lip out and arms crossed. "No bus," she declared, glaring at the nearby rainbow-colored crosswalk. A tiny dictator in tie-dye tights and pink ballerina flats.

"Yes bus," Kristen replied. "And that's enough of your attitude. We're going to Aunt Teresa's to see her and Aunt Victoria. T is going to make some yummy food for us, like always."

Teresa wasn't a blood relative, but a sister to Kristen and Victoria nonetheless. Many of their gatherings focused on food. Teresa cooked at a homeless center, and she liked experimenting with different ingredients on a budget. She also considered it a personal challenge to create exceptional vegan meals for Kristen.

The bus pulled up and Kristen shifted her knapsack higher, then lifted Daisy to one hip. She greeted their driver, Manny, who looked disappointed at missing out on a sunny smile from Daisy.

"Sorry, Manny, she didn't even dance for our f-i-s-h today."

"It's a tough old world," he mock-sympathized as Daisy hid her face in Kristen's shoulder. "Don't worry, sweetie. We all bounce back, especially the little ones."

As Kristen got them settled, she wondered what happened to her cheerful baby, the one who usually goggled and smiled at their fellow passengers. Since her own mother had died when she was two, Kristen paid special attention to Daisy's responses to her world. She was curious how she herself had been as a toddler, and Daisy gave her a window into that.

Despite her insistence on "no bus," Daisy remained quiet during the ride, staring out the window at the wide variety of people and buildings they passed. At their Bernal Heights stop, Kristen settled Daisy on her hip for the two-block walk to Teresa's flat. As they headed down the hill to the converted Victorian, Daisy fussed and shimmied around, rubbing her face against Kristen's shoulder.

"No," she said.

"You don't have to eat," Kristen told her. "But you do need to be kind."

"No."

With great cheer, Kristen said, "I think that's my favorite word right now." She stopped at the pretty pale blue door of Teresa's ground floor studio.

"*No*."

"It is. I love it. I think I'll write a song about it." To the tune of "You Are My Sunshine," she sang the word 'no' over and over.

Daisy grumbled against Kristen's neck. Kristen had a key and knew she could pop right in, but with her hands full of child and baggage, knocking was easier than searching for her keychain.

Teresa opened the door into the small living/kitchen space, and Kristen embraced her warmly with her one free arm. Teresa wore red capris with a black and white-striped boatneck top, and had recently chopped her micro braids and opted for an afro. The short style accented her high cheekbones and tilted cat eyes.

"You look amazing," Kristen gushed.

At the exclamation, Daisy's head popped up and she beamed at Teresa. "T!" she squeaked, holding out her arms.

Teresa and Victoria had nicknamed each other "T" and "V" respectively, and Daisy had picked up the names, too.

"Hey, baby." Daisy leapt to Teresa and wrapped her arms around her neck, beaming at the room in general.

"Where were *you* hiding, Perfect Child?" Kristen asked her, then turned to hug her older, shorter sister. As usual, Victoria had dressed as if attending an event, but recently she'd moved away from her Corporate Woman in the City style. She'd kept all her three-inch-plus heels, but instead of trousers, now wore tailored gray jeans with a soft pink blouse.

In contrast, Kristen topped knee length tights and flat sandals with a flowing green dress. Growing up, she'd often wondered if one of them had been switched at birth, but they both had generous figures, similar facial features and thick wavy red hair. Kristen's was lighter and curlier than Victoria's. They both also had round blue eyes which Daisy had inherited.

Kristen hoped Daisy had inherited only the best from Michael, which meant...well, she couldn't think of anything at the moment. But Daisy had, of course, inherited *something*, and one day would want to know about her father. After Michael's betrayal, Kristen had expressed her anger by acting like Daisy was the result of some immaculate conception. But continuing in that vein was childish and helped no one.

"I want to tell everyone about her father," she announced.

"Well, that's one way to start the party," said Teresa. She handed Daisy off to Victoria so she could pull a quiche out of the oven. The tiny kitchen was tucked away in an alcove off the main living area, but the entire space was so small they could all still hear each other.

"You want to talk about that right now?" Victoria looked down at Daisy, who grinned at her and patted the collar of her shirt.

"I've been thinking about it for awhile, but I want to do it with all my family there. Both of you, of course." She pointed at Teresa. "Gabe." Then she gestured to Victoria. "Luke. Cort. Indica. It can be another good reason to get together and eat."

Teresa took out a smaller dish and set it on the stovetop. "We never need an excuse for that." Hands on hips, she glared at the dish. "I swear, soy cheese just isn't normal."

"You made a special quiche for me?"

"I want to put quotes around the word 'quiche' for this since it doesn't have eggs or cheese, but I've been experimenting. We try to offer healthy stuff at the shelter, but we have to use what's available. And honestly, people want comfort food. But I thought I'd give it a shot since you love it so much."

"And you love it now?"

"Oh, no. It's terrible." Teresa poked at the topping. "But I think this will taste good."

Kristen appreciated T speaking her mind; until a year or so ago, that had been hard for her. "If you made it, I know it will."

They beamed at each other.

Victoria set Daisy down near the dark wood coffee table with some paper and fat crayons. "Can we get back to the subject at hand?"

"Soy cheese?" Kristen asked.

"Mutual admiration society?" Teresa added.

Kristen added, "So what's the subject at hand? And, actually, what does that phrase mean anyway? A subject at hand. What does a hand have to do with a subject? I mean..." She stopped at the stern expression on her sister's face, the "you can't be serious" one. "You're so easy," she told Victoria. "Yes, I finally want to tell everyone. It's time. But I also want everyone there so I only have to do it once."

"Why now?"

"Keeping it a secret was wrong. I was so hurt by everything, I wanted to shove it all aside. I could have, except for..." She glanced at her daughter, who sat quietly rolling crayons back and forth on the wide plank flooring, then smiled at her sisters. "I'll go over everything when we all get together. And before you say anything, I shoved it aside because of Daisy, but if it hadn't been for her, I'd have immediately told everyone his name, and just how small his penis is."

Teresa let out a snort. "Was it small?"

A crease appeared between Victoria's eyebrows. Kristen knew she'd never quite gotten comfortable with "girl talk." Meaning, talking about boys. And their various-sized parts.

With a huff, Kristen said, "*No*." She settled on the comfortable blue sofa in the middle of the room. "It was kind of wide, actually. But it did have a gentle curve so it hit all the right places."

Now Teresa looked pained.

"*Anyway*," said Victoria.

"Anyway," Kristen continued. "Mr. Just Right Penis is also called Michael, and you'll hear the rest with the group." Since she met Danny she realized that "just right" was just that. Middle ground. Bland. Which meant there could be something better. And that was Danny, of course. She thought of his abrupt exit at the café. Well, that hadn't been so great.

Teresa pressed the tips of her fingers to her lips. "Will you be talking about his penis when the guys are in the room?"

Kristen shrugged. "If it comes up."

"Then the guys won't be in the room very long," Victoria said dryly.

Teresa snorted another laugh, and pulled plates from a narrow hutch. Victoria took them from her, and Kristen popped up to take a set of flatware from the drawer. She set a knife and fork down next to each plate on the coffee table.

"Just make sure this calling out party doesn't happen mid-April since Gabe and I are going to his friend's wedding in New York then."

"Noted. So how is your world?" Kristen asked her sister.

"I'm bored. The band is on hiatus until we head back to Nashville to record. Can you watch Frog then, by the way?" Frog was Luke and Victoria's cat. At Kristen's nod, Victoria continued. "Luke is writing songs and working at the bar." Luke and his best friend Cort owned a small sports bar called Blitz. "I need a project."

"You could always go along with Luke's idea and have a baby."

Victoria shrank away, a napkin clutched to her chest. "There's too much going on in our lives for that."

"You just said you were bored and needed a project."

"Short-term. Not an eighteen-year-plus project."

"Feel free to babysit your niece for a week or more. It might even cure some of Luke's baby lust."

"Nothing seems to do that." Victoria turned toward Teresa. "Hey, what about you and Gabe? Any talk in that department?"

"Oh, no you don't," Teresa said, setting one of the quiches on the table. "No distracting Luke's desires with someone else's baby."

Kristen asked, "Is it the baby part or the pregnant part?"

"A, B, and C," Victoria replied. "C being the 'giving birth' part."

"It's so amazing," said Kristen, rubbing at her belly.

"And should be physically impossible," Victoria retorted. "A woman's uterus is the size of a *pear*. Not of a small child. There's really got to be a better way."

Daisy trotted over with a piece of paper in her hand. "Mama!" she said, shoving the paper at Kristen. "I dwaw you! All!"

Kristen took the drawing and said, "That's beautiful, baby. You drew your family."

"Wuv!" Daisy shouted, throwing her hands in the air.

"Yes, love," Kristen agreed, her heart melting for the umpteenth time since Daisy blessed her life.

Teresa examined the picture. "Talented girl. She even got my brown tone just right."

She set more food in front of them. Teresa and Gabe's apartment was too small for a dining table, so the four of them clustered around the coffee table, serving themselves and oohing over each dish. Along with the quiche, Teresa had roasted asparagus and spread out mandarin slices.

"The pregnant part doesn't last forever," Kristen told Victoria. "And it's fascinating to experience." Kristen sat next to her daughter on the floor and hugged Daisy to her. "And the baby part is pretty special." She took a bite of vegan quiche. "You know, if it's just the pregnancy/childbirth you're afraid of—"

"I didn't say I was afraid."

"—I'd be your surrogate."

Teresa dropped her fork.

Victoria gripped the edges of the plate balanced on her lap. "You're serious."

"Of course I am. I'd never joke about something like that."

"Do *not* say that out loud in front of Luke."

"I can't make promises like that. If Luke brings it up, I'm not going to bite my tongue because it scares you."

"*I am not scared.* Subject change."

Teresa stage-whispered to Kristen, "She's gritting her teeth, mama. Better to change the subject. What's going on with this TV show you were talking about?"

"Did you actually have lunch with Danny Linstead yesterday?" Victoria added. "I looked him up. Did you know he—"

"No," Kristen interrupted. "And I don't want to know."

"—lost all of his own, his parents' and his brother's money in an investment scam?"

"That's terrible."

"It wasn't his fault. It was that investment broker guy, I can't remember his name. Lots of people lost their fortunes. His brother's kind of skeevy, but other than that..." Victoria sighed. "He seems like a decent guy."

"He is."

"For an actor."

"I've seen it in his eyes. He's a good person. And he's made me go zing again. And, remember, it's been *three years*. We literally create sparks when we touch. But he seems...reluctant."

Teresa settled back against the cushions, patting the one next to her for Daisy to snuggle under one arm. "You'd better start at the beginning."

Kristen walked them through the yoga class with Danny and Liz, then the filming and the awful producer. Victoria gnashed her teeth at that, but kept silent. Kristen didn't leave anything out, including the sparks, before moving onto the audition at the warehouse, but she wilted when she thought about her lunch with Danny yesterday.

"His mood changed." She snapped her fingers. "Just like that. No, actually, his attitude changed."

"So what happened right before his attitude changed?"

Kristen ticked things off on her fingers. "Victoria called to make sure I hadn't been murdered by the TV people and dropped in the bay. He heard the entire conversation because I held the phone away from my ear so I won't get brain cancer."

"You *always* do that," Victoria muttered. "I'm getting you another set of ear buds."

"Daisy will just turn them into an art project, but thanks. I taught him how to do belly breathing. He's a little impatient, but I can work with that. I told him about Mom dying when I was two, and how you were—and are—my protective big sister."

"Well, that's true." Victoria nudged the plate of mandarin slices toward Kristen.

"Then I asked him if his parents were alive and did he have any other siblings besides his twin, and he told me all of these fascinating things that just made me want to know more, so I asked him a bunch of questions about his life, and then he got weird and—what?"

Kristen caught Victoria and Teresa giving each other a look. "What?" she repeated.

"You asked him a bunch of questions," Victoria said simply.

"But I was curious. And we'd been telling each other all sorts of things, and he'd already seen how I am and didn't run away then."

"If it's too many questions at once, maybe it was overwhelming and scared him."

Kristen *hmphed*. "*Your* men haven't been scared."

Victoria and Teresa both laughed. Daisy laughed, too, as if she were in on the secret, then mashed her fingers in a piece of quiche. Kristen boosted herself up on the couch and squashed herself between the two women to clean Daisy's hands before her daughter spread the food all over Teresa's outfit and furniture. She leaned against the cushions, holding the dirty napkin in both hands.

Victoria said, "They got scared plenty. They just hid it. Or tried to. But we knew each other better at that point. You've only met this man—"

"Danny."

"You've only met Danny three times. And like I said, he lost his money in an investment scam. He's filming a pilot, and that's incredibly stressful in itself. He's probably focused on all those things right now, and not on a relationship."

"You may think he's meant to be your man," Teresa added, "but it still takes awhile to learn people's cues, and what sets them off."

Kristen nodded, thinking that through with what she knew about Danny and their interactions so far. "You're right, you're right. We obviously need to spend more time together."

"Maybe don't ask so many questions at once," Victoria said. "And maybe…try just being friends with him first."

Kristen wrapped an arm around her sister's shoulders. "It's like you don't know me at all."

CHAPTER THIRTEEN

On a mission, Danny strode up the alley off of Harrison Street. He usually loved all the movement around him on a set, but today he barely saw the crew rolling dumpsters away from the camera lines, erecting light poles, and measuring the alley from side to side. He fist bumped Glen, who called out that he needed to talk to Danny when he had a second. Danny responded that he'd be in touch later, but continued past the graffiti-lined walls in his search for Kristen.

He had a big apology to make to her, and he needed to do it in person. Soon.

The L-shaped alley would represent the side exit Kristen and Danny escape through, but was actually across the city from Club Nuance. They were working double time to film the additions Jenkins had demanded, including Danny and Kristen running from the thugs, and a series of shots of Kristen looking over her shoulder before walking away.

Keesha had told him Kristen's character disappears after an explosion and Danny's character thinks he sees her everywhere.

"She dies?" he'd asked her.

Keesha shrugged. "They're leaving it open. If it works out, she could be a returning character. If not, then it's recurring drama for Seth."

What went unsaid was that all of this depended on Jenkins's whim. And it was all the more reason for Danny to find Kristen and apologize to her as soon as possible. He tried not to think about that conversation he'd overhead between Liz and Jenkins, but it kept creeping back on him. Not only could Kristen be gone tomorrow, but so could he.

At least today's shots didn't require much dialogue. It was only the short exchange from Kristen's audition the other day. The rest was action and reaction shots. He could handle those.

Still, he flinched when Samantha Jamison-Gallagher showed up just as he reached the alley entrance. *Not today*, he pleaded to himself. He stepped aside and gestured her ahead, but she stopped in front of him.

"No script changes today," she said with a grin. "I just wanted to let you know about a wardrobe update. Olivia's on her way."

Over Samantha's head, he caught a glimpse of wavy red hair, and his mind skittered to a halt. What had Samantha just said? "Great." He forced himself to look her in the eye. "That's great. Fine. Thanks."

Samantha patted his arm and moved on. Danny stood at the corner looking up the alley, mesmerized at Kristen chatting with Liz.

She wore jeans that made him want to run his hands over her hips, and her red hair curled around her shoulders and down the back of her yellow top. Even in her usual platform shoes, Liz had to crane her neck to look into Kristen's eyes. Danny imagined himself standing there instead of Liz, their heights matched, holding Kristen's gaze to see the gray flecks in the blue, her pupils dilated in response to the heat between them.

Kristen said something now to make Liz double over with laughter. They giggled together, hands clasped, and Liz gestured Kristen up the alley and around the corner. Then the production designer caught Liz's attention, and Kristen turned away from them both, still smiling.

When her eyes locked with Danny's, her smile broadened. His stomach flipped, and he had to remind himself he needed to apologize to this woman and not just stand there gaping at her. He was planning his speech, deciding the right thing to say, when Olivia stepped in front of him, layers of clothing draped over one shoulder and in her arms.

"Wardrobe change today, handsome. They don't want you in a suit for the ghost segments after all."

She flipped her hair back from her face in a long hard sheet and held up first a dark blue shirt and then a green one, tilting her head back and forth at each.

"They couldn't decide," she said with a sigh. "Rashika thinks the blue will be better, go with the mood of each segment." She slung the green one over her shoulder and held the blue close to his face. "I heard you had to go to yoga, of all things. How was *that*?"

"It was all right, actually." He glanced over her shoulder and saw that Kristen hadn't slowed her forward trajectory. It had been more than all right, but he couldn't quite put it in words yet, and he didn't know Olivia well enough to try. "I met some cool people."

"At *yoga*?" When he didn't respond, she went on. "Anyway, you should know that Glen and I—"

Kristen reached them, and Danny took a step back from Olivia.

"Hello," Kristen said cheerfully. "I'm so happy to see you again," she said to Danny, before turning to Olivia. "I'm Kristen. Dancer and escape artist. You have the most amazing skin. I'm envious."

She held out her hand, and Danny watched as Olivia gave it a brief shake with just the tips of her fingers before pulling it away to hold the bundle of clothing tighter to her front. "Olivia Chester," she said flatly. "Costume design." She seemed to realize her response and loosened her hold, shaking the clothes out and draping them smoothly over one arm again. "Pleasure."

"What a cool job. Once you're done," Kristen said to Olivia, "I'd like to steal Danny away. We have a few things to discuss," she added with a smile at him.

He couldn't help but smile back. Kristen's bright personality and presence dimmed everything else around her. Even though Kristen was treating him as if he hadn't peed all over the end of their lunch the other day, he itched to apologize. No, he hadn't recovered from all of her questions, and yeah, he realized they barely knew each other, but when she stood in front of him—hell, when he just thought about her—she tugged him in so hard, he could barely breathe.

But he didn't need to breathe when she was around, when she looked at him the way she did now, completely open, lovely, and welcoming.

Her lips parted, and her eyes crinkled as she smiled at him. "Are you about to cross yourself and say 'Holy Mary Mother of God' again? You have that same look on your face."

He shook his head, grinning like an idiot. He didn't know why he'd done that when he caught her dancing for the camera in the warehouse; it had been automatic. Her sinuous swaying had been both sinful and prayerful and he'd actually been respecting her at the time, as well as expressing his surprise. And man, had he been surprised.

A rough throat-clearing caught his attention and he broke his gaze from Kristen's sweet face to see Olivia scowling at him. "Be in wardrobe in ten." She lifted her chin at Kristen. "He's all yours," she said, and stalked away.

"Thank you," Kristen called cheerfully after her. Then she turned back to Danny. "Is that true? Do I have you for the next ten minutes?"

He nodded. "I owe you at least a ten minute apology for being such an ass yesterday."

She studied him, neither confirming nor denying. "Is there somewhere private we could go?"

"Not much privacy on a set," he told her. "And I'm sharing a trailer with two other people today since there's not enough room on the street for all our vehicles."

"Then how do all of those affairs happen between celebrities?"

What was she asking for here? "It's kind of 'don't ask, don't tell,' and 'what happens on the set stays on the set.'"

At that, a small vertical line appeared between her brows. Before he could even think about it, he pressed his thumb to it, then smoothed it up and over her forehead, his fingers lingering at her temple.

"I don't like secrets," she said.

Well, hell. "I don't, either, but everyone has them."

Two carpenters shuffled past, carrying a long board up the alley, a reminder that he and Kristen stood among a bustling television crew.

He lowered his hand from her face. "C'mon, I have an idea."

Danny led Kristen down the street to a supply trailer. One of the prop guys stood in front of it, frowning at a clipboard. "Hey, Jon," Danny called to him. "Okay if we use this space for a minute?" He gestured around them. "No other room to talk."

Jon shrugged. "Sure. Just for a few, though. We're on double time these days."

"Yeah, I hear you. Thanks."

Danny bounded up the steps and flapped the door back and forth. "Is this all right?" he asked Kristen.

"I'm the one who asked if there was somewhere private we could go."

"And I'm the one who acted like an ass the other day."

"You did." She was no longer smiling as she closed the door behind them.

Okay, small punch to the gut, he thought. *And deserved.* "I'm sorry about that," he told her. "I'd like to explain."

"There's something I'd like to explain first," she told him.

"You don't owe me anything."

"No, I don't. But I do want to tell you a couple of things. You already know about my daughter. What you don't know is that her father was an ass. Is an ass. I assume he still is one. Leopards don't change their spots that easily." She huffed and put her hands to her hips. "I shouldn't put leopards in the same category as that...that..."

"Jerk? Asshole? N'er-do-well. Loser. Oaf. Imbecile." He'd just called himself an ass. His thoughts switched from "on-set affair" to "massive smackdown" at this point. And he'd take it.

"All of those," she said with venom, a tone he hadn't heard in her voice before.

But he wanted to. Even while she ranted about leopards and assholes, and he braced for the smack-down, he wanted to be there. He didn't know what to do with this new revelation, but some of the tension in his body lessened in response to it.

She covered her stomach with the flat of one hand, took a deep breath, held it, then let it out again in a loud "whoosh." She repeated the process one more time, then said, "Belly breathing," and he remembered he hadn't tried it since she'd shown him the process the other day. "Anyway, Daisy's father was married, although I didn't know it then, a big-time developer. He told me he worked for Habitat for Humanity. He found out I was pregnant, I found out he was married, and I haven't seen him since before Daisy was born. Seen, heard from, nothing."

She moved a box of spray paint and slumped on a stool. He had no idea why she was telling him all this, but he wanted her to keep talking.

"I let him get to me more than anyone else who's lied to me or broken up with me. Probably because of Daisy. Maybe because I felt so vulnerable at that point. I don't know. Either way, it hurt, and I wasn't even in love with him. I don't ever want to go through that again, even though I know it's possible. But now I have Daisy, and I have to make good decisions for both of us."

"And you think I'm a bad decision." He didn't pose it as a question. She might not be saying it outright, but he got her point.

No idiot leopards who ran away and left without an explanation. No Danny. That was better, considering how his life was going these days. Right?

When she spoke, her voice came out gentle, but firm, and she looked him right in the eye. "You're a great decision."

"Then why all the leopards and assholes talk?"

"Because friends share things like that with each other, and I want us to be friends."

"Friends."

"Yes." She took another deep breath, her chest expanding. "Although, with you looking like that..." She shook her head. "You're a very handsome man."

"And you're a very direct woman." Even so, he wasn't sure how to feel right now. She was telling him what he thought he wanted to hear—friends, no entanglements—but his body said otherwise. Friendship was a side hit to the knee.

"I think it's healthier to express yourself than hold things back. So. Friends?"

"Yeah." He took her hand, but didn't shake, just stroked his thumb along the soft flesh of her palm. "Sure."

"Oh, boy. The universe really did send me a challenge," she said, squeezing his fingers.

"You said that before." He'd barely heard it this time; an electric current had just run up his arm. "At yoga," he added, shaking his head to clear it. "What challenge?"

"You."

"How is it me?"

"I've never been just friends with someone I'm insanely attracted to." She stepped closer to him, still holding his hand tight.

"And just friends is better because...?"

"Because of the leopard. And my daughter. And you scare me."

And she scared the hell out of him, but he was more concerned about her feelings at that moment. "I don't want that. That's never an option."

"It's actually a good thing. I'll explain someday."

"Okay."

They'd continued to move toward each other until they now stood a breath apart, eyes locked. All the air left the space again and he could think of nothing but pressing his lips to hers and breathing her in.

CHAPTER FOURTEEN

Kristen gasped, forcing herself to take a step back, and let go of Danny's hand. What had she been thinking? Friends? She couldn't be *just friends* with this man. He electrified everything in her body.

He seemed to regain some composure when she moved away, drawing in a deep breath. "You were right."

"I was?"

He nodded. "Friends is a good idea. Yeah." He ran a hand through his hair, half-turned from her. "I'd like to be friends. With you." He looked like he might charge through the door like a cartoon character. "Yeah. Friends."

"Damn. I was hoping to get some sex."

"Uh." He bumped into the stool and grabbed it to keep it from toppling.

"Are you okay?"

He righted the stool and straightened. "Yeah. Listen—"

Someone banged on the door, startling them and they both turned to look at it.

"I gotta finish my work, Linstead. I need the trailer back."

"Yeah, man, just give me a sec," Danny called back. He turned to Kristen. "I like you. And I haven't met a lot of people here yet. It would be nice to have another friend."

She laughed. "The universe has *such* a sense of humor. So, my friend, can I have your number so I can call you some time?"

He dug into his back pocket, swiped a few times on the phone screen, then held it out to her. "Type yours in. If you give me your phone, I'll give you my number."

She dug into her bag and pulled out her trusty flip, handing it to him before she took his. She carefully typed in her name and number, saved it, and held the phone back out to him. He still stood staring down at hers, the case unopened.

"What's wrong?"

"I keep forgetting you have a flip phone. I don't know how to use this."

She switched his phone for hers, brought up her address book, and typed in his number while he recited it to her.

"C'mon, Linstead," said Jon from the other side of the door. "My stepmother just fakes it to get my old man to finish. I got—"

Danny flung the door open and grabbed Jon by the shoulder, jerking him toward the open door. "Apologize," he demanded.

Kristen stood in the doorway, amazed at how quickly Danny had moved, and at his anger toward the other man. "You're holding him a little too tight for him to talk," she said. She taught her daughter that you could go through the world without violence, but something about Danny's immediate reaction to defend her sent bubbles of primitive satisfaction down her spine.

Danny loosened his grip enough for Jon to rasp out, "Sorry, lady—"

"Kristen," Danny told him. "Her name is Kristen."

"Sorry, Kristen."

"That was uncalled for," Danny said, and Jon repeated the words to Kristen.

"I'm sorry," he said again.

Danny let him go.

Jon straightened his shirt and glared at Danny, although Kristen could see that even before Danny grabbed him, there hadn't been much fight in him. "I really do gotta finish my work."

"Yeah." Danny held his hand out and helped Kristen down the steps.

"Tell your stepmother a vibrator works just as well." Kristen beamed at him. "Thank you for letting us use the space."

Jon gawped at them as Danny set a hand on her lower back and led her back to the alley, moving swiftly down the sidewalk.

"Where did you learn to react like that? To grab someone like that?"

"Grew up on a set, but Denny and I had to fight for ourselves most of the time," he said. "My dad left when we were nine, and Ma was in her own world."

She stopped and he strode ahead a few stops before turning to look back at her.

"I'm sorry," she said. "About your parents."

He shrugged. "We managed. And sometimes we had to deal with assholes like that."

"And sometimes you had to defend women from them?"

He looked at her for so long she wanted to interrupt and ask what was going through his mind.

"Yeah," he finally answered. "This is a great business, with awesome people. But it's not perfect." He ran a hand through his hair. "C'mon, let's get you back to the set."

CHAPTER FIFTEEN

Over and over, Danny stepped out of the doorway into the graffiti-covered alley and asked, "Which way?" as Kristen took his hand.

And over and over, Gary called "Cut!"

Danny could sense the crew's frustration building, but everyone kept it together. Not only did they have to cram these extra scenes into an already tight schedule, but they were filming this one "day for night." The moment Danny and Kristen's characters leave the club takes place late at night, and it was possible to film during the day for that, but it took special camera filters and the right outdoor lighting to make it look like one a.m.

Everyone waited for the clouds to drift back over the sun; filming in direct sunlight created harsh shadows, ruining the night look. Kristen's words from their talk in the trailer ran through Danny's mind again.

"I've never been just friends with someone I'm insanely attracted to."

He agreed with her wholeheartedly. They'd shook on it, and he respected that. He'd also made an agreement with himself to protect her from Jenkins. He didn't want to be *just friends* with her, so why had he agreed to it? He'd put himself in a hell of a position.

Finally the DP gave the all clear and the crew went through the protocol.

"Rolling..."

"Scene 4A, take eight." The slate clicked.

"Settling…and set."

And finally, from Gary: "Action."

"Which way?" Danny asked.

Kristen took his hand in hers. "Over here."

Together, they ran up and around the corner of the L-shaped alley. Gary called, "Cut! Print that!" and they practically skidded to a stop.

From the far end of the alley, Jenkins emerged from a limo blocking the opening. While he adjusted his jacket, caressing the lapels, Nicole slid out in a tiny skirt and stilettos. Jenkins grabbed her by the waist to pull her close and she teetered on her heels as she bumped into his side.

Kristen's fingers tightened on Danny's.

"What is she doing?" she whispered.

"Hopefully not making a big mistake," Danny responded.

Jenkins called out, "My two favorite dancers are here."

I guess his money-maker is out of favor, Danny thought. He felt no satisfaction in the idea of less interest from Jenkins.

As he and Nicole got closer, Jenkins waved his chubby, be-ringed fingers at Kristen. "Come join us, sweetheart."

"No, thank you," she said politely. She stepped closer to Danny. "Nicole's my friend, and I don't interfere in friends' relationships."

"And you're my dancer and I want my dancers at my side."

Nicole's face turned sour. Kristen's body had gone rigid next to Danny.

"Thanks," she repeated. "But we have work to do. On your orders, I think?"

"Hey, what's going on, people?" Keesha called from behind them. "We've got a new setup to do. Wardrobe changes, and—oh." She came around the corner and saw Jenkins. "Mr. Jenkins." She gave a short nod. "Nicole. Nice to see you, would you like to come watch the filming?"

She'd directed her question to Nicole—Danny assumed to get her away—but Jenkins responded. "That's why we're here, sweetheart. Don't you need to be getting on it if we want to keep on budget?"

Keesha cut her eyes to Danny and Kristen and said to them, "Wardrobe's waiting." Then she turned her back on Jenkins and said into her walkie, "Hey, PA Nation, we're rocking and rolling."

Danny knew that was the crew's new code for "Producer Jenkins is on set," and that "PA Nation" meant for the production assistants to spread the word.

Keesha stalked around the corner and Danny tugged at Kristen's hand. "We should get going."

"But Nicole—"

"Knows what she's doing," Danny said in a lower voice, although he wasn't so sure. He wanted to help, too, but he was at a loss.

Jenkins stood glaring at Danny and Kristen, his face red, while Nicole smoothed her hand down his sleeve and whispered something soothing at him. They'd defied him, and men like Jenkins hated that. Danny wondered what the repercussions might be.

Still holding Kristen's hand, Danny led her around the corner and through the crew. They all looked more tense than ever as they moved everything to the next location, out of the alley and into the street. No one joked or laughed, there was barely even any talking.

Glen stood at one corner of the wardrobe trailer next to Olivia, who perched on the bottom step.

"You hear?" Danny asked, trying to sound casual.

They both nodded.

"I can stay," he said.

"I got it," Glen told him. "Last time he was here, we put some protocols in place."

Olivia tilted her head to the next-door trailer, hair and makeup. "We're trying to get this next one done ASAP, so they'd rather have you over there now."

Danny hesitated, looking at Kristen.

"You're sweet," she said. "But I bet Olivia can kick some pretty good ass. And I can take care of myself."

"I believe you." Reluctant to leave, he bent his head as if to kiss her, and her eyes went wide.

"I wish," she said, and slipped away from him and past Olivia up the steps.

I've never been just friends with someone I'm insanely attracted to.

\# \# \#

WHILE KRISTEN ENJOYED MUCH of the filmmaking process, it was also repetitive and a little dull. And at least on this set, the machinations everyone had to go through because of Jenkins were appalling. She wished she could talk to Nicole.

While Olivia helped her out of her dance outfit and into bootcut jeans and a filmy purple top, Kristen asked, "Is Jenkins really that bad?" Despite what she'd seen, she hoped he was all talk.

Olivia slipped a black ankle boot on Kristen's foot. "I shouldn't talk about it," she said. "But yes." She yanked down on the pants legs. "Just don't make him mad."

"My friend Nicole—"

"I know." Olivia crossed her arms. "She made her choice."

"That doesn't make it okay."

Olivia huffed out a breath. "It's like…think of it like dealing with an addict. Only it's addiction to power. She has to be the one to make the choice. You can try to talk to her. But she has to make the decision to leave."

"I don't like it." And she didn't like feeling so helpless.

Olivia's eyes softened for a moment. "None of us do." She turned business-like. "You're ready to go."

"I'm not really the skinny jeans type." Kristen peered over her shoulder to look at her butt in Olivia's full length mirror. "Too enhanced in the girl parts department. And no more flat belly after giving birth." She straightened. "Not looking for compliments."

"Not giving them." Olivia moved a roll of fabric, her expression stern, but her voice not unkind. "But I still wouldn't leave any woman open to that asshole. Even one who…" She shoved the roll of fabric onto a shelf.

"One who's completely disrupted everyone's work on this show? I'm sorry about that." When Olivia didn't respond right away, Kristen said, "Or maybe one you're not so thrilled with in general?"

"No. Not that." Olivia crossed her arms over her chest and stared out the window. "One who flirts with the crew members even though she has a perfectly great guy lusting after her."

This pronouncement stunned Kristen. "I hope the lusting guy is Danny. He's the only one I've flirted with."

"Also Glen."

"Which one is Glen?"

"The boom operator, Danny's roommate? One of the few guys

who makes a man bun look sexy?" She waved a hand at the window. "The one waiting outside to make sure we're not harassed."

It all clicked into place; the moment had been such a small blip, she'd barely registered it. "Oh, *that's* Glen. He seems like a natural flirt, and so am I. He said something complimentary the other day, and I started to respond, but I wasn't feeling it. I haven't been since..."

"Danny?"

Kristen nodded. "I'm really sorry. I don't mess with men if someone is already interested in them. Is it that obvious?"

Olivia snorted. "You're both gaga. But thanks. Anyway, you should get going. Glen will walk you to the makeup trailer. He'll probably have to be on the set soon, but Danny will be ready by then."

"I'm not too thrilled my daughter's growing up in a world where these kinds of protective gyrations have to happen all because of one predator. The universe needs some balance here."

"Did you grow up in some sheltered backwoods with no men around? Every woman I know has had to deal with this kind of shit in one form or another throughout their lives." She snipped a thread from Kristen's sleeve. "You didn't hear this from me, either, but...let's just say some things are getting put into place to take care of said man." She waved a hand when Kristen opened her mouth to ask a bunch of questions. "You didn't hear that."

Kristen paused. She wanted to know more, but not if it caused trouble for anyone on the set. She already felt guilty about the crew's extra work. She nodded and Olivia and Glen ushered her over to makeup.

Awhile later, Kristen ran down the blocked-off street, followed by a cameraman and a guy rolling a fan on a cart. They had spent at least twenty minutes adjusting the fan settings so her hair would billow around without getting too much in her face. There had also been a long discussion about whether to get a smoke machine for a more ethereal effect, but when Keesha reminded them they were losing daylight, Gary declared they would "deal with it in post," whatever that meant. There were a few grumbles at this, but everyone continued the setup. Under Gary's direction, Kristen ran in a variety of ways—slow, fast, skipping, side-to-side—and quite a few times she looked over her shoulder. Smiling, wistful, teasing. She assumed she got the expressions right, since every time she reached the line of tape at the end of the street, Gary said, "Great, come back and do it again. Keep rolling. Back to one, everyone."

One of the things that made it fun and easy for her was that Danny stood behind her so she could see him when she turned. She certainly *felt* happy, wistful, and teasing when she saw him, especially since she noticed those emotions mirrored on his face.

The last time she jogged back to the starting point—another line of tape near where Danny stood—everything stuttered to a stop when Jenkins called out, "I want a kiss."

From his side, Nicole said, "Well, if that's all you need."

"Nicole." Kristen started to walk toward her, wanting to rescue her friend from this mess, despite how much she realized the truth of Olivia's words. Nicole had to be the one to make the decision to leave. Danny stepped in front of Kristen with a shake of the head.

"You can't win this one," he whispered.

"But—"

"Please trust me on this."

Jenkins bellowed out, "Those two! There should be a kiss. You should take advantage of that chemistry, Mr. Fancy Director."

Danny's eyes went flat and Kristen saw him clench a fist, his back still to the producer. He swiveled in Jenkins's direction, and Kristen grabbed his clenched hand with both of hers.

"My turn to say 'please,'" she said. "It's not worth it."

"Are you okay with a filmed kiss?"

His fist shook and she gave him what she hoped was a reassuring smile. "With you? It's about time someone suggested it."

Danny turned to Gary, who seemed to be trying to convince Jenkins a kiss wasn't necessary.

"She's not a professional actress," Gary said.

"She's doing all right," Jenkins insisted.

Gary straightened all of his five-foot-seven height. "We're running out of light, Mr. Jenkins. You're going to have to leave my set if you're going to keep interfering."

"You forget it's actually *my* set, Twinkletoes."

"It's okay, Gary," Danny called out. "She's okay with—"

Kristen stepped in front of him to look directly at Jenkins. She held the producer's eye before turning her gaze to Gary. "I'm not a professional actress, but I do know how to kiss. I'm fine with doing this."

Gary nodded at her, and Keesha said, "Okay, everyone, let's do a setup here in the street."

Everyone mobilized, and Kristen whirled on Danny. "I am very capable of speaking for myself," she said in an even tone. "Don't make me regret agreeing to kissing you."

And she didn't regret it.

Well, she did at first, because it wasn't about kissing, but about all of the technical aspects. She stood in the blocked off street with Danny, Gary, Samantha, Hans, Glen, and Keesha while Gary walked them through the process without them ever touching. Hands here, head tilted that way—but not quite that far—this foot ahead of the other, don't open your mouth too much.

When Gary broke away to discuss lighting with Hans and Glen, Danny said to her, "I've done this before. I can be as neutral as you need. Whatever you're most comfortable with."

"I need a 'big, fat, romantic, passionate, grab each other by the ass, get lost in it' kiss, is what I need," Kristen told him.

Sudden silence around them. Kristen winked at Gary. "But I didn't think that's what you were going for."

He smiled at her. "Not in this scene anyway."

Finally they got to rehearse it, and Kristen expected a jolt the first time their lips touched, but instead she melted into him with a sigh. He was warm, soft, and firm all at the same time. He grabbed her hips to keep her from falling into him and she murmured, "Yes, please," against his mouth. She forgot all her instruction and wound her hands around his neck, his hair silky-smooth against her fingers. A noise of desire bubbled out of her, and she stepped closer, hooking one heel around his ankle.

His hands tightened on her hip bones and his lips parted. She had just flicked her tongue against his when—

"Yes, that!" Gary cried with joy. "Do that when we film."

Reality crashed back in and Kristen bumped into Danny, dizzy with lust. They fell into each other, laughing in surprise and shared desire. The laughter stopped abruptly as they caught each other's eyes. Kristen couldn't look away, her belief they should be just friends shifting so firmly to affirmation of him as a desired lover, she knew she'd never be the same again.

CHAPTER SIXTEEN

Kristen spent the next few days busy with Daisy, yoga classes, and trying not to act like a teenager and check her phone every five minutes. She didn't do so well with the latter. Actually, she was able to set her phone away and concentrate on her students and classes, but outside of them, if she was shopping at the farmers' market, cooking dinner, helping Indica and Star with their handmade bath items, anything that didn't take her full concentration, she was thinking of Danny. And if her phone rang, she jumped as if she'd been prodded with a hot poker, her heart beating double time until she saw the caller's name on the screen. Whether it was Victoria, Teresa, Gail, or Unknown Caller, it might as well have flashed in neon: NOT DANNY.

She knew she'd freaked him out with her questions, and thrown him off with her suggestion to just be friends. And then that kiss! That heavenly, skyrocketing, life-changing kiss. When Victoria had asked if she'd ever been just friends with a man she found attractive, it was like a lightbulb had lit up over her head. It was the perfect solution. Except that she wanted much more with him.

So what to do about it all?

After her Thursday afternoon yoga class, she and Daisy trooped the few blocks to the Victorian. Daisy insisted on walking most of the way, which was fine with Kristen's tired arms, especially considering she also carried a pack of child supplies and a mesh bag from the corner grocery with that night's dinner. Daisy would charge

89

ahead, little legs churning, then dash to the right to pet a dog someone was walking, or to the left, close to tumbling off the sidewalk and into traffic. Kristen fully understood leashes for children.

After the fifth—or one hundredth—time commanding, "Stop!" she switched her grocery bag to the other hand and swept her arm around Daisy to pick her up.

"No!" Daisy yelled. "Down! Down, Mama. Down, down, down!"

Kristen hoisted her ungracefully to one hip, but Daisy shifted and wriggled, straightening her arms and pushing with both palms against Kristen's chest. "Me walk, Mama. Walk."

"Walking is great." Kristen tilted her head away from Daisy's pushing hands. "But listening is better. And you didn't listen to me when I said not to run into the street."

Their duplex was now one house away, and Kristen saw Indica step out to check the mail, Kim and August's toy Yorkies dancing around her feet. With their landlords away, Hamilton and Peggy were temporarily part of the family.

"Uppies!" Daisy cried.

Indica turned at Daisy's call, immediately going to her knees and setting down the mail before holding her arms out for Daisy. The dogs yipped and twirled as if performing for treats.

"Would you like to say hello to Aunt Indica and the puppies?" Kristen asked.

Daisy clapped her hands. "Yes!"

"Okay. You can run to her, but only to her, okay?"

Daisy nodded, returned now to a model child.

Kristen slipped her down the side of her body until her tiny feet touched the ground. As soon as they did, Daisy shot off in her side-to-side way, shouting, "In-ca! In-ca!" which was the closest she could come to saying "Indica."

Whenever Kristen tried to correct Daisy, Indica hushed her and said she loved it. "It's her special word for me."

Kristen stopped on the sidewalk a few feet away, throat tight. She had the best family. Friends, team, tribe, village, whatever words you wanted to use for them, they were her family, and she couldn't get through this world without them.

Indica swooped Daisy up and stood, then twirled in a big circle, both of them shouting with joy.

Kristen nodded to herself. How could she have gone this long without asking for her family's help with the Danny situation?

"Time to call in the tribe," she said to herself. "And have some food."

She walked up to Indica, who now held Daisy against her chest, letting the girl slide backward so she could look at Kristen upside down, her hair hanging in wild curls, giggling madly. Then she'd lift herself up and fling her arms around Indica's neck before going through the whole routine again.

"I wish I was that flexible," Indica said, looking at the curve in Daisy's back.

"Be two again," Kristen said with a smile. She scooped up the mail and held the front entry door open. "Or do lots and lots of yoga."

Indica herded the dogs ahead of her, then stepped inside the tiny foyer created from the house's original front room. Kim and August's door was to the right, and their own door was straight ahead at the top of a set of stairs. A small half corkboard, half chalkboard for notes let them know if someone had stopped by, or signed for a package for the other. The small space currently stored construction supplies for the insulation work being done while the landlords were out of town.

Kristen led the way up the stairs. "I need to call the girls over."

"Which girls?" Indica asked.

"Gail, Star, Teresa, Victoria." She caught Indica's surprised expression. "I know. Gail and Victoria in the same room. Remember when they each said they thought the other was kind of bossy and I said that made sense since they're so much alike?"

With a grin Indica said, "And they both said 'No, we're not' at the same time."

They laughed at that, and Kristen added, "They're both practical, and I need a double dose of that right now." She walked through the open door, then closed it once Indica and the dogs had stepped inside.

"So what am I, if I'm not practical?" Indica covered Daisy's eyes in a variation of peek-a-boo they'd invented. Daisy giggled, then tried to cover Indica's eyes, but pressed a palm to her mouth instead.

Kristen set the mail on their small side table, and slid her knapsack to the floor. Heading to the kitchen, she said, "Well, Star and I are dreamers, and you and Teresa are somewhere between dreamers and practical."

Indica switched her hand from Daisy's eyes to her mouth, and Daisy moved hers to one of Indica's ears. Following Kristen into the kitchen, she said, "Can we come up with a better word than practical? That's so..."

"Dull?"

"Kinda."

"You're anything but dull. But you do have a reasonable side."

"Reasonable," Indica repeated, as if it left a bad taste in her mouth.

Kristen pulled items out of her bag and set some aside for that night's dinner while putting others in the cupboards and refrigerator. "Do you have a preference?"

"Exotic. Charming. Endearing. Quirky."

Kristen smiled at her. "Good words, and all you. None of them are synonyms for 'practical.'"

Indica pointed at her. "Exactly." She made a raspberry on Daisy's cheek, eliciting a giggle and Daisy's thrilled little voice saying, "No, no, no."

"No?" Indica asked, pulling away. "No more raspberry kisses?" She shrugged. "Okay. No more raspberry kisses." She turned back to Kristen. "Looks like you're making dinner."

"Mac-and-cheese. I need comfort food." She considered Daisy, now bobbing in Indica's arms and insisting she *did* want raspberry kisses. "She needs a bath," she said.

"I can do it." Indica twirled around the room with Daisy, humming Ed Sheeran's "Galway Girl."

"It's not your job."

"I like to help. I wish you'd let me help more."

"You take care of us in so many ways," Kristen said, knowing that Indica meant money more than parental tasks. "You keep the kitchen stocked with vegan staples; you let me waitress at your café even though I'm terrible at it; you and Nella watch Daisy when I'm busy. And I know some of those gorgeous clothes you bring home for Daisy don't come from the thrift store. Or the ones for me, for that matter."

Indica pressed her face in Daisy's hair. "Some of them are." She leaned toward Kristen and bumped her shoulder. "I have all of this money thanks to my brilliant mama. You have a child, and they're expensive."

Kristen snorted. "In gummy worms alone. But this is my way of letting you know that I know about it, and I'm grateful."

"So why don't you let me give you some—"

Kristen clapped a hand over Indica's mouth and Daisy put a hand on Kristen's. "Don't finish that sentence," she said around Daisy's fingers. "I don't know why I won't let you give me some money. It doesn't feel right. If something comes up where I need a kidney or something, we'll talk. But let's just...let it go otherwise."

Indica nodded, and Kristen lowered her hand. "Thank you."

"I'd give you my kidney, too, you know," Indica told her.

"I know." This time Kristen bumped her shoulder. "I already think what you do is wonderful." She kissed Indica's cheek, and then her daughter's.

Indica started twirling with Daisy again. "Well, tonight, I'll give her a bath, since you're making dinner. Even though I still think it's mildly indecent to make mac-and-cheese in any vegan form, you're the one who does it the best. Can we have a veg, too?"

"I can put together a salad." Kristen watched Indica whirling with her daughter, the puppies trotting around randomly. She set down the box of elbow macaroni and joined them in their dance.

CHAPTER SEVENTEEN

Prompt as always, Victoria and Teresa showed up together, just as Kristen and Indica were setting dishes on the table. After enthusiastic greetings with Daisy and the dogs, Kristen pulled out two folding chairs and they crowded around the table.

"Gail and Star are coming a little later, so they said to start without them," she said.

Victoria set the garlic bread she'd brought to warm in the oven, then scooped some salad. Teresa let them peek at her dessert offerings: vegan lemon bars and peanut butter cookies. As Kristen set them on top of the refrigerator, far away from small fingers and dogs, Teresa added both salad and mac-and-cheese to her plate.

Once everyone had settled and started to eat, Teresa said, "Gabe says hello to you all. He's looking forward to the picnic on Sunday. We want to see everyone before we go to his friend's wedding in New York."

Kristen bounced in her seat. "I feel like I haven't seen you all in ages. This TV show is taking over." She encouraged a bit of salad into Daisy. "So how's Luke?" she asked Victoria. "And Cort. I haven't heard from him in ages, either."

Victoria and Teresa exchanged a look.

"What?" Kristen asked.

"He's been kind of quiet lately," Teresa finally said. "Not secretive, exactly..."

"But secretive," Victoria said.

"What do you think is going on?" Kristen peeked at Indica and Teresa, relieved to see the subject didn't seem to bother either woman. Teresa had had a fairly intense fling with Cort before meeting Gabe. Then Cort and Indica had done their off-and-on dance before calling it quits recently.

Teresa said now, "I think it's a woman."

"But he's never been secretive about women before," Kristen said. "He talks about them all the time. He kind of lives for them."

Victoria said, "He hasn't even said anything to Luke. Not that Luke has encouraged him too much. He just says 'leave him be, and he'll come around when he's ready.'" She said it with a slight twang in her voice, echoing Luke's Southern accent.

Footsteps on the stairs set the dogs off in shrilly barks and a mad rush toward the door. A couple of brisk knocks gave them paroxysms of excitement, and they turned in circles, yapping happily.

"They know it's Star." Kristen got up and, halfway to the door, she called out, "It's open."

Gail and Star came in, holding their bags away from the dogs, who charged at them, dancing around their feet.

"Back, you little yapping mop-heads," Gail commanded.

Star lifted her package high up while she went to her knees to greet the dogs. Kristen took the package from her, so Star could scoop the tiny dogs up and give them kisses even as they licked her chin and wriggled with happiness. "Hello, sweet puppies," she cooed at them.

Daisy wriggled in her highchair; she loved Star's greetings as much as the dogs did. She tried to slide under the tray to the ground, but a bar between her legs stopped her. She shifted around, trying to free herself, and whined when it didn't happen.

"Sar!" she whimpered, pushing at the tray and giving Kristen desperate looks. "Sar!"

"Oh, please let her out," Star said, still cuddling the dogs close and looking as pained as Daisy.

Gail plunked a large can of caramel popcorn on a side table and said, "Yes, please, let her out. Everyone's angst is hurting my ears."

Kristen lifted Daisy up and out, and set her on the ground. Daisy went from full stop to full go, crashing into Star so that everyone fell over in a heap, laughing, barking and giggling.

"That doesn't seem very angsty to me," Kristen said. "That

sounds like joy."

"Okay, their joy is hurting my ears." Gail pulled the popcorn canister into her lap and ripped at the plastic around the lid. When it stretched but didn't give, she growled at it, and tugged harder.

"You don't seem at a good place for me to hand you a weapon, but here, let me help." Teresa sliced at the plastic with her knife.

When it fell to the carpet, Gail pried off the lid and stuffed a handful of popcorn in her mouth. "Fanks."

Kristen sat next to her and draped an arm around her shoulders. "What's going on, honey?"

"My publisher isn't taking my next book," she said through a mouthful of popcorn. "And they're dropping my Naughty Nights in Nashville series. And Star made me promise to keep quiet about something on the way up here, and you know how much I hate secrets."

From her spot on the floor, Star admonished, "*Gail.* You *promised.*"

"I didn't actually tell them anything." Gail grabbed another handful of caramel corn.

"But now that you mentioned a secret, everyone's going to be intrigued and I'll have to tell them."

"No, you won't," Kristen told Star. "It's up to you if you want to."

"*I* want to know," Indica said. "And besides, I think she told Gail on purpose, or at least subconsciously, because she knows Gail can't keep a secret, and she actually wanted us to know, but didn't know how to tell us."

Everyone turned to Star, who went pink. "I'm not in third person," she said.

"You're right," Indica said. "I'm sorry. But my argument is still valid." When Star didn't say anything, she said, "Right?"

"Maybe," Star mumbled into Daisy's hair. The dogs had settled down and lay with their chins on her ankles. They looked up now at the squeak in her voice, and Hamilton crawled up to balance on her thigh. "But isn't anyone going to say they're sorry about Gail's publisher?"

Everyone started talking at once, saying how sorry they were, and what a drag, and what happened, and they obviously didn't know what they were giving up by letting her go.

"And I didn't know you wrote that series," Teresa told her. She added in a whisper, "I read it to Gabe sometimes..."

Gail nodded morosely, staring into the canister. "Thanks. They can go suck eggs, I'm going to self-publish. And I don't want to talk about it anymore." She nudged Teresa in the shoulder. "But, thanks. It's kind of hot that you do that."

Teresa nodded, staring down at her hands.

Star announced, "I'm seeing Cort."

"What?!" most of them said in unison, turning toward her.

Star nodded and smiled, but then tears tracked down her cheeks. She didn't make a sound, just shook her head, and bowed it over Daisy's red curls.

Gail abandoned her popcorn and scooted over to sit as close to Star as Daisy and the dogs would allow. "Did he hurt you? 'Cause I'll kick his ass if he did."

Star shook her head more vehemently.

Kristen lowered herself to Star's other side and Indica joined her. Teresa slid next to Gail, and Victoria perched on the edge of the coffee table, crossing one booted foot over the other.

"What happened?" Victoria used her gentle producer's voice, the one that commanded an answer, while calming any chaos.

Star wiped at her cheeks with the tips of her fingers. "He said I was like a true Southern belle, sweet on the outside and steel inside."

Kristen, Gail, and Indica all looked at each other, wide-eyed, and Kristen noticed Victoria exchange a similar surprised expression with Teresa. That would explain Cort's attitude lately.

"And that's bad because?" Victoria prompted.

Star lifted her face and said, "He's been with so many women, how can I know if he thinks I'm special or not? He probably says that to *everyone*."

"I've never heard him say that before," Kristen told her.

This time, Teresa and Indica—the two women who had dated Cort—looked at each other, shaking their heads.

"He never said that to me," Indica told her.

"Me, either," said Teresa.

Star blinked, the tears damp on her lashes, then stared at Teresa. "Really? He was so in love with you."

Teresa shook her head again, but didn't say anything. Kristen knew she wouldn't want to deny any feelings Cort had had for her, but the end of their relationship had been difficult, and she was so happy with Gabe now. He had become her all, where men were concerned.

"Were you afraid to tell us?" Kristen asked.

Star twirled one of Daisy's curls around her finger, concentrating on the motion as if her life depended on it. She nodded, her tears flowing again.

Kristen hugged her tight with one arm. "Is it because of what we said at dinner the other night? That he's a dog and a..." She stopped, remembering that Indica had called him a "woman eater." She caught Indica's eye and knew the other woman was remembering that night, too. "And a serial dater," she finished.

"Those things," Star admitted. "But also because two of you have already dated him, but Indica didn't sleep with him—"

"Oh God, did *you* sleep with him?" Gail asked.

"None of your beeswax," Star said sharply.

"Honey," Gail started, "when you say things like that...that's why—"

"It's why you think Cort wouldn't be right for me," Star snapped. The dog on her thigh yipped, and she scooped Peggy up with one hand and set her next to her brother. "You don't think I can take care of myself, or pick the right man for me." She wasn't shouting, but came as close to the Star version of yelling as she seemed capable.

"We don't want you to get hurt," Indica began.

"And David hurt you," Kristen said, referencing Star's ex-boyfriend, who had brought her to San Francisco from Oklahoma, then left her.

"David was a weenie," Star said, her expression fierce as she looked at them all, as if daring them to contradict her. "And Cort's a *man*. A real man. And because I'm from some hick town, and I'm little and cute, you all think you have to protect me, and that I can't handle a real man." She hugged Daisy closer to her. "Well, I can."

"Who are we to tell you who to date?" Victoria said reasonably. "I dated a weenie before I met Luke. I didn't have enough sense to realize Luke was the right one for me, and thought I was better suited with the weenie." She shuddered.

Star straightened. "Thank you." She looked at Indica and Teresa. "Are you okay with me dating Cort, seeing as how you went out with him?"

They both nodded, and Indica said again, "We really don't want you to get hurt, though. It's not about what you can or can't handle, it's that you're a sensitive soul, and Cort...he's..." She flapped a hand around, then looked at Teresa.

"Cort's rougher around the edges. He might not notice if he's said or done something that would hurt your feelings. Plus, he's had so much experience, and David was only your second boyfriend."

"Haven't you two considered that his being with you, and with the other women before you, that it affected him in a good way? That your relationships helped him grow as a man?"

Indica opened her mouth, then pressed her lips together. "Umm..." she hummed.

"To some degree, I suppose," Teresa said.

Star stared at nothing across the room, her expression gone soft. "And all of that experience means he's an exceptionally good kisser."

"Can't argue with that one," Teresa told her.

Indica looked a little dreamy herself. "Preach."

"So why aren't any of you worried that Kristen will get hurt?" Star finally asked.

"We are," Victoria said. "Isn't that why we originally agreed to gather here tonight? Because you decided you liked him, but realized you'd never been friends with a man before?"

"A man I found insanely attractive." Kristen scooted around Star and reached for the caramel popcorn. She peered into it. "Not vegan," she muttered, then handed it over to Gail, who shoved another handful in her mouth. Kristen decided to cuddle a dog instead, holding Hamilton near her face until he licked her chin, then settled in her cupped hands. She held him close to her collarbone while she gave them a quick rundown of what had happened between her and Danny.

"His good producer had a bunch of people take yoga classes at Priya. I adjusted his downward dog and zinged like I've never zinged before with just a touch. Then we filmed at the club and he was protective and alpha and offered to help me with the audition the nasty producer wanted me to do. We had lunch, I scared him away with a bunch of questions, Victoria suggested we just be friends, he seemed okay with that, although I wasn't sure. Then that creep producer demanded a filmed kiss, and we did, and..." She let out a very long breath. "I don't know what to do next."

Everyone turned to Victoria, who seemed to have taken charge of guiding the emotional portions of the evening. But it was Star who spoke up.

"You call him. You tell him to meet you and Daisy at Dolores Park for a picnic this weekend." When everyone turned to her, she went pink, but tightened her grip on Daisy and added, "As friends. Tell him to be there or be square. We'll all go, too. Right?"

"Sure." Victoria shrugged. "Sounds like good advice to me. Maybe you need to stop underestimating this woman."

When Gail, Indica, and Kristen began protesting that they didn't underestimate their friend, Victoria simply stood and adjusted her blouse. She looked around the small room, then strode to where Kristen had dropped her knapsack. "Your phone in here? At the bottom as usual?"

"It's in the side pocket, actually," Kristen told her. "You convinced me to start keeping it there, in case I needed it for a Daisy emergency."

Victoria fished it out, strode to Kristen and held the phone out.

Complete helplessness flooded through Kristen, which she was pretty sure would have happened whether she had a tiny dog in both hands or not. What puzzled her was why? She had no fear of calling a man, or even of having her loved ones overhear her conversation. "I'm scared all of a sudden," she admitted. "Why is that?"

"Because he's so important to you," Star said.

Kristen blinked back a sheen of tears. "You're right. How did that happen so fast?" She took a deep breath, set Hamilton next to Peggy, and accepted the phone from Victoria. She took another steadying breath. "Okay. I'm putting it on speaker." She dialed, and they all listened to it ring.

It only rang one and a half times, before that sound was cut off and replaced by background buzz—voices, music, a car driving by? Then—

"Kristen?" Danny's voice came through.

She only got the word "yes" in before he continued. "I'm glad you called," he said in a rush of breath. "I really want to talk to you. You scare the hell out of me, but I've been thinking about you non-stop since the shoot at the alley, hell, since we first met, and I haven't had a chance to call. That kiss...You said you just wanted to be friends, and I think...I didn't mean to screw that up. Plus, you're right, I shouldn't have spoken for you. Shit," he said. "I'm rambling."

"Danny..."

"I'm really sorry, Kristen. I do want to talk to you, but I'll have to call you back. I'm about to go on set for a night shoot."

"I can verify that schedule," Victoria said from her perch on the edge of the coffee table.

A pause. "Am I on speaker?"

"I tried to tell you," Kristen told him. "My sister Victoria is here."

"Oh. Hi, Victoria," Danny said.

"And my friend, Teresa."

"Hey—"

"Also, my friends Gail, Indica, and Star, my daughter Daisy, who's half asleep right now, and my landlords Kim and August's dogs, Hamilton and Peggy."

"That's...I lost count. But hey, everyone."

"Hi," they all chorused, except Daisy, who twitched in Star's arms, but settled back again after a few pats. Even one of the dogs gave a tiny yip.

"Why would you verify my schedule?" Danny asked.

Kristen answered for Victoria. "To make sure you're not lying about being busy, and thus getting out of calling me back."

Instead of responding directly to Kristen, Danny said, "Hey, Victoria?"

"Yes?"

"I hear you know Samantha Jamison-Gallagher."

"I do."

"Then you know she doesn't mess around when it comes to filming schedules."

Victoria nodded. "That's absolutely correct."

"Well, ladies...and dogs...you're now on speaker with Samantha Jamison-Gallagher."

"Um....hi?" said a voice on the other end.

"Sam," Victoria said. "It's Victoria Clausen. Tyler." She rolled her eyes. At Kristen's look, she said, "I'll figure it out."

"Hey," Samantha said with great cheer. "You need to come visit us. But why am I on speaker with a group of women and...dogs, apparently."

Danny's voice said, "Kristen's friends and family and landlord's dogs would like confirmation that I'm about to go on the set, which is why I can't talk to her right now."

"That's true," Samantha said. "In fact, he's late, and I'm going to hear about it from my director and our AD."

"AD is Assistant Director," Victoria clarified for everyone.

"When will he be able to call her back?" Victoria asked.

"You know I can't give a definite time on that, as much as I would like to."

"What's the end time on your call sheet?"

Without pause, Samantha said, "Nine-thirty."

Victoria nodded. "He'll call you at ten," she told Kristen.

"Signing off," said Sam. "You have one minute."

"Kristen?" Danny said. "I really am glad you called. I wasn't sure if you wanted to talk to me after what I did."

"What did he do?" Star said, her wide-eyed innocence returned.

"He presumed to make a decision for me," Kristen told her. "It surprised me," she said to Danny now, "but I understand why you did it. And I did still want to talk to you. I *do* want to talk to you."

"And do you still want to be friends with me?" he asked.

"Yes."

"Then I'd like to ask you, and your friends and family and landlords' dogs' forgiveness."

Kristen looked around the room. "Well, everyone?"

"Yes," they chorused, with the dogs yipping along.

"Forgiven," she said into the phone. "And I would like to ask my friend to a picnic in the park to meet all my other friends so that he can make more friends. Are you filming on Sunday?" When Danny said no, she added, "I'll give you the details when we talk later."

There was a pause and, if not for the background sounds, Kristen might have thought they'd been cut off. "More friends," he said, as if talking to himself.

CHAPTER EIGHTEEN

Danny looked at the blue Victorian with pink gingerbread trim. He glanced at his phone to confirm the address Kristen had given him. This was it. Landlords downstairs, she, Indica, Daisy, and the landlords' miniature Yorkies upstairs. Because the house was set back from the street, it had room for a one-car garage and space for more cars off-street, a highly coveted setup in the city. He noted a Jaguar, a beater truck next to it, and a Prius at the end before his gaze drifted to the top floor.

They'd talked for hours the other night. He confessed about losing his family's money, talked about Vince dying, and his mother and brother not speaking to him. She told him about growing up in Illinois and studying yoga in India. She'd also told him she and her friends played a version of football that she knew he'd love. Her bedroom was in the back, but he pictured her at the bay window in front, just behind the filmy curtain, waiting for him. He wiped his palms against his shorts.

He waved the rideshare driver off, and strode toward the front steps. Halfway up, the door opened and a big guy in a Bulldogs ball cap stepped onto the porch. He crossed his arms over his chest, but Danny kept going. Another man stepped out and stood next to him, but Danny didn't pause even though they now occupied the total square footage of the porch. The new guy, blond and just as big, copied his buddy's pose, and Danny figured this wasn't the welcoming crew, but the vanguard, judging his worthiness to be "friends" with Kristen.

He took the final two steps up, forcing them back when he stepped onto the porch proper. He lifted a chin at first one, then the other. "Morning," he said, then copied their poses, feet slightly apart, arms over his chest, hands fisted. He didn't think things would go there, but Danny Linstead hadn't got this far in life without being prepared.

A sense of the ridiculous drifted over him when he pictured this scenario from an outsider's perspective: three tall guys crammed chest to chest on the blue porch with pink accents. He searched his mind for reference points and finally found one, noting the V tattoo on the pumped biceps of the dark-haired guy in the hat. "You must be Luke Tyler," he said with a nod.

The guy's stance relaxed a millimeter, and he nodded back, but didn't say anything.

The front door swung wide and a curvy woman in wedge sandals marched out, shoving between Luke Tyler and the blond guy. "For heaven's sake," she said to no one in particular. "Haven't we gotten past these peeing contests? If Gabe were here—"

"On his way," the blond said. Then he held out his hand and said, "Cort Landry. Think of us as Sunshine's brothers and protectors."

"Sunshine?" Danny gave Cort's hand a firm shake.

"Fits, don't you think?"

Danny nodded, then something clicked. He looked from Luke Tyler to Cort Landry. "Hell. Tyler Landry? I've got your album on my workout playlist. Kristen never said."

"She wouldn't have," the woman said. "My sister has no sense of celebrity. Everyone is equal to her. I'm Victoria."

They also shook, and while Victoria didn't look like her sister at first glance—darker, wavy hair, shorter in height—on closer inspection Danny saw the similarities. Both curvy, fair-skinned, blue-eyed, their lips the same size top and bottom, with a little dip in the middle of the top one.

Victoria nudged Luke and he finally held his hand out. "Hurt her, and I kill you," he said.

"I get that," Danny said seriously. He wouldn't embarrass any of them by claiming to be "just friends" at this point.

Victoria rolled her eyes and opened the door again. She snapped her fingers and said, "Get the lead out, gang. We have a two-year-old and two Yorkies to gather up, and a picnic to get started." She glanced behind her at that last, and Kristen came up behind her sister.

Danny relaxed all over when he saw her, even while his gut tightened and his breathing accelerated like he'd been running uphill. He caught sight of her face as she stood in the doorway between the "bodyguards" and when she smiled at him, he couldn't help but grin back. He wanted to elbow aside Tyler Landry, hold Kristen tight and swing her around in her tie-dyed outfit.

Everyone turned to look at Kristen, then back at Danny.

"Well, that says it all," Victoria said, before grabbing Luke's hand and pulling him inside. Then she gently smacked the back of her hand against Cort's arm until he got the clue and went inside with the others.

Kristen stepped outside, shutting the door behind her. Danny closed the gap between them until they stood bare inches apart.

"Hi," they breathed at the same time.

"There's time for me to show you around upstairs and for you to meet Daisy again," she said.

Danny nodded, never taking his eyes from hers.

"Sorry about the welcoming committee."

"It doesn't matter." He thought if he couldn't kiss her in less than two seconds he might burst. Since they were so close, it would only be a matter of bending his head forward. Now that he knew what he'd been missing, he wanted to spend his days kissing her to make up for lost time.

"They figured if they intimidated you, you weren't man enough for me."

He nodded again.

"At least—" She stopped. "Why do you look so funny?"

He jerked back. He'd zoned out her words and had actually been about to kiss her. "Sorry. Distracted. Let's go upstairs."

She led him through a quick tour. Small living room with a comfortable couch and chairs. Electric fireplace. A couple of fish peering out of a bowl. A wide doorway to a colorful kitchen and a hallway presumably leading to bedrooms. Luke stood at the top of the stairs holding Daisy, playing some kind of peek-a-boo, and Victoria and Cort faced off near a square dining table. It looked like she was lecturing him, if his hangdog expression meant anything, the opposite of his tough guy stance downstairs.

Kristen leaned toward Danny and whispered, "Cort just started dating one of my friends. There's a little consternation about it. She'll be at the picnic."

She held her hands out to Daisy, then squeezed the girl's face. "You get to help us with the puppies at the picnic, okay? And I'd like you to—"

"Uppies!" the girl cried, bouncing in Luke's arms.

"Well, we know what's most important," Kristen said sardonically to Luke.

He wrapped an arm around her shoulders and kissed her temple. Kristen slid a large paisley bag over his shoulder.

"Daisy. This is Danny. Danny is coming on the picnic with us."

"Uppies!" Daisy cried again, not even looking at Danny.

"Again, priorities."

"Can I help with anything?" Danny asked. "Take things downstairs, load the car?"

Kristen led him to the table, which held some small knapsacks. "It's only a few blocks away, so we're walking."

Still managing to look tough with a pink-clad girl in his arms and a purple diaper bag on his shoulder, Luke held a hand out to Danny and gave a firm shake. To Victoria, he said, "Let's go, darlin', you can school Cort on the way down."

Cort took two of the knapsacks, and Victoria held the leashes of the tiniest Yorkshire terriers Danny had ever seen, and they headed downstairs. Danny took the remaining pack.

Kristen put a hand on his arm. "Wait." He set the pack down and turned to her. "That kiss. On the set."

"I'm sorry about that."

"It was one of the best kisses I've ever had. I wouldn't mind another one."

"What about being friends—"

She swooped over and grabbed his face, clearly meaning to kiss him. Before their lips even touched, his arms swept around her. One hand splayed at her back, the other caressed her neck, simultaneously tender and possessive. Their mouths met, open and inviting, and she flicked her tongue across his upper lip, eliciting a gasp, a tightening of his grip. Sparks raced up his spine and heat coursed through his body. Her arms around his neck, a heel hooked at his calf…closer, he wanted her closer, for every inch of their skin to be pressed together, and right at that moment, that impossibility felt possible.

As if she read his thoughts, her hand glided down his chest and abs to his belt. "I want you," she whispered hot in his ear. "Inside me. Hard inside me."

His hand tightened on her neck, and he groaned. He wanted that, too, wanted that contact, her skin, their bodies, to be driving inside her in rhythm to the beat of their desire—

Footsteps and a wailing sound carried up the stairs. Kristen flew away from Danny and pressed her hands to her chest. He gasped. What had just happened? An eternity had passed in a few seconds, and yet it hadn't been nearly long enough. Her expression mirrored his feelings. Lust, confusion, and that shift in perspective that meant you'd never see the other person the same way again. He held up one finger, asking for a moment, then bent over his thighs, breath still coming in gasps. It took him a few seconds to return to reality.

San Francisco. Victorian. Living room. Standing on a carpet. A child crying. Someone coming up the stairs. He hadn't fully recovered himself, but he needed to get a grip, fast.

"Danny?"

"Yeah," he rasped, straightening. "Go ahead."

Kristen opened the door a little. Victoria appeared in the doorway.

"What's wrong?" Kristen asked.

"Everything's fine. Daisy's fine. But we forgot Fuzzy Bunny."

Kristen still had a hand pressed to her chest. "I was sure I put Fuzzy Bunny in her bag."

"Believe me, we looked everywhere." From the doorway, Victoria peered around Kristen at Danny. He didn't know how he must look at that moment, but something on his face must have registered with her. "Oh. Sorry for the interruption."

He raised a hand to convey it was no problem, but still couldn't speak, his body pulsing from that kiss. He gave a short nod instead.

"We got...sidetracked." Kristen looked at Danny, but he couldn't read her expression. He hoped it was something along the lines of: this isn't over. He nodded again. Kristen opened the door wider. "Come in. We'll look for Fuzzy Bunny."

Victoria looked between Kristen and Danny as a heavier set of shoes headed up the stairs. "Are you sure we didn't interrupt—"

"Darlin', if we're interrupting, you think they're going to tell us that?" Luke asked as he came inside, ducking his shoulders because Daisy rode on top of them.

"Just some of the best kissing ever," Kristen told him, then looked down at herself. "Hey, my bra's unhooked. That was some good work."

Danny caught the unspoken exchange between husband and wife as Victoria and Luke glanced at each other. Apparently, Kristen did, too, because while she reached under her top to fasten her bra, she added, "Did you forget who you were talking to?"

"Temporarily discombobulated on account of a certain rabbit gone missing," Luke told her with a wink.

Daisy raised her hands up in the air and Luke tightened his hold on her legs. "Fuzz bun!" she exclaimed.

"We'll find her, baby," Kristen told her.

"Sorry again," Victoria said. "We thought you'd be on your way down. We'll find FB and we can go ahead and give you some time alone."

"Why don't you leave Daisy here?" Danny suggested. At Kristen's questioning look, he said, "Let's get to know each other. Didn't you say the park was only a couple blocks away?"

"Park!" Daisy crowed. "Parkparkparkparkpark!"

"We still spell and use covert language," Kristen told him. "I figured we'd all be going together, but then that kiss made me lose consciousness and we lost some time." She captured Daisy's hands to keep her from clapping them against Luke's ears and said, "Yes, we're going to the park. But you still have to be good."

"Good," Daisy pouted.

"Are you sure you don't want to be alone?" Victoria asked.

"Absolutely." After Luke knelt down, Kristen lifted Daisy from his shoulders. "Where are the dogs?"

"Probably peeing on the construction equipment," Luke said. "The little nippers."

"We'll take them, too," Kristen said. "We'll meet you down at the p-a-r-k and help you set up."

"Are you sure?"

Kristen gave her sister a one-armed hug, and kissed her cheek. "Positive. With Daisy and the dogs as chaperones, we're relatively safe."

CHAPTER NINETEEN

Danny walked the little nippers, the pack slung over one shoulder, while Kristen held Daisy's hand. A collection of blue bags was tied to one of the leashes, and Danny didn't relish the idea of having to use them, but that concern disappeared when Kristen slid her fingers into his.

He watched Daisy dance around at the end of her mother's hand, the notorious stuffed rabbit clutched to her, looking everywhere but at her feet. She seemed like Kristen, carefree, but wanting to examine everything around her at the same time. She hummed to herself, but every once in awhile sang a few words. Danny listened in, trying to place the song.

"...put our lizard to the tents..."

Danny raised an eyebrow at Kristen. "Isn't it 'put our service to the test'?"

She looked at him. "You know the song? Indica's mom plays it when she babysits."

He sang a few more lines, then hummed for awhile, enjoying her shocked expression.

"How do you know *Beauty and the Beast*?"

"My brother and I got in trouble a lot. My mom got DVDs from the library." He eased the dogs away from a sidewalk café table. He'd confessed to Kristen the other night about losing his family's money, but he still burned with shame at the thought of saying why Ma didn't just buy the DVD. She'd been so careful with the money they earned, and he'd lost it all. He cleared his throat. "See, Ma thought Disney would teach us manners and respect, things like that."

"Did it work?" By the glint in her eye, Danny figured Kristen already knew the answer.

"She made us watch *Beauty and the Beast* so much, one day after filming, she'd gone to the store, and we took the DVD out to an empty lot near our friend Frankie's house and practiced shooting BBs through the middle hole."

"And how'd you do?"

"Let's just say my mom made all of us go around asking our neighbors if they needed help with anything so we could earn back the library fee she had to pay. And apologize to the librarian. We were making a lot of money then as child actors, but she said that wasn't the point. That taught me more than Disney ever did. Still..." He trailed off, remembering what seemed like such innocent times now.

"Still what?" Kristen asked, her voice quiet as if she didn't want to disturb his reverie.

"We watched that movie so many times, Denny and I learned all the lyrics." They stopped for a light, then crossed the street linked together. "And I think Ma made us watch it partly because *she* loved it. So we'd put on these dumb shows...just to make her laugh, you know? And 'Be Our Guest' was one of her favorites. We even dressed up like Belle and the Beast. She really loved that." He stopped. He'd told variations of this story in interviews where he and Den sang for their mom, but he hadn't given so many details before. Especially how they traded off dressing up like Belle. Who was this woman that she got him to open up so much?

Kristen's expression turned soft and he expected her to say something about how sweet he and Denny were or what a lovely story and memory. Instead she said, "Would you ever want to dress up as Belle again?" Before he could respond, she added, "Sometimes I think it'd be fun to dress up as a pirate. A real one, you know, not a sexy girl pirate like those Halloween costumes they have. But something a real pirate would wear." She patted her head. "Tricorn hat, those breeches type pants, socks with garters." This time she leaned down to pat her knee. "Of course, pirates were sailors, and a lot of times they didn't wear shoes or socks." She stepped close to him, taking his hand again, and said in almost a conspiratorial whisper, "Did you know some male pirates wore women's clothes?"

Just last week, Olivia had sat next to him and put her hand on his bare forearm before she revealed some gossip about a crew member. He'd wanted to brush away her cool, smooth fingertips; he wasn't interested. At Kristen's touch, his breath stopped and he closed his eyes as if he'd just stepped from a cold room into sunlight, the warmth radiating on his face.

Still basking in the sensation, he opened his eyes. "I'd heard of women dressing up as men, but not the other way around, no. And just for the record, I have no urge to dress up as Belle these days. Hope that doesn't disappoint you."

She grinned, swinging their clasped hands. "Not in the least. But it would be okay with me if you wanted to."

He stopped on the path and studied her when she turned to face him—those crazy curls, her round, bright blue eyes and open expression. "You're extraordinary, you know that?" He leaned forward, thinking he could lose himself in her eyes, that he wanted to kiss her again. And again...

A small foot stamped between them. "Mama!"

Danny and Kristen pulled apart and looked down at Daisy. She pointed and announced, "Inca!"

They'd crossed the street and walked along a path halfway through the park and Danny had barely taken in the details.

Kristen waved their clasped hands at a group of people standing near a large blanket; all were turned toward them. Daisy tugged at her mother's grasp and the dogs did the same on their leashes. Kristen commanded the dogs to be still and they immediately sat, but their tiny rear ends wiggled with emotion. Then she eased Daisy closer and told the little girl to look her in the face. "Go straight to Inca."

Still looking at her mother, Daisy pointed behind her. "Inca," she pouted.

"Yes. Go to Inca. And take the puppies." She let go of Daisy's hand, and Danny had never seen someone that small and wobbly move so quickly. The dogs shot to their feet and Kristen unclipped them. "Go get Daisy," she said, and they chased after, yipping.

Danny and Kristen watched until Indica swooped up Daisy. When a short blonde woman patted the dogs to her side, Kristen turned to face Danny, still holding his hand. "When I asked you to the picnic, we were friends. Since that's changed, you should know they'll all be watching."

"I said 'yes' hoping to be more than friends, so I get it. I'm expecting full scrutiny."

When he lifted his hand, she tilted her head to it, fitting her cheek to his palm. Closing her eyes, she said, "I know I shouldn't say things like this, but no one's touched me like that in almost three years." She opened her eyes and looked straight at him. "I've really missed it."

He hadn't touched a woman in true affection and desire in longer than that. Normally he wouldn't admit it, but Kristen's honesty didn't push him away or shut him down. It scared the hell out of him, but it also allowed him to open up. "I have, too," he said, brushing his thumb along her cheekbone.

"We're sounding like we missed *each other*," she whispered.

And there it was: that feeling of being so comfortable, of already knowing each other, while at the same time, her smooth skin under his thumb fanned the flames and sent his senses reeling. "You confuse me," he admitted.

"I get that a lot." She stepped close enough that he felt her breasts push through the thin material of his shirt, and his gut tightened.

Someone called from the field, "Hey, Linstead, you playing or what?"

Yanked from his anticipation, he recoiled as if socked in the stomach, and turned to see the big guy, Cort Landry, football under one arm, waving them over. The woman who had gathered the dogs now elbowed Landry in the side, and he responded in dramatic fashion by falling to the ground with a loud, "Ooph!"

Kristen shook her head and Danny looked at her.

"When it's just the guys, they play flag football with some serious tackles. But when it's the whole group, we play NRUF." She pronounced it *en-ruff*. "No Rules Unicorn Football." she explained. "Gail thinks it's sexist that we don't play the same as the guys, but this way we can play in heels if we want to and Daisy can play, too."

"Do the dogs play, too?"

She grabbed his hand and led him toward the group. "You're going   to   do   just   fine."

CHAPTER TWENTY

At sixteen, Danny and his brother starred in a film called *My Brother the Addict*. They'd grown out of their "adorable kiddos" roles on *Double Trouble*, and the network canceled it after eleven seasons, the last three of which had been filled with painful jokes about their gawky teen years. After acting and modeling his entire life, Danny wanted to go to a public high school, but his brother and mom wanted the wagon train to continue. So he agreed to the ridiculous film in which Danny's character goes to great lengths and makes a lot of speeches to save his doomed brother. It tanked, but since his character was the star quarterback, he did learn how to play football.

He'd continued to play over the years with friends, but today's game with this group of outgoing, generous people resembled nothing like anything he'd played before. There was a football involved—two foam ones, actually, one lime green and the other neon purple—but that was the closest it got to official.

As Kristen said, no rules applied, but as they chased each other around, laughing and tossing footballs at random, Danny noted the respect and teamwork always in play. Kristen's sister Victoria refused to remove her high wedge sandals, so if someone tossed her the ball, her husband Luke flipped her over his shoulder and ran to the end zone, which was designated by two garden gnomes stuck in the grass. He slid her to the ground, then took one hand and spun her in a dance before pulling her up against him for a smoldering kiss. When that happened, Gail ran in to steal the ball, dodging and weaving both Indica and Kristen as they chased her, and growling at Danny if he tried to block her. Once he scooped up a dog and held it out to her as she ran at him. It yapped so high-pitched that Gail slid to a stop, then fell on her butt laughing. Danny set the dog on her stomach and the other dog and Daisy piled on top of her while Teresa swooped in to steal the ball.

Daisy had unicorn duty, wearing a headband with a plush rainbow horn and multicolored streamers. Star stole the ball from Teresa, ran in a circle around Cort, dropped a curtsy in her cute sunflower print dress, then stole the other one from him. She raced to the other end zone, and stood there beaming with her face flushed and the footballs clutched to her chest, while the women surrounded her and fell into a group hug, cheering.

For her "win," Star was presented with her own a unicorn horn, and the game was declared officially over. Everyone dropped onto the large circle of overlapping blankets, mostly keeping to couples, but shifting around to share in the amazing array of food. Danny stood at the edge of the group, watching, with a lump in his throat. He and Denny had played like this—well, no one he knew actually played *quite* like this—and before his mom remarried, she had joined them in their games. They'd been the Three Musketeers, and after Vince came into their lives, they'd dubbed him D'Artagnan and he'd become one of them. That fun companionship had stopped long before Vince died, but he couldn't remember exactly when or why. And he didn't realize how much of a gap it had left until today. His mother had been pulling away for years, and he hadn't noticed.

Someone thrust a bottle of beer at him, and he turned to see Luke Tyler watching him from under his ball cap.

"You've played before," Tyler said in his gentle Southern drawl before taking a swig and switching his gaze to the picnicking group.

Danny accepted the beer with thanks and took a swallow. Part of the lump in his throat remained, a reminder of the loss of his family. "Can't say I've ever played like *this*." He spread one hand out to take in the two footballs, dogs, unicorn horns, and heeled shoes. "But, yeah, I've played some ball in my time."

Luke nodded, smiling. "It shows." He turned to face Danny again. "My wife's gonna charge over here in less than twenty seconds, so I'll be quick." He tilted his beer toward Kristen and Daisy, who sat between her legs. "They mean the world to us and one good game of football isn't enough to prove your worth."

Danny tried to hide his smile when he caught Victoria approaching them just as Luke said she would. Luke held up an arm and she slipped under it. She patted his chest, then pointed at Danny. "No more threats, Luke Tyler. That gets old fast."

Luke lifted his arms up to indicate his innocence, then pressed the beer bottle to his chest and held her closer. "I do not break my promises, darlin'."

On the blanket, Daisy crawled from Kristen's lap to Star's, and Kristen swiveled to face them. "I can hear everything you're saying, you know." She shifted to her knees, then stood and sashayed to Danny's side.

Luke nodded. "I know. No secrets."

She smiled at the three of them. "Exactly. No secrets. And a reminder that I can take care of myself."

"Never doubted that for a second," Luke said.

He kissed Kristen's cheek and led Victoria back to their blanket.

Danny noticed other park visitors taking pictures of the group with their phones—probably video, too—but no one had approached them so far.

"You should be hungry after all that running around and sweating." Kristen traced a finger from the side of his throat, along his clavicle, down to the top of his shirt, easily distracting him from the onlookers.

"Hungry," he repeated, mesmerized by the smooth pad of her finger against his salt-roughened skin.

"My cauliflower steak sandwich will reduce you to tears."

From nearby someone said, "You're doing that already with your teasing touch."

Kristen laughed and dropped her hand, but grabbed Danny's and sat down with him near their food. She addressed Gail, the one who had interrupted them. "You can use that in one of your books." She opened up a small cooler and said to Danny, "Gail writes erotica."

Gail plopped down across from them, the cooler in between. "Cauliflower steaks are not sexy. Although I will admit that yours are pretty sexy in the taste department." She took the one Kristen offered her.

Danny took his own wrapped sandwich. Kristen had introduced

him to everyone when they first arrived, but since the football game happened right away, he hadn't had a chance to really talk to anyone. He watched them moving from blanket to blanket. "Are you all into each other's business all the time?"

"You betcha." Gail took a big bite of sandwich. Danny noticed that her bright pink t-shirt read "Feminist AF" in curly script. She growled at him again when she caught him watching, and he saluted her with his sandwich.

"We're family," Kristen added. "We're in each other's lives. If one of us knows something, we should all know about it so we can support each other."

"And she makes us *talk* to each other." Gail sighed as if it were a huge drama, but the corners of her lips also tilted up. "It's the most functional relationship I've ever been in."

Danny waved his sandwich around to include the whole group. "Functional with everyone?"

"Yes," Indica said, settling herself so close to Gail their shoulders touched and one woman's cross-legged knee overlapped the other. "We're a unit, but we're not a closed unit."

Bemused, Danny bit into his sandwich to collect his thoughts. He'd forgotten it was vegan, but it didn't matter. The crispy, sweet, garlicky flavor rolled over his tongue as he crunched the bun, cauliflower and toppings together. After he swallowed, he said, "What's in this?"

"Seared cauliflower steak, garlicky greens, and romesco sauce. That's almonds, roasted red peppers, paprika, more garlic, and olive oil."

"Someone's talking my talk." Teresa squished herself close to Indica. Kristen had introduced her as a chef who had been in a reality TV cooking contest. She currently worked in the kitchen of a local homeless center.

"Food is everyone's talk," her boyfriend Gabe said. He tucked himself behind Teresa and reached a hand out to Danny.

Before he knew it, everyone had formed a tight circle around Kristen and Danny. Daisy sat nearby, pulling up blades of grass, the dogs at her feet. He got their protective point and decided to let them have their moment. He liked how much they cared. He finished his sandwich and was about to tell Kristen it was the best thing he'd tasted in a long time when his phone buzzed. Everyone had continued their conversations, mostly focused on food, but Danny knew they were also keeping one ear and/or eye on him.

"It might be the production," he said in apology to Kristen as he leaned to one side to pull out his phone. He read the text and held back a curse. Instead, he sighed and shoved the phone back in his pocket.

"What is it?" Kristen asked.

"Nothing." He stared down at the blanket, and when he looked up, he found a few too many sets of eyes on him. Right. No secrets or evasion with this group. Kind of like being on a film set, only more intimate. "My roommate. Letting me know he's having company tonight." He ran a hand through his hair. "There were a few too many, ah, loud encounters, so we came up with a system. He texts me if he's bringing someone home." He raised his beer in salute to the group. "Apparently it's two someones tonight."

There was an awkward silence, broken only by Daisy singing to herself.

Teresa cleared her throat. "Well, this might be a good time for a change of subject." She looked over her shoulder at Gabe, who nodded. She reached into her shirt and pulled out a necklace. "We're engaged," she announced, lifting the necklace so everyone could see the diamond ring swinging from it.

The group erupted, hugging the couple and shaking their hands in congratulations.

When Kristen sat back down next to Danny, her chest rose and fell and her cheeks went pink like they had when she played NRUF. She smiled at Danny. "This was a long time coming," she said, gesturing at Gabe and Teresa.

"How long?"

"A couple of years, and some heartache."

Danny's brother had been engaged to Lorelei for almost six years. He couldn't imagine finding the woman you wanted to spend the rest of your life with and not making it permanent as soon as possible, but he knew part of Denny's engagement was drama for the cameras. Who knew what Gabe and Teresa had been through?

Daisy had gotten caught up in the joy and now charged over to Danny and Kristen.

She stood with one hand on her hip, the other held out toward them, a dark oblong object on the palm, smiling big and proud. "I pick up a poo!"

Danny cringed back with a low sound.

To his shock, Kristen looked delighted. "Good for you, baby. But we talked about that. Remember germs? We'll need to get you washed up."

"Juuurrrmms." Daisy drew the word out with great relish, then thrust her palm at Danny. "Here! For you!"

He recoiled, holding up his hands in defense. "No. Nope. I'm good."

Daisy's face crumpled, and her arms dropped, the poo sliding to the blanket. As it fell, Danny saw how small and hard it was. Not even a petrified poo, just a rock.

A small sound similar to a stomach rumble rose up from Daisy's chest, building in volume and intensity, while her face got more squashed together and her cheeks turned dark red.

"Steam kettle," Kristen said in a warning tone to Danny. "Thar she blows!"

At that a high-pitched scream erupted from the tiny person at his feet and he automatically pressed his palms to his ears. "Whoa."

Everyone else turned to look, but went back to their conversations, just a little louder this time.

"I usually have to let her wind down before I can reason with her," Kristen said, her voice raised above the din. "We're working on that."

Danny couldn't quite believe the range and volume of sounds emanating from something so tiny. He'd noticed heads starting to turn, people shaking their heads at each other, moms with their own kids offering sympathetic looks.

"Should I have just accepted the poo?" he asked with a small grin.

She smiled back, but the skin around her eyes had tightened, and the smile disappeared quickly. "It was a good lesson for someone to say no to an inappropriate gift." She let out a sigh, barely heard above the roar of the Kraken. "But, yeah, it would've made things easier."

Daisy fell in a heap at Kristen's feet, now just bawling instead of screaming. Kristen slid closer to Daisy and said, "That's enough."

"No," Daisy howled. "No no no no no."

"Never in my life did I think I'd be saying these words," Kristen said, although she didn't seem to be speaking to anyone in particular. She leaned toward Daisy, who had her head bent over her arms.

"You stop that right now, young lady, or you're getting a time out."

"No," came the muffled reply.

"I'm going to count to five, and if you aren't quiet and sitting up by then, then I'm picking you up and we're going straight home. And you're still getting a time out."

"*No.*"

Waves of childhood flashbacks washed over Danny. He remembered being small, feeling misunderstood, having what his Ma called a tantrum and he thought of as expressing himself. He could never do anything like that on the set, but he tried it plenty at home with his mother. She didn't use the same words that Kristen used now, but his mother definitely gave him time outs. And ultimatums. Strong ones.

"Daniel Anthony Linstead, you shut your yap this instant or you get the belt."

He'd never been so great at shutting up. He knew Kristen wouldn't hit her child, and he *really* hadn't wanted the poo present, but he still felt some sympathy for Daisy. He found himself easing closer on his knees opposite Kristen, who had started to count, with Daisy shouting "No!" between each number.

Danny put a light hand on Kristen's upper arm, tense and strong under his fingers. "I used to pitch fits at my Ma," he told Kristen in an easy tone.

"Not really the time," Kristen told him over the wailing.

"I wanted something from her, I just didn't always have the words."

Kristen looked ready to respond to that, maybe to remind him in a not-so-nice way that this wasn't his business, but Daisy had stopped her litany of "No," and turned her head; he could see one eye peeking up at him.

Face still pink, a cheek streaked with tears, crazy curls like her mom's stuck to her temple. And that big blue eye watching him, waiting.

"I don't want the poo," he told her gently, and that eye narrowed. "Because I don't want juurrrms," he added, copying the way she'd said it. "But I wouldn't mind a hug."

Before he knew what had hit him, Daisy had flung herself at him, arms tight around his neck, warm, solid body against his chest. He automatically put his arms around her to support her, and risked a look at Kristen.

She didn't speak at first. "Well played," she finally said with a nod. "Neither one of you listens, but at least you're both quiet."

Danny almost said, "For now," but decided not to push his luck. He just nodded and let Daisy snuggle closer to him. She felt heavier and more substantial than he'd have thought, and a piece of the true "weight" of being a parent hit him. She had a lot of help, but Kristen was still doing this on her own.

His phone buzzed again, but he ignored it, cradling Daisy closer. Some things were more important.

CHAPTER TWENTY-ONE

Kristen heard Danny's phone buzz multiple times, and finally took Daisy from him so he could check his messages and she could wash Daisy's face. The Petrified Poo Incident seemed to signal the end of the picnic, and everyone started to gather their belongings. Kristen noticed more people than usual taking pictures and a few came forward to ask for autographs from Luke, Cort, Danny, Gabe, and Teresa.

After watching the distressed expressions flash on Danny's face and the way his shoulders lifted up after checking his phone, Kristen made a decision. She and Danny each held an end of a blanket and when they came together to touch the corners, she said, "You can sleep on my couch tonight. If you don't want to deal with your roommate and his someones."

They stood facing each other, hands touching, the blanket draped between them. He took it from her and finished folding it. He held it to his chest and stood nodding as if to himself. "That's...Do you...?"

"Indica is going to her parents' house and Daisy and the dogs are staying with Star tonight." She took the blanket from him. "I know what I'm suggesting. I also know it can be exactly what I said. My couch for you to sleep on."

"I'd like that."

He smiled when he said it, but she didn't miss the fact that he hadn't addressed her options—sex or no sex—but she understood.

He'd dealt admirably with her family's openness with each other, but she knew it wasn't everyone's preference.

"Star lives around the corner. I'll ask if she needs us to drop her off or can just take Daisy and the dogs from here."

They said goodbye to the others, offering more congratulations to Teresa and Gabe. Danny noticed less side-eye from Kristen's friends and received more friendly handshakes and hugs. He didn't know if it was the football game or the poo incident, but he seemed to have passed a test.

Danny held the dogs' leashes and hooked both knapsacks over one shoulder while Kristen gathered Daisy close.

"Star wants to spend the night with you and the puppies. Doesn't that sound good?"

Daisy wiggled back and forth on the grass. "Uppies!" she announced, her free hand shooting up in the air.

"I call that a yes," Kristen said.

Danny smiled at her. "You have good friends."

"I couldn't get by without them."

He eased closer to Kristen and they watched Daisy charge on all fours to Star, who sat cross-legged on the grass next to Cort. The dogs strained at their leashes and Kristen told Danny he might as well let them go or they might strangle themselves.

"She's like a tiny things whisperer. They can't keep away from her." Kristen stood hands on hips, smiling as she watched them. "They won't even miss us if we scoot away down the path," she told Danny, though she didn't move.

Star sat up, hugging the tiny ones close. "Of course we'd miss you. But we're also going to have a delightful time singing along to *Frozen* and cuddling in bed and eating treats."

"Eats!" Daisy announced.

"Makes me wish I was staying," Cort said with a wistful sigh.

"No, you're helping me get everything back to the apartment, then you're going to your shift at the bar, and we"—she looked down at the trio in her lap—"are having a girls and puppies night."

"Do you have everything you need?" Kristen asked her. "Extra clothes and diapers for her, and food for the dogs?"

"You left plenty last time." She made a shooing motion with her hands. "Go. Have fun."

"But not too much," Cort said. He stood and held his hand out to Danny. "Good game today."

Danny nodded, and they shook. Kristen noticed that each of them squeezed hard enough to silently announce they were still assessing each other.

Kristen crouched in front of Daisy, who sat in the middle of Star's crossed legs. "Hey, daughter, you and the puppies be good for Star."

"Mama!" she cried with joy, throwing her arms around Kristen's neck. "'Night, Mama."

"Goodnight, baby. I'll see you tomorrow. Have fun with Star."

Daisy peeked over Kristen's shoulder.

"'Anny," she whispered.

"You want to say goodnight to Danny?"

Daisy nodded. "Unh." She climbed out of Star's lap and peered up at Danny. "'Night," she demanded, holding her arms up.

Danny crouched in front of her and hugged her close while she flung her arms around him. "'Night, germy girl," he told her.

"No," she said, pushing against his chest and smiling before she crawled back into Star's lap.

"She is such a flirt," Kristen said with a head shake.

At the same time, both Star and Danny said, "Like her mom."

Kristen laughed and reached for Danny's hand. "That is our cue to go. Call me when you're ready for us to pick her up."

Star sketched her a little salute, but was clearly focused on the tiny trio snuggling with her.

Kristen took Danny's hand to lead him toward the sidewalk. "So are you ready for dessert?"

CHAPTER TWENTY-TWO

Danny's most recent texts didn't distract him from Kristen's innuendo over the word "dessert." Thoughts of whipped cream, cherries, and frosting won out over a text from Jenkins stating "Stay away from the yoga teacher, keep your job," but the words still curdled in his stomach.

Glancing around at the fans still aiming their phones at the group, it was easy enough to guess how Jenkins had heard about today. Pictures and video had probably already circulated on social media. He'd made peace with online gossip concerning himself a long time ago, but he didn't like it for Kristen. Or Daisy.

He bristled at the threat. What the hell did seeing Kristen have to do with his job? Jenkins had Nicole, as wrong as that relationship was. He didn't want Kristen, too, did he?

Knowing Jenkins, the answer was yes.

Kristen squeezing his hand brought him back to the present.

"I just made a super obvious innuendo about sex, and you look like you just stubbed your little toe."

He stopped where the path turned into the sidewalk, and edged her away from a group of people heading into the park. "Are you sure?" he asked, staring into her eyes. "About dessert?"

"I've never been more sure." She didn't blink. "And I hardly ever waffle." She giggled. "Sorry. Food. Sex. They seem to go together. Are *you* sure?"

"You had me at waffle."

He let her set the pace as they walked, still holding hands, but he wanted to swoop her up like Superman and fly to the Victorian. He was so focused on reaching that candy-coated house, he walked a couple steps ahead when she stopped on the sidewalk. He spun back to look at her.

She pointed to a sign on a shop. *Dessert Delights, Ice Cream & More.* "Dessert," she said. "Now, and later."

Well, hell. He hadn't thought about ice cream. He nodded and they stood in line behind another couple and a family of four. He glanced at the menu. "Wait. *Vegan* ice cream?"

"Well, as a vegan, I don't eat ice cream with actual cream. I promise you'll like it."

She could feed him sawdust and he'd agree to it right now, but he wouldn't say he liked it. He kept it simple with a scoop of chocolate, and Kristen went for strawberry. As soon as they hit the sidewalk and he watched her lick her way up from the bottom of the cone to the top of the pink scoop, he charged back into the store and got a pint to go.

He didn't remember the rest of the walk back, but once inside, they both ran up the stairs and stood facing each other. He could barely think, but he managed to get out, "Birth control? I have condoms, and I've been tested."

"IUD, condoms, tested." She crunched into her cone.

He dropped the packs he'd been carrying. His chest constricted and he bit into the last of the chocolate, swallowing it fast and ignoring the brain freeze. Her tongue curled into her cone, lapping up the ice cream along the edges. He thought his head might pop off.

"Whatever you want, slow, fast, or somewhere between," he choked out. "Here, the bedroom, the kitchen counter. But if you don't finish that ice cream soon, I make no promises."

Still holding the cone in one hand, she stepped close and kissed him. Her lips were as cold as his, but they warmed the longer the strawberry-flavored kiss lasted. The lyrics of an old song went through his head: lips like sugar. Sugar kisses. She was sweet and salty, tender and firm, and he couldn't get enough of her.

He dropped the bag with the pint and swept an arm around her to pull her closer. She squeaked in surprise, laughed, and kissed him harder. Then she pulled away to take another bite of ice cream before holding the cone up to his mouth.

"Would you like some?"

He finished it in one bite, then kissed her again. Chocolate and strawberry, the sweetness melding together to form one mouthwatering flavor.

Wrapped around each other, they drifted to the floor, hands roaming, hair stroked from the face here, a hip cupped there. When Kristen slid her hands under his shirt, Danny pulled away only long enough to whip it over his head while Kristen shimmied out of hers. They stopped to appreciate each other, no hint of shyness for either of them, then leaned in to kiss again, now stroking the bare skin of arms, backs, and bellies. Danny traced a hand from Kristen's neck to her shoulder, sliding one bra strap down before unhooking the back. She tossed it across the room, then leaned back to wiggle out of her leggings.

He moved with her, and as he kissed his way down her body, he felt her squirm under him. "What is it?" he asked, lifting himself up.

She was reaching into her bag with one hand and fumbling with the button of his shorts with the other. "Condom," she gasped.

"I have—"

She pulled a condom from her bag, face lit with triumph, and pushed his shorts and underwear down with the other hand while hooking one foot around his leg.

"How are you—"

"Flexible," she panted. "Yoga. I want you now. Fast. Hard. Now."

Even as the tip of her tongue traced a warm line down his arm, her hands curved around his back and he heard a package tearing.

"Don't tease me," he said.

"I mean it. Slow later in the kitchen." She grasped him with one hand and slid the condom on without looking, now licking circles on his chest. "In the bedroom. Kitchen. Hallway. I don't care."

"Are you sure?" He caressed the side of her neck with his tongue, trailing it down to the top of her breast. "I want to spoil you, learn every inch of you—"

"It's been almost three years." She bit his nipple; he gasped at the bite. "I'll be fine. Fast now," she repeated, her voice insistent. "Hard."

He wanted her so badly his body trembled at the thought of taking her hard and fast. And he would, but first he couldn't resist a taste of her breast, circling his lips around her nipple and flicking his tongue against it. He could still taste strawberries.

She cried out, and her back arched. She grabbed his ass with both hands and he slid into her, the hot, tight warmth of her freezing him in place with a groan. But when she started to move under him, his body took over and he thrust with her rhythm, hard and fast like she wanted. They entwined arms and legs together, pushing hard against each other, and rolling to the side until she straddled him. She rose up, her hair wild around her shoulders, and he grasped her hips to experience the strength, the cadence, the wonder of her.

He matched her pace, wanting to share this with her forever, but the urgent way she rode him shot desire throughout his body until he felt about to burst. Then she moaned in his ear, "Now now now," over and over until she convulsed around him. He let himself go then, free-falling into waves of bliss while she continued to rock her hips, purring little moans of pleasure in his ear.

She finally collapsed on top of him, her hair billowing everywhere. After a few minutes, she whispered, "I forgot what an orgasm with a man is like."

She slid to the side and he disposed of the condom in its wrapper before gathering her close to nuzzle her neck. He trailed his lips along her jaw to her mouth, lingering over a long, sweet kiss.

"I'm glad I was that man," he murmured against her mouth.

"I can't imagine anyone else," she whispered back, her eyes closed. They flew open the next second. "Oh, does that scare you?"

He stroked a finger along her cheekbone. "I don't scare easy."

"That's good. Because I tick a lot of boxes in the scary department for men. I have a child, I speak my mind, I'm tall and strong—"

He stopped her list with another kiss. "Then they weren't the right men for you." His lips lingered over hers, soft and teasing, his tongue darting to hers and away while he explored the rest of her body with his hands. "And I like all of those things about you. Including how you eat ice cream." He trailed the tip of his tongue down her collarbone, as if lapping her up.

"Mmm…" She sank into the sensations, warm from the glow of sex, just like him. Then her eyes flew open again. "The ice cream!"

Danny continued his explorations. "Hmm?"

Kristen twisted to look for the carton of ice cream. "It's melting."

He held her by the hips, tracing her navel with his tongue, then slipped down to taste her thoroughly, inside and out. Kristen drifted back to the floor. "I'm melting," she sighed.

This time, Danny lingered, spoiling both of them.

THEY HELD HANDS on their way from the living room to the small, bright kitchen Kristen loved. A row of cheerful mugs hung from wooden pegs under a cabinet. Alphabet magnets at a two-year-old's height on the refrigerator spelled nonsense words like "guh," and "mizleput." Multiple overlapping pictures showed Indica, Kristen, Daisy, and their friends and family, including one of Kristen at Victoria and Luke's wedding and clearly pregnant. Daisy had been born the next day.

She and Danny shared the smiles of new lovers who have discovered a delicious secret. He wore just his shorts and she had on a flowy shirt. Kristen set the bag with the ice cream on the counter, and Danny circled an arm around her waist while he kissed the side of her neck. She kept thinking she should do something with the ice cream, but then Danny would distract her.

She turned in his arms and held up another condom, beaming at him.

Bemused, he said, "It has a smiley face on it."

"Pleasure in all things," she told him.

"You're more flexible than I thought," he told her.

She nodded sagely. "Yoga sex."

He kissed her forehead, eyelid, cheek. "I'll never miss another class," he whispered, and slid the condom from her fingers. He tucked it in his shorts pocket, but her dismay turned to delight when he removed the lid of the ice cream container and dipped a finger in it. "You might not want to get ice cream on your top," he said, his voice husky.

It fell to the floor without her even remembering taking if off. He slid his finger down the slope of her breast to her nipple and she shivered as the chill increased every sensation. He caught a drip with his tongue, then licked the ice cream from her breast before taking the nipple in his mouth, lingering enough that she wanted to command him to take her fast and hard again. But this was too delicious, and she let herself fall into his generous care as he lifted her onto the counter and trailed kisses from the inside of her thighs all the way down to her toes and back up again.

Then he licked at her center as if she were the ice cream, and she rode the waves of another orgasm, barely hearing him ask if he could join her.

"Yes, please," she murmured, head back, eyes closed in bliss.

His shorts dropped to the floor and the heat of his body suffused her and she realized she wanted to see him. She opened her eyes, wrapped her legs around his hips, and they watched each other as they rocked together and both melted into oblivion again.

HAVING RECOVERED FROM the latest round and put the ice cream away, they stood wrapped together, reveling in their newfound discovery of each other. Kristen could have stayed there forever.

"What made you change your mind?" Danny asked. "About being just friends."

"I started to trust myself again. Plus, that kiss on the set."

"Mmm, that kiss was magic." He ran a thumb along her bottom lip. "I can't imagine you doubting yourself."

"After Michael left..." She made a noise. *"Ugh.* I don't want to bring him into the room right now, but after he left, I did start doubting myself. Especially when Daisy was born and I was now responsible for this little person. But when I met you, you scared me."

"I don't ever want that."

"It wasn't anything you did or didn't do. It was me, wondering if my radar had gotten scrambled after Michael. That's what I meant earlier, that day in the trailer, when I said it was a good thing and I'd explain it to you later. So I—" she stopped. "Do you want some popcorn?"

He blinked. "Will it be just as much fun as the ice cream?"

"Maybe better. Serious talk can sometimes flow easier with food." She pulled out some ingredients: popcorn, coconut oil, and what looked like light cocoa powder. She shook the jar. "Cacao with cinnamon, in case you were wondering. The combination is messy, but divine." She turned to face him, clearly waiting for his answer.

His stomach rumbled. "Obviously works for me. But what were you saying? About the friends thing?"

"I can't remember. Your abs are distracting me. Usually sharing an orgasm with someone makes me even more chatty with them. Give me a minute." She pivoted to point to a small drawer. "We have a ton of napkins from Indica's Suzy Homemaker stage. Could you get a couple out?"

He opened the drawer and pulled out two napkins from the colorful stack. "Her Suzy Homemaker stage?"

Kristen started on the popcorn. "She likes to keep her life interesting, to try out multiple passions. For a couple of months, she made a lot of things for the house. Curtains, pot holders, candles, and those napkins. If she has extras, Star sells them at her shop."

"And they own the flower shop together."

She was in the process of shaking the pan over the stove as the first kernels started to pop, but glanced at him with a smile. "You remembered."

She had not only made introductions that afternoon, but she'd also told him who was part of a couple, and given a brief bio on each person. He may be having trouble with his lines recently, but the fact he remembered information about her family was more important to her.

"I like your friends and family," he said over the frenetic popping sounds

"I consider them all my family. But I agree they're very likable."

"They're very protective of you."

The activity subsided, and Kristen shook the pan a few more times before turning off the heat and setting it on a cool burner. "They seem stuck on the idea that I can't get through my life without some help."

Danny reached up for a large bowl at the top of one of the cabinets and set it in front of her. "I think everyone needs some help to get through life."

She nodded at the bowl. "Point taken." She reached one hand up and touched the ceiling with her fingertips. "But I can still handle a lot on my own."

"I don't doubt that in the slightest." He grabbed a couple of colorful pot holders and upended the pan over the bowl. Kristen poured some of the cacao/cinnamon blend over it and mixed it with a large wooden spoon.

When she held out a few kernels, he opened his mouth and she popped them in. He chewed, and his eyes widened at the burst of flavor. She took some herself, savoring it: bitter, rich and sweet at the same time.

"Okay," she admitted. "I have a little coconut sugar mixed in here, too." She handed him two cold beer bottles from the fridge, picked up the bowl, flipped the napkins over her shoulder, and said, "C'mon. Let's eat and enjoy each other some more."

They settled on the couch with the bowl between them, sitting almost sideways to face each other.

"You're not as restless as usual," she said.

"We just had sex three times in a row."

"I like the 'we.'"

"Are we a 'we'?" he asked.

"It's early, but I hope so. I can see it happening." She pushed a lock of hair behind her ear. "Does that scare you?"

"Like I said before, I don't scare easy." He took a handful of popcorn, but didn't eat it, just stared down at the coated kernels. "My life is unsettled."

"The money?"

"That, and no guarantee on this pilot." He shrugged and finally looked at her. "Uncertain future, but that's the life of an actor."

"Are you warning me off?"

"I just found you, I don't want you to go anywhere. But you're always straight with me, and I want to be the same."

"I can work with that as long as we're together on it."

He leaned over the bowl to kiss her. Spicy. Salty. Sweet. "I knew I could never be just friends with you," he said.

They stared at each other over the popcorn bowl. It went flying as they reached for each other and once again tumbled into that sweet abyss together.

CHAPTER TWENTY-THREE

Kristen, Daisy, and Gail walked up Castro Street past La Tortilla. The red and white sign for the Castro Theater loomed ahead of them, but their destination was the bright green building two shops up: Dog Eared Books. Gail visited about once a week to buy, recommend her own books, and sign any copies in the store, and Kristen often joined her.

Kristen wore an orange sundress, patterned with large flowers, over leggings. She'd dressed Daisy in rainbow striped tights and a purple shirt with a unicorn on the front. Gail wore black jeans, black boots, and a white t-shirt with pink sleeves that read "Ask Me About My Radical Feminist Agenda." She'd spiked her hair more than usual, and purple streaks mingled with the blonde.

Kristen thought they were pretty low key on the San Francisco scale.

She'd been telling Gail about her night with Danny, and while she left out some of the more private conversation and toned down certain words because of Daisy, she'd just gotten to their make out session on the living room floor.

Gail stopped on the sidewalk. "We can't go in the store until you tell me if he's a good kisser or not. Ever since my publisher dumped me, and Casey decided he didn't want to have sex with girls anymore, I haven't been able to write one single smutty thing. Please give me something to work with."

Kristen, holding Daisy on one hip, pulled them closer to the building and away from sidewalk traffic. Daisy held a hand up toward Gail and Gail high-fived her.

"It's like the kid knows what I'm saying."

"She does. She's two. She walks and talks and thinks and everything."

"No, like she knows the depth of it. It's creepy."

"I know you're not calling my child creepy."

"Not in the least. Seriously, though, good kisser?"

"Well…"

While Kristen tried to come up with the best description for Danny's kissing style, two teenage girls scuffed by in flip-flops, staring at their phones.

"Pick up your feet!" Gail barked at them.

They started, clutching their phones to their chests, and stared at her.

"What's wrong with you?" one of them demanded.

Gail gave them a charming smile and said, "You'll live longer if you do," before sweeping into the bookstore.

Kristen shifted Daisy in her arms so she could press her palms together and give the girls a slight bow. "Namaste," she said, before following Gail.

"Stay!" Daisy called after them.

Gail kneeled in front of a small round table, furiously scribbling on the back of an old postcard. A sign indicated you could express your opinion to your elected officials and the bookstore would mail them for you. Kristen set Daisy down and peeked in the box of completed cards. She saw more than a few drawings of crude gestures and bare backsides.

Gail scribbled another line and muttered, "Next I'll be telling those teenagers to get off my lawn."

"Kids these days," Kristen said playfully.

"Right?" Gail stood and dropped her card in the box. "And no one talks to them the way they need to be talked to. With any sort of authority. Everyone caters to them, afraid that every second of their existence won't be stellar." She handed a dollar to a passing store clerk, indicating it was a donation for postcard postage. "We're raising a generation of rude, spoiled crybabies."

"Amen, sister," the clerk said on his way past. He waved the bill and thanked her.

Kristen looked down at her daughter, who sat trying to tie Fuzzy

Bunny's ears in a knot. "Is that what I'm doing with Daisy?"

"Well, sometimes you give in to her, like when she has a tantrum, but overall, no. You're an outstanding parent."

"I always appreciate your honesty, Gail."

"It's what I'm known for."

Kristen waved her hand around. "I don't have the words for how he kisses. You're the writer…"

"You're not even giving me one end of the spectrum here." Gail peered at the shelves, then headed for the "Local Lit" section.

Kristen gathered up Daisy and followed, glancing at the shelves as she went. Beyond picture books, she didn't have time to read for pleasure these days, but she missed it. Her sister insisted that film and TV won out, but Kristen always thought books were better.

"Good kissing," Kristen told Gail. "Beyond good. The best I've ever experienced."

Gail pulled one of her own books from the shelf and held it to her chest. "This never gets old," she said with a sigh. "And neither does good kissing. Exemplary," she said, then shook her head. "No. Exceptional? Why am I stuck on 'e' words?" She signed her name in the book and put it back.

"Sometimes the words don't matter." Kristen handed her another copy of her book.

"The words always matter." Gail signed this one with more of a flourish, adding a couple of Xs and Os. "So now that we've covered the extraordinary kissing, how was the sex?"

"I also appreciate how your words are always straightforward."

"It's the only way to be. You taught me that." She replaced the book and turned toward the counter. "I'm going to give them a couple more copies." She waved a finger at Kristen. "I want all of the details you can manage in front of your brilliant offspring."

Kristen smiled at her. "We'll be in the children's books."

She sat Daisy on a tiny chair and settled next to her, pulling out a copy of *Knuffle Bunny*, one of Daisy's favorites. Bunnies were a big deal right now. This was a story about a little girl with a stuffed bunny going to the Laundromat with her father. Then the bunny goes missing.

She started reading aloud, but Daisy insisted on doing it herself. Kristen handed the book over and listened to her daughter making up words and a story as she flipped the pages, her own bunny tucked tightly against her body.

How long before Daisy's own questions about a daddy came up? How long before she started feeling the lack of a parent or siblings in her life? Kristen surrounded herself with people who saw Daisy as their own, including strong male role models, and Kristen herself didn't feel the need to fall into the traditional idea of family. Still, she couldn't step away from simply being a mom and wanting her daughter to be happy and feel complete in her life.

Gail came back with a stack of books in her arms. "We need to leave before I buy any more books. Do you want food?"

They ended up at a nearby café, settling at a table in the window. Kristen sat Daisy on her lap since there weren't any booster seats. Even though Kristen draped her in napkins, Daisy managed to get peanut butter in her hair, on her shoe, and one elbow. But she was happy, able to eat the bagel on her own, so Kristen let her go at it while she ate her own roasted eggplant chipotle sandwich. She set Fuzzy Bunny on the windowsill to watch over them.

Before Gail dug into her pepperoni pizza and diet Coke, she said, "I have two subjects to cover: the sex, and this revelation about Star and Cort."

Kristen wiped a smear of peanut butter from Daisy's shoulder. "You know I don't like to talk about my friends when they're not here."

"So we're going to talk about Danny's performance prowess?" Gail bit off the end of her pizza slice with a happy growl. "Or maybe his birds and bees bewitchery?"

"Touché. I already told him this, so I can tell you: he kisses like an angel, he has as much stamina as me, and he fully understands a woman's body." Her spine tingled as she remembered the night before, but it dissipated quickly. "But I'm confused. And I really need to talk to someone about it."

"I'd rather have more naughty details, but I can live with that for now. But first I want to say, I think Star could tame cowboy Cort. Doesn't mean I won't be watching him. He steps out of line for a split second, and I'm all over his ass."

Kristen smiled. "I'd expect no less. I agree with Victoria that we shouldn't underestimate Star. I think Cort's been growing up, and he has a good heart. But we'll both be watching."

Gail nodded. "So what's going on with Danny?"

"He rearranged some of the letters on the refrigerator."

"Scandalous."

"He had to leave early this morning. He left Daisy's words, but he wrote out 'miss you already.'"

"Was 'you' spelled or just a letter?"

"Spelled."

"Damn." Gail shoved a large bite of pizza in her mouth. "Keeper just for that," she mumbled.

Daisy's fingers opened so the section of bagel she'd been eating dropped into her lap. "*Danny*," she said in a serious tone, staring down at the mess.

Kristen leaned around Daisy to try to see her face. "What about Danny, baby?"

"Danny!" Daisy announced it this time in the voice she usually used for something joyful.

"Do you like him?" Gail asked.

"Yes," Daisy said, and picked up her piece of bagel again.

"Well, that's a good start," Gail said with a wry grin to Kristen. "So spill. What's going on with you two?"

"You were right. About the teacher becoming the student." Kristen twirled a lock of Daisy's hair around one finger. "He fits all of the criteria for my soulmate list, but I actually never thought through the fear part. That fear of messing up because the stakes are so high. He's a *soul mate*. It's much scarier than I imagined. But he's so...and we're...I mean, last night, was..." She sighed, images of the night before flooding her mind, stealing all of her words.

"Full of o's?"

"So many o's."

"Oh." Gail sighed, too, a piece of pizza drooping in one hand. "I so miss the o's. Can you get over the fear part? Or is it too much."

"I think I can. It's...that's not my biggest concern."

"What is?"

"He's on his phone all the time." She stopped. "No, that's not right. His phone is buzzing with texts all the time. He tells me about some of them, like his roommate Glen bringing home two women in one night—"

"I feel my next book starting to come alive."

"—but with some of them, it's like there's a secret. He gets this guilty look on his face after he reads them, and then he shoves the phone in his pocket. And I know we don't know each other well enough to be sharing everything, but…"

"But you had enough secrets with Michael. Or he had them with you."

Kristen sighed, looking at the top of Daisy's head. She caressed the curls back from her daughter's face. "Exactly."

Gail tugged at her own spiky hair. "You need to ask him. Directly."

Kristen took a drink of water, and held the glass for Daisy to drink while she considered Gail's suggestion. "You're right. But what if I don't like the answer?"

CHAPTER TWENTY-FOUR

Danny strode up Washington Street at Baker, running lines through his head. Samantha had given him a good tip about associating words with movement.

"I've heard taking a nap can help, too," she'd told him. "But that's not in your wheelhouse."

So he charged up the block and back down to the intersection where the crew was setting up for the next scene, which would take place after he and Kristen escape through the alley. He stopped on the corner to practice belly breathing. He felt like an ass doing it, but he wanted to let Kristen know he was trying.

He shucked his jacket and draped it on the doorknob of his trailer. The fog had crept in that afternoon and remained in the street, touching the edges of trees, cars, and his exposed skin. He could have gone into his trailer, but walking had heated him up and he liked the brisk air and watching the crew. They were filming day for night again since it was supposed to be after one a.m.

And who was he kidding? He'd gotten here an hour before his call time, and was standing on this street corner with a wide view, for his first glimpse of Kristen when she arrived. The lines were coming easier, not slipping from his mind as they had been the last couple of weeks. Still, he needed to work off some excess energy while he waited.

Just as he turned on his heel to go down the hill, a vehicle pulled up across the street in front of a nondescript apartment building. His heart skipped until he saw it was a small beater pickup with a toolbox in the back. He was looking for the Prius Kristen shared with Indica or maybe a rideshare vehicle, not another crew member's car. He took a few steps down.

Heels clicked on pavement and a car door slammed. Danny glanced back at the truck again, pausing at the sight of a short, elegant woman in a business suit and leopard print boots. Interesting choice of vehicle, he thought with a smile, then his body electrified when he realized it was Kristen's sister Victoria.

The passenger door opened and his gaze was riveted across the street as Kristen's strawberry curls came into view. He remembered those curls floating across his face and shoulders as she panted above him, her nails digging into his chest. Had that been episode three? Or four? They all blended together in one stunning, overwhelming memory.

Her friend Cort had called her "Sunshine," and it was a fitting nickname. But she'd done more than brighten his world; she'd tilted it sideways.

Kristen scanned the area while Victoria said something to her. As he crossed the street, Danny looked neither left nor right as his good Ma had taught him, his focus laser-sharp on the woman across from him. She laughed at something Victoria said, then brushed windblown hair from her face, and turned, finally, in his direction.

He felt his grin match hers, and he even laughed a little as she rounded the car, her pace increasing as they closed the gap. They rushed to each other, then stood inches apart, their eyes locked.

"Hey," he said.

"Hi," she breathed.

He couldn't think of any other thing to say. His entire being was filled with only her: cheeks and nose pink from the cold, hair shimmering around her face in the same breeze that drifted the fog toward them. He took in the flecks of gray in those bright blue eyes, her rounded top lip, a tiny mole at her left temple that he wanted to kiss.

Victoria let out a gentle cough.

Danny turned to Victoria in apology. "Hey, Victoria, sorry. It's nice to see you. I had a good time at the picnic."

She smiled as he gave her a one-armed hug. "You passed a few tests you probably didn't even know you were taking the other day.

I'm just here to drop off Kristen and say hi to Sam. Is she around?"

He did a slow turn, seeing the crew setting up lighting, taping down cords, and assembling portable reflector shields. "Across the way there," he said, pointing. Samantha Jamison-Gallagher stood around a clump of monitors with Gary, Keesha, and Hans. "At video village."

"Thanks. Have fun," she told Kristen, and marched across the street.

"Do you have your lines with you?" Danny asked Kristen.

She patted a large orange bag hanging from one shoulder. "I'm nervous. Victoria helped me with them last night, but I'm worried I'll forget everything."

"Let's go through them together." He took a step to head to his trailer, but Kristen stayed put.

She tilted her face toward his. "That might not be very productive."

He shook his head. "Why not? We—" Sunlight flashed on her hair and in her eyes. "Right." He'd been so focused on seeing her, his brain had shut down what his body never forgot. Just standing next to her wasn't enough. He stepped so close their chests brushed, and he caught a lock of hair that danced in the breeze, holding it lightly so the ends tickled his palm. "May I kiss you?"

"I don't know why you haven't already."

It took only a slight tilt of the head and their lips touched, feather-light, almost hesitant, but still shooting fireworks off through his entire body. She gasped against him, and they moved closer, solidifying the contact. He still held a lock of her hair in one palm, and pressed the other against her cheek. He let his fingertips stroke the edge of her ear, strong and delicate at the same time. Her lips parted and she flicked her tongue against his upper lip.

His skin tightened, heating up.

He had no idea how long they kissed before Kristen pulled back. They stared at each other, gasping, as if awed by what had passed between them, from just a kiss.

Then Kristen giggled.

"I don't think anyone's ever laughed at my kissing," Danny told her. "Blow to the ego."

She pressed a hand to his chest. "It wasn't the kissing. It's me. I think I'm maturing."

"And that's funny?"

"No, it's good. What's funny is that I'd rather kiss you than sleep with you." She paused. "Well, okay, I want both. But you kiss like an angel. And the way we just kissed here in the street? I could do that all day."

He could do it for the rest of his life, he thought, and tucked her close, pressing his face into her hair. She'd probably already seen it, but he wasn't ready to reveal such strong emotions to her. Or was it that he wasn't ready to realize them himself?

He cleared his throat, but could still hear the gruffness in his voice when he spoke. "You'll need to check in with Keesha. Then you'll go to to hair and makeup."

"What about reading lines?"

"You're right. We should probably do that outside."

"It's warmer in the trailer..."

He didn't respond. He knew he should say something, stop standing there like an idiot in the middle of the street, holding her like he wouldn't be able to breathe if he let go.

She tilted her face up until he finally had to look at her.

"Trailer." She brushed her hair from her face after saying that one word. "Do we have time to *read lines* in the trailer?"

His body heated up again. "Depends."

"On what?"

"On whether you want it slow, fast, or in between."

CHAPTER TWENTY-FIVE

After hair, makeup, and a wardrobe change back into her glittery halter top, gold boy shorts, and go-go boots, Kristen walked with Keesha to the filming spot. Kristen counted seven other people besides herself, Keesha, Danny, and Samantha. She recognized them from the previous filming, but couldn't remember all their titles. She waved and smiled, and a few waved back, but most looked serious as they watched Gary, who stood on the sidewalk in front of a narrow alley. They were in a completely different part of the city from where they had filmed the last couple of scenes, but Danny had told her the editors would use filmmaking magic to make it all look like the same area.

"We don't have a lot of time with the light, so we're going to do some quick blocking, then move on." Gary turned to Kristen. "You'll stand out of sight at the edge of the alley. When you run out, you'll be holding hands, Kristen in the lead because she knew the secret way out of the club and through this alley to get Seth away."

He showed them where to stand, then walked them through the actions. "You'll run to this point on the sidewalk, then Danny will pull you to a stop. While the dialogue is going, Kristen, you should be pulling at his hand, like this." He grabbed Danny's hand and stood facing him, tugging while Danny planted his feet. "You're desperate, you're scared, and you're steaming mad at him for putting you in this position."

"And kind of cold in this outfit," Kristen interjected.

Gary laughed and nodded. "And when he won't budge, you'll say your line about needing to get to safety. Danny asks where, you point up the street, and say your place is nearby. When he still refuses, and you're torn between safety and going back to face the bad guys, you finally let go and run up the street. We'll tell you when to stop."

"And when does the explosion happen?" she asked him.

"That's another day and another dollar," Gary told her. "Our special effects team will take care of that."

"TV is much more complicated than I thought."

The crew members around them all nodded, even as some of them were scribbling notes, taking out tools, or adjusting handheld cameras.

"So let's go through it once," Gary told them.

Danny led Kristen to the alley, stepping back into the shadows until Gary told them to stop. He had Kristen take one step forward, and after consulting with Samantha, even rearranged the placement of their hands so that Kristen's overlapped Danny's more.

"You were holding hands like that at the last location we filmed," Gary told her. "Plus, she's a strong woman, she led him outside. She's on top."

A laugh bubbled out and Kristen clapped her free hand to her mouth. She was having fun, but she knew this was everyone's job, and they took it seriously. She nodded.

Gary told them to go ahead, and she and Danny raced from their hiding spot, her boots clacking on the sidewalk. When she reached the tree Gary had indicated, she felt a hard tug on her arm and stopped.

"What?" she said with great impatience.

"I think we're clear."

Kristen stepped back toward the street, stretching out their linked arms. "I know those guys. We're not clear."

"You know them?"

"Please. Let's go." She pulled again, but he stood firm.

"We need to talk."

"My place is right up the street. We can talk there."

Danny shook his head.

"Your funeral." She dropped his hand and ran past Gary, the cameraman, and the crew until she reached the opposite side of the street. She turned, pushing hair out of her eyes. "Good?"

"Great," Gary told her. He turned to Hans, the director of photography, and they talked with their heads together, gesturing broadly. Hans looked at the cameraman as he joined the huddle.

Kristen glanced at all of the crew still standing around. Whoever said filmmaking was exciting was nuts. Just as Danny said, it was a lot of hurry up and wait. She had thought maybe the more scenes she filmed, the more the pacing would increase, but that hadn't happened. And she was freezing. She was about to trot back across the street when one of the crew members shifted and she could see Danny again. He was watching her, and the breeze blowing in from the ocean barely cooled her newly heated skin.

Hans broke away and shouted, "Mark 'em," and the crew came alive again. Terry, one of the assistant cameramen, gestured Kristen back to their starting point in the alley, and positioned her with Danny, their hands clasped. He pulled a roll of pink tape from around his wrist and slapped one piece in front of Kristen's boots and another in front of Danny's.

"It's for camera focus," Danny explained to her when another assistant cameraman stuck one end of a tape measure at Kristen's nose and measured out a length to the camera lens.

Terry then walked them through the action again, taping at each starting point, and waiting while the other cameraman measured. Keesha draped a borrowed coat over Kristen, who sighed with pleasure at its warmth, thanking the AD with a smile.

Kristen stood patiently, not minding the wait so much at this point because she got to hold Danny's hand. She hadn't realized she'd squeezed his fingers until he squeezed back, looking at her.

"What?" he asked quietly, to keep from disturbing the crew.

She shook her head, but gave him a reassuring smile. "It'll keep." She wasn't even sure she could express her happiness at that moment.

He pressed a quick kiss to her temple, straightening as Gary broke out of his huddle. He nodded to Keesha, who told Kristen and Danny they could break while the crew finished setting up the lighting.

Still holding hands, Kristen and Danny walked away from the set.

"Could we go to your trailer now?" At his look, she said. "Just to warm up."

"I'm pretty warm already."

She turned to him at the bottom of the stairs. "I might need to get hotter."

Inside the small space, Kristen slid the coat open. "With or without the coat on?"

His eyes roved up and down her body. "Oh God, with."

She leaned back against the table, slid aside her shorts, and reached for his belt. She was ready for him, but he bent in front of her for a few teasing caresses with his tongue. She clenched his shoulders and tugged his shirt at the same time.

"Now," she panted. "Right now, so good…"

When he slid into her, she couldn't hold back a moan, and wrapped her legs around his hips, urging him harder and faster. The waves of pleasure rose through her and consumed her body. She continued to gasp with an excess of bliss as he finished, but he suddenly froze and slipped a hand over her mouth.

"Shh…"

She tried, but it was so hard to keep quiet after that explosion.

A shuffle of steps, then someone knocked on the door.

"Mr. Linstead? You and Miss Clausen are wanted on set."

Kristen giggled into Danny's shoulder. "I don't think I'd ever get used to that."

Danny gave her a squeeze before letting go. "I definitely haven't." He helped rearrange her clothing, then held out his hand. "Miss Clausen? You're wanted on set."

He started to lead her down the steps, but paused, his body blocking her view from the doorway. She peered around him and thought she saw that creepy producer, but couldn't be sure. Then Danny flipped around, grimacing as his phone buzzed, and said, "Hey, sorry. I forgot something."

"What is it?"

"Just this." He angled her so she faced away from the doorway, then kissed her long and slow. When they headed back outside, the street was empty.

CHAPTER TWENTY-SIX

Her illustrious acting career ended with that day's scene, but Kristen agreed without hesitation to meet Danny on the set for lunch a few days later. During one of their many late night phone conversations, he reminded her the caterers always had vegan options available.

"You're not going to try to convince me to go carnivore?" She said it lightly, but she'd dealt with people who didn't understand her choice to be vegan. She'd long given up trying to explain. They either accepted it as part of her or they didn't.

"You're a light-hearted person, but you don't make life decisions lightly. I wouldn't ask you to change that."

Kristen blinked, toying with the cord of the latest ear piece Victoria had given her. She knew he wasn't too good to be true—no one was—but the good kept stacking up. She pulled her comforter tighter around her shoulders, staring out at the lights of the city from her spot on the back deck. The fog had rolled in, but it only added to the atmosphere and beauty of her adopted home. She didn't know what else to say, or express how much what he'd said meant to her, so she settled on, "Thank you."

They finalized their plans for lunch on the set, and reluctantly hung up. Kristen enjoyed the view for a few more minutes, before going inside to lie on her bed and daydream while she listened to her daughter's rhythmic breathing.

After her mid-morning yoga class, she left Daisy at the center's daycare and took the bus to a short block of Waverly in Chinatown that had been blocked off for the filming. Even having been a small part of the production, Kristen was still astonished by the amount of equipment, vehicles, and people involved in the filming.

Colorful awnings stretched across the top of a variety of businesses, from restaurants to florists to a jewelry design and repair shop. Red and gold Chinese lanterns strung between buildings swayed in a light breeze.

As Kristen stood watching the activity around her, a short woman dressed in platform Mary Janes, a black skirt, and plaid bustier approached her. She held two takeout containers in front of her.

"Hi, Kristen."

"Liz, the producer! I think that's amazing, by the way. You kick butt, and so do your outfits."

Liz stared at her. "I forgot how straightforward you are."

"I tried being crooked, but it didn't work out."

Liz burst out laughing. "Then I'll come right out and say Danny sent me. He's stuck in a meeting and asked me to keep you company for lunch." She held out the containers. "Vegan for you. Old-fashioned falafel for me. That okay?"

"That's great. I'd love to hang out with you."

Liz pointed behind Kristen to a section of sidewalk. "There are chairs we could use. Or there's a spot around the corner by the catering truck."

"I like curbside. And I just watched someone clean this area as if his job depended on it."

"We have a good crew. Curb, huh?"

Kristen smiled at Liz and settled on the edge of the sidewalk. "Different perspective," she said, accepting the container with her thanks.

Liz plopped down next to Kristen, tucking her skirt under her. "Works for me." She pulled napkins and cutlery from her huge purse and handed some to Kristen.

Someone had taped a hand-written note on top of her container: Cauli QM. She took a bite and moaned.

Liz poked at the falafel, then speared one and lifted it up, holding it there.

"No good?" Kristen asked her.

Liz shook her head, staring at the speared falafel. "This town is full of gay men," she sighed.

"Mmm." Kristen took another bite. "But we have great food."

"And you're vegan?"

Kristen nodded.

"That's not really eating. That's suffering."

"Your caterers know how to do it right. Cauliflower with quinoa and turmeric coconut sauce. Sweet, earthy, with great texture. And I'm not sure I could even pick out all of the spices. Garlic, ginger. Cinnamon?" Liz still looked skeptical, and Kristen wasn't going to argue that Liz's falafel was probably vegan. She returned to Liz's apparent dilemma. "So are you trying to find a straight man here?"

"Here, there, anywhere. I haven't had sex in two years."

"I went for almost three years." Kristen offered up some of her dish.

Liz shook her head. "You win." She shoved the falafel in her mouth.

"Oh, it's not a contest. I was sympathizing. Plus, my streak was broken recently."

"So miracles happen." Liz stared across the street for awhile, then seemed to shake herself. "Everything's a contest with me, but I'm losing in the love game. Ick." Liz made a face. "I can't believe I just said 'love game.'" She pointed at a tall man across the street with his back to them, wearing jeans, a t-shirt, and a utility belt. He had medium-length blond hair pulled back in a ponytail. "Do you think that boom operator's gay?"

"What's a boom operator?"

"Microphone. The tall guy with amazing shoulders. What do you think?"

Kristen studied the man as he adjusted a microphone on a tall pole. "Oh, that's Glen, Danny's roommate. Not gay."

"How do you know?"

"He flirted with me the other day." Kristen ate another bite, wondering who she could ask for the recipe.

"Shit."

"I thought that would be good, since it proves he's not gay. But—" she started, wanting to tell Liz about Olivia liking Glen.

"But I can't compete with you!" Liz flipped a hand up and down. "Did you flirt back?"

"Actually, I didn't." The statement surprised her. "Normally, I'm a big flirt, but I'm not interested in him. And—"

"Well, I can't grow three feet," Liz said, as if that might have been an option, "but I could dye my hair red and get some extensions."

"Why would you do that?"

"He likes you, so maybe he likes redheads."

"If that's all he wants, then he's not right for you anyway. Plus, I know someone on the crew who's already interested in him."

"I should just give up." Liz shoved the falafel around in the container. "Listen…" She looked around the general area, then scooted closer to Kristen. "PJ? The producer? He's got crazy-scary power, and not just in Hollywood. It's the kind of thing you only hear about in movies and can't believe is true. But it is." She glanced around again, as if they might be overhead.

"Why are you telling me this?"

"Because he disrupted our entire production to see you more. It sounds like a cliché, but he's got his sights on you, and he's like a steamroller when that happens. I know you're here to see Danny, but now that you're finished filming, you should keep clear of the production. He could show up at any time."

"I appreciate the warning, but I choose not to be afraid of people like him." She waved her fork around. "I also choose not to make stupid decisions around men like him, and to keep them away from my daughter, but I can't live in fear."

"And I can't stress enough how dangerous he is. Just…be careful. And you can come to me or Keesha if there's a problem."

Kristen nodded her thanks, but didn't say anything. She would only have been repeating about choosing not to live in fear. But she would definitely watch out for him. She didn't need that kind of energy, or person, in her life.

"On a lighter note," Liz added, "I never thought I'd like yoga, but I enjoyed your class. You should make a video or something."

"A video?"

"Yeah, to sell. Or download online. People love self-help videos and not only do you have a distinctive visual style, but you're really good. I don't think I've ever seen anyone as bendy as you."

Kristen laughed. "You should see some of the more dedicated yogis. They have amazing control over their bodies. But a video could be fun. I've never thought about it."

"You could make buckets of money. Include women with real-life bodies in there, but it doesn't hurt to have a sexy man, either. Something for the rest of us to watch when we're feeling unmotivated."

"You know, I know lots of straight men. I'll introduce you if you'd like."

Liz stared at her. "Oh. Thanks. That's...Thanks." She took another bite of falafel.

Kristen wondered if Liz was really ready to meet a man, or just wanted sex. Either way, she'd be happy to connect her with someone interesting. "You know, men don't always have a type. Some men..." She trailed off when she caught sight of a particular man making his way through the crew members from the other end of the street. He wore his character's outfit—a sharp suit, skinny tie, and shiny shoes—and moved with authority and purpose. Kristen's breath caught in her throat.

"Some men, all right," Liz said, catching sight of Danny herself. "Those freaking abs of his."

Kristen tore her gaze from Danny and looked at Liz. "I'm sorry. I don't believe in ignoring friends just because a person you're wildly attracted to takes over your entire being." She took a breath. "But he makes that difficult. What I was saying was, not all men have a type they always go for. Some of them, many of them, just like women. So if you don't mind a little advice, just be yourself."

She turned to smile at Danny, who had reached their lunch spot. He stood with his hands in his pockets, smiling down at them. "Thanks, Liz. For bringing Kristen lunch and keeping her company."

"No worries." Liz closed her container and took Danny's proffered hand. "It was enlightening." She turned to Kristen. "Think about the yoga thing. And that thing you said earlier? I might take you up on it. Let me think about it."

Kristen beamed. "Any time."

Liz patted Danny on the arm before winding her way through the crowd. Kristen saw her pointedly ignore Glen and wave to one of the carpenters, who gave a manly chin lift and wave back, but continued watching Liz as she sashayed up the street.

"The world is a good place," Kristen said to Danny.

"Sometimes." He nodded down at her. "Would you like to sit somewhere more comfortable?"

"No. I'd like you to sit with me." He settled next to her and she held up her container of food. "Would you like some?"

"Thanks. I had a sandwich during the meeting. I'm sorry I invited you out here but didn't get to spend time with you. And it looks like I'm going to be busy with the scene changes we just talked about. We have to cram in more today than we'd thought. The merchants aren't thrilled with us blocking the street for so long."

Kristen set her cauliflower to the side and wound her arm through Danny's. "It's okay." She leaned into him and he turned to kiss her. A long, tender, let-the-world-fall-away kiss. When they parted, she said, "That more than made up for it. Are you filming this weekend?"

"I'm free. Why?"

"Everyone is gathering at the Barn Sunday night so I can finally tell them about Daisy's father. I wanted to get it all out at once. No more hiding it like it's some dirty secret. You don't have to be there…"

"I want to. I want to support you. But what's the Barn?"

She laughed. "I forget you don't know everything about me. The Barn is where Luke and Victoria live. And Cort. They have apartments upstairs and a rehearsal space downstairs. We use it for big gatherings."

She normally loved parties and being the center of attention, but she was ready for this particular event to be over even before it started.

CHAPTER TWENTY-SEVEN

Danny rode to the Barn in the shared Prius. Indica drove, Star next to her, and Danny and Kristen held hands in the back. Kristen had confirmed she wanted him there, sealing it with a kiss. Or three. Daisy was with Indica's mom, Nella.

They picked up Gail on the way, and when Danny got out to open the door for her, she squashed in close to Kristen, laid her head on Kristen's shoulder, and grabbed Kristen's hand with both of hers. She wore a leather jacket over jeans and a black tank top that read "If Daryl Dies We Riot."

"What's going on, honey?" Kristen asked.

"I can't use my pseudonym for my self-published books. It's like starting all over again." She turned to glare at Danny as Indica rounded a left turn. "Could you not rub your thigh against mine? That'd be great."

Danny held up both hands in apology, even though he hadn't done anything wrong, and squashed his legs as far to his side as possible.

"Gail, don't take out your frustrations on Danny. He's a good guy, and wouldn't feel you up while you were down."

"Kristen, do you ever realize you're often unintentionally funny?"

"All the time. Not always in the moment, though."

They parked in a small lot next to an old brick garage with two roll-up doors and a red entrance door between. The downstairs rehearsal space had a white van parked on the left, surrounded by shelving cluttered with a variety of items. To the right sat musical equipment, a weight bench, couch, and chairs, including two loungers. A table in the center held platters and containers of food, while beer, soda, and water chilled in an open cooler next to it.

Since they lived upstairs, Victoria, Luke, and Cort were already there. Cort sat in one of the loungers, an arm around the waist of Star, who perched on the chair's edge. Taking up the other lounge chair, Teresa sat in Gabe's lap. Luke and Victoria both stood, arms around each other. Luke held the neck of a bottle in two fingers, but switched it to shake Danny's hand in greeting.

Kristen hugged and greeted everyone, introducing Danny to anyone he didn't already know: Marty and his wife, Miranda; Parker and his significant other Marrakesh. Her landlords Kim and August.

Kristen settled in the middle of the couch, patting the cushion for Danny to sit with her. He shook his head. "This is your story. But I'll be close." He settled on the arm, and set his plate and beer bottle on a small round table nearby; he might need a drink while Kristen spoke, and his stomach rolled at the thought of what she would reveal.

His phone buzzed. His agent. There'd been some talk about a Warhawk sequel. Danny would believe it when he saw a contract. Another nasty text from "Unknown Caller," which he knew had to be Jenkins. And his brother. Of all the times to finally get in touch with him. *Hey, brother-man*, was all it said. Danny itched to respond, but didn't. He put the phone on silent and turned to Kristen.

"I love you all." Kristen looked around the room. "And I love being the center of attention, and I know I'm the one who asked you all here, but this is admittedly a little weird." She looked at Danny, as if they were a tag team and it was his turn to add something, or to give her some encouragement. It was disconcerting, not only because it called them out as a couple, but it also revealed her current vulnerability. He'd never seen her turn to someone else for encouragement.

He nodded, and she released a long breath and turned back to the others. "I wanted to tell everyone about Michael because I wanted it to stop being My Big Secret. I've dragged out my refusal to talk about him for too long, and you're probably going to be underwhelmed at how this will just sound like yet another story of a woman who got pregnant and the jerk left her.

"But Daisy is getting older and even though she's got so many great men in her life, she's going to start asking questions. And what I want—and what I hope you'll all help me with in the same way you've helped me raise her—is to just be matter-of-fact about her dad. Her father."

She sucked in her lips, pressing them hard together. "He's her father, not her dad." She pulled her legs up and sat cross legged, tucking her feet under her thighs. The longer Danny knew her, the more he saw how brave she was. She might claim she couldn't do her life without her people, but he thought, if tested, she'd come out just fine.

"I met Michael right after I moved here. I was staying with Victoria and Teresa and figuring out my place here. And with them. I was really lonely, and I didn't even realize it. I think because I'd never felt that way before, not really."

Danny glanced at Victoria, then Teresa. Both of their faces showed surprise and guilt. Teresa pulled her boyfriend's arm tighter around her waist, and Danny bet she didn't even realize she'd made the gesture. He could see from Kristen's face that she'd caught the reactions, too.

"I always felt welcome. And loved. Never doubt that." She waved at Victoria, who had her arm around Luke's waist, and his over her shoulders. "You were busy with your job. And falling in love." Kristen smiled at the couple, then turned to Teresa. "And you were finding yourself. That's always so hard, and I supported you all the way. But I knew you had to do some of it on your own."

Teresa nodded, but to Danny, she looked close to crying. As if to back that up, she flung Gabe's arm away from her, and rushed to Kristen's side. She threw her arms around Kristen's neck, and Kristen gathered her close, like a parent comforting a child. Teresa's legs ended up over Kristen's. As they sat like that, murmuring to each other, Victoria disentangled herself from Luke, squeezed his hand, and tap-tapped more sedately to the couch. She sat on Kristen's other side, and the three of them clung to each other, alternately crying and soothing.

"Well, hell," Cort announced, as Star got up and joined them, soon followed by Gail and Indica. Even Miranda managed to find a spot. They all piled together, on couch cushions, back and arms, and Danny found himself pushed to the side. He suspected Gail, but he didn't mind. Their responses solidified his thought of what good people they were.

Victoria lifted her head, wiping at one cheek, and said to Kristen,

"We didn't know. You're always so self-possessed."

"No, honey, that's you." Kristen kissed her sister's cheek. "But until things settled down a little, like when you and Luke stopped dancing around each other and finally had sex..."

From across the room, Luke snorted a laugh, and Victoria shook her head. But she was smiling. "Anyway," she prompted Kristen.

"*Anyway*...until then, and until I got my yoga classes going, and met these lovely ladies..." She looked around at Gail and Indica perched on the couch, and at Star, tucked next to Victoria. "I was lonely. And a little sad. And I wasn't sure if I'd made a mistake moving here."

Not wanting to interrupt, fascinated as much by the tableau in front of him as with Kristen's revelations, Danny lowered himself slowly into a folding chair, one hand on the edge of the seat to keep it from making any noise.

"Then I met Michael."

And her life changed, Danny thought to himself, his stomach tensing.

"It was so mundane. I was walking through the park, he was sitting on a bench, drinking coffee and reading some boring financial article in the paper. In fact, that was my opening line, as I sat next to him."

SHE'D NEVER FORGET IT. He'd had one arm draped over the back of the bench, and she'd tucked herself next to him as if they were close friends, or already lovers. "There are so many more interesting things you could be doing right now," she said.

He hadn't missed a beat, continuing to at least appear to be reading. "I could give you a double entendre reply, but I won't, since I'm a gentleman."

She could hear the teasing tone in his voice, despite his almost deadpan response, and she said, "Pity. That can be pretty boring, too."

He finally lowered the paper and looked at her. He was maybe in his early 40's, by the crinkles at the corners of his eyes and across his forehead, but otherwise, his skin smoothed over strong cheekbones and a firm chin. He looked like a former surfer, with his faded blue eyes, tan skin, and close-cropped blond hair that might once have flowed around his face.

The arm draped over the bench now shifted closer to her

shoulders, almost but not quite touching, and he bent close to her. In a deep whisper, he said, "I bet you're *never* boring."

"May it be my last day on earth if I am," she said sincerely.

He laughed, and tucked his paper away. "Can I buy you a drink?"

"It's eleven in the morning."

"Feels like we've been together much longer," he murmured, and she caught him unabashedly reviewing her from head to toe. She'd left the house without a destination, wearing a yellow v-neck tunic over orange leggings and sandals. She gave him the same casual perusal. Light hiking shoes, tan carpenter shorts, and form-fitting black t-shirt. One that looked so soft she wanted to run her hands over it to feel the silky material and his firm muscles underneath.

He caught her eyes when they finally reached his, and smiled at her. "How about a coffee?"

"Caffeine makes me hyper. More hyper." She shrugged. "But I love herbal tea."

He nodded, as if making an internal decision. He dropped his paper and cup into a nearby garbage can and held out a hand to her. She took it and they walked to a local coffee shop, where they sat outside and talked.

"I SHOULD HAVE KNOWN at the time," she told her friends now. "First, he didn't recycle his paper, he *threw it away*. We held hands on the way to the coffee shop. His was a little sweaty, but I figured that's because *he* figured he was going to get laid and hadn't thought that might happen when he woke up that morning. But I can deal with a sweaty hand. The problem is there was no *zing*. None. Not like with you," she told Danny, "when we first touched." She saw every head swivel his way, and he gave a tiny wave, shifting in his seat. He didn't seem embarrassed. Maybe caught off guard, but still focused.

To get the story finished, she continued. "And as we talked, Michael said all the right things, was still very funny. But he only talked about himself. All about him." She shook her head. "Of course, later I found out most of it was lies."

She shifted on the couch, pulling Teresa's legs up higher on her own thighs, then reached behind her to squeeze first Indica's hand, then Gail's. "If Miss Gail had been with me at the time, I know her bullshit meter would've redlined. His list of lies included being single, with no children, and working for Habitat for Humanity. He also said he lived alone, which was technically true, because he had a separate apartment for his..." She wrinkled her nose, unable to think of any good word. "Liaisons," she finally said. "Again, I should have known. His place was too sterile, too much like a hotel room. I found out later it was in a building for corporate rentals. I also found out later, in one of my few forays on the Internet, that he'd been married for twenty years, had three kids..." She stopped, because her throat had tightened and she'd noticed her voice getting high-pitched. Someone rubbed her back.

Victoria took her hand and muttered, "Asshole," under her breath.

Gail added, "How do we find him? Beat the shit out of him."

The men in the room made noises of assent, shifting in their seats or where they stood. She looked at Danny. How had he ended up so far away, in that metal folding chair? He was leaning forward, elbows on his knees, and clenched fists hanging between them, eyes on her. She couldn't quite read his expression. There was no pity for her there, but she sensed sympathy for her situation. Mixed with anger. And that restless edge he always carried with him, like he was ready to jump up and follow Gail.

"No beating. I hope I never see him again. But I know that's not realistic." She looked at Victoria. "Maybe we can talk to an attorney, protect myself somehow if he comes back and wants to see Daisy, wants some kind of custody."

Victoria already had her Blackberry out. "I'm on it." She stood, phone to her ear, and paced away from the group. Kristen smiled after her. Taking charge, in the moment, was so very Victoria.

"This hasn't been very organized," Kristen said to the group. "And I've gone on too long anyway. The short version is: we didn't have sex that first day, despite all the signs pointing to it, but we obviously did later. He had told me how much he loved kids, and was sad he'd never had any, so when I told him I was pregnant, he was so happy. He said we had so much to talk about, so many plans to make. I believed him. Because I wanted to.

"He got me a cell phone, did I tell any of you that?" she asked. "We texted a lot. Although I didn't love it, I got caught up in it. The whole emoji thing..." She shook her head. "Anyway, we were supposed to meet at his place, to make all of our grand plans..." She stopped, not wanting to fall into dramatics or sarcasm. "He texted he was running late. I wrote back that I was, too, no problem. Stupid thumbs up in response. That was the last communication I got from him. When I got to his place, the doorman was thrilled to tell me all about Michael's wife finding out about his 'love nest'—that's what the doorman called it—and that Michael was gone. No note for me, no forwarding, just...gone. Even in the age of the Internet, I couldn't track him down. I eventually gave up."

"Did he give you his real name?" Gabe asked.

Kristen nodded. "When I looked him up, I found the website for his company, with a little bio about him and all of the high-end developments he'd been part of, 'beautifying' the Mission by tearing down workforce housing and replacing it with modern, 'affordable' housing. Affordable for the millionaires. The little bio was pretty generic, brief mention of wife and kids, not that I had any reason to doubt the doorman. He was so...gleeful about the whole thing. When I called Michael's office, they said he'd taken a leave of absence and was unavailable. So I had Daisy, I've been raising her with you all, and I moved on with my life. End of story."

Teresa hugged her, and Kristen hugged back.

"Well, not quite end of story. I want everything out in the open now. No more secrets going forward, so that as Daisy grows up, she'll know she has a father named Michael and he was with us for a really short period of time, but that he also has another family he's with. And when she's old enough, I'll try to explain that he's not with us because he's a shit heel, without using those words. But I'm not sure how best to do that yet."

She took a deep breath, feeling her lungs expand, then let it out in a whoosh. She patted Teresa's legs, and gently moved them aside so she could stand. "And now I really, really need to do some sort of releasing yoga pose, and then I want to stuff my face with the vegan amazing-ness T brought." She turned to Danny, who stood at the same time she had. He looked at her as if she were the only person in the room. "And definitely hug my new boyfriend."

CHAPTER TWENTY-EIGHT

When Indica drove them home, Gail sat in the front seat with Star on her lap. "I'll let the lovers have their space," she said. She didn't smile at Danny, but she at least looked less sternly at him. He wasn't convinced that she liked him any better, but he figured compared to Evil Incarnate Michael, Danny the Actor wasn't looking so bad.

Kristen sat in the middle section, one leg over his, her chin on his shoulder. Both of their hands twined together, and he found himself bowing his head toward hers, not certain exactly what he wanted—to talk, to kiss, feel her breath on his face?—but he knew he needed to be closer to her. And that was challenging in the back seat of a Prius.

They dropped off Gail first, then Star, and after Indica pulled the car into the small driveway, she left it running, and turned her head to look at them. "I'm going to mom's. We'll keep Daisy tonight. She's probably asleep by now anyway. You two can have some quiet time."

Danny shook his head, not so much in negation, but in awe over the generosity of Kristen's friends. "You don't have to do that," he told her. He glanced at Kristen. "Maybe you two want to talk after tonight's revelations anyway?"

Indica reached between the seats and squeezed Kristen's knee. "We got plenty of time to talk. My mom, however, does not have any grandchildren yet, and she might disown me if I take away her substitute granddaughter." She lifted her phone from the center console and waved it at them. "I already texted her about it."

"Indica, you're the best ever," Kristen told her. She looked at Danny. "Okay with you?"

He nodded, and they got out of the car. While he waited on the bottom step, Kristen urged Indica out of the car and they stood hugging for a long time, swaying side to side, arms tight around each other, long hair draped over the other woman's arms. Danny could only admire the dichotomy of women's absolute strength and tenderness.

The women parted and Indica gave Danny a wave before hopping back into the car and reversing into the quiet street. He waved back and turned to Kristen, who still stood in the driveway, watching Indica leave. With her back to him, in the darkened area of the drive, it took Danny a moment to realize Kristen's shoulders were shaking. And she sure wasn't laughing.

He leapt from the step and wrapped his arms around Kristen from behind. As tightly as he held onto her, she still managed to turn in his embrace and slide her arms around his waist, squeezing so hard for a second he gasped. She burrowed her face in his neck and her warm tears wet his skin.

"That was harder than I thought it would be," she said with a snuffle.

"I can't imagine what you've been through, or how that bastard could've left you." He squeezed her tight. "If I ever see him, I'll be happy to—"

She shook her head, her hair tickling his face. "No. No violence."

He sighed. He understood that, but he wasn't sure he could honor her request if that jerk ever showed himself. "Next to my ma, you're the bravest woman I know."

"I like that you included me with your mother. Men should always respect their mothers."

"You're shivering. We should go inside."

She shook her head, burrowing closer to him. "I'm not cold."

He held her away from him, just enough to look in her eyes and brush at her tears with his thumbs. "Neither am I, but I don't want to hold you out here in the street." He laid the fingertips of his hands along her cheeks, his thumbs caressing her chin. "I'm selfish, I want to be alone with you."

Her eyes moved left to right and she whispered, "There's no one on the street right now."

He laughed, wrapping an arm around her shoulders and led her to the front steps. As they walked up, he leaned close to her ear and said, "I want to be alone so I can undress you, layer by layer, celebrating every inch of skin as I go. When you're completely naked, I'll lay you down with your hair spread out like a cloud of golden red around your shoulders and—"

They'd reached the front door, and Kristen shivered under his palm on her low back. Before he could finish his sentence, she whirled around, hands on his face to pull him close. She kissed him hard and pressed her body full length against his. They kissed for a long time, lingering over each caress.

He pulled away just enough to groan, "Inside."

Kristen continued to kiss his face, moving her lips down his neck to his shirt collar, sending jolts from his spine to his feet. She traced his jugular with the tip of her tongue, and he practically felt the pulse of his heart there, beating harder and faster the more she kissed him.

"Inside *now*," he growled, ready to pull off all their clothes and go at it right there, never mind what he'd just described to her. But he couldn't stop kissing her long enough to reach the doorknob.

She backed them up to the door, pulling him with her, and took one hand away to open it. They fell inside, still wrapped tight and kissing, pawing at each other like teenagers. He kicked the door closed with one foot, and maneuvered her toward the stairs.

"Stairs," she said to him.

"Mmm hmm." They were headed for the stairs, indeed.

"Now," she said, echoing his earlier sentiment, when he'd wanted them to get inside, *now*.

He let her pull him toward the foot of the stairs. They pirouetted in their grappling dance until the staircase was at his back. Just as he started to swivel to get them up the stairs, Kristen gave him a light shove. He stumbled back, fell on his ass, and Kristen toppled onto him so his breath rushed out with a "whoof!"

She held his head between her palms, kissing him again with such intensity he forgot his lost breath and kissed her back. She reached between their bodies and undid his belt buckle, then slipped the zipper of his jeans down before he'd realized what she was doing.

"Whoa," he managed. "Here?"

She nodded, maneuvering her dress out of the way, then reached between them again. He felt her hand on his cock, pulling it out from his underwear, then she shifted up so her breasts rose heaving above his face, before she slid on a condom and lowered herself on him.

They both gasped at the contact, him deep inside of her, her thighs outside his, pressed against his jeans. Her panties, pushed to one side, brushed against one side of his cock when she lifted herself up, adding heat to an already fiery situation.

He made a sound, something like "Ohh, God," unintelligible even to him, and thrust his hips up to meet hers. He had to brace one boot against the wall and the other against the railing to keep them both from sliding down the stairs.

Kristen rose up and down, her breath increasing, and he lifted his head to kiss her neck, then slid his hands under her sweater, slipping them up her sides to cup her breasts. Her nipples hardened and peaked under his thumbs as he rubbed circles around the tips.

Her breathing became more ragged and high pitched. He already knew her sounds, and could tell she was getting close. He flipped her sweater up, shoved aside one bra cup, and pulled a nipple into his mouth while wrapping one arm around her waist to hold her tight.

She moaned as he flicked his tongue along her nipple, and moved faster. He met her thrust for thrust, pushing high into her, while sucking hard on her breast.

"Yes," she moaned. "Yes, and yes, and more yes."

She froze for a split second, body and breath, before moving faster and tightening around him so firmly he came hard and fast. One foot kicked against the railing and he thought he heard an answering thud. Had Kristen kicked out, too?

Danny fell back against the steps, minding the sharpness of their edges more than he had in the past few minutes, and Kristen collapsed on top of him. To keep them in place, he braced his boots more firmly and hefted her up with one hand on her ass.

"That was the most amazing stair sex I've ever had," Kristen breathed in his ear.

Still catching his own breath, it took Danny a second to process what she'd said. "The most? You've had stair sex before?"

A tiny yip sounded near their feet, and Danny jumped, tightening his hold on Kristen. "Jesus, what was that?"

A miniature growl followed the yip, and Danny felt the bottom of his pant leg tugged to one side. "Hey." He tried to jerk his leg back, but the Yorkie had a firm grip.

Kristen shifted in his arms and tilted her head toward the foot of the stairs. Danny's continued attempts to dislodge the terrier caused him and Kristen to bump down a step. She giggled, dropping her head on his chest. "Peggy is being territorial."

From the side door, someone said, "She hates it when no one pays attention to her."

Danny yelped like one of the dogs when he realized Kim stood in the doorway of his flat. Danny caught sight of him through the stair rail, dressed in a red and gold kimono, arms over his round belly, a knowing smile on his face. When he caught Danny's eye through the gap, he added, "August and I tried stair sex once. We kept sliding down. You'll have to tell me your secret to staying in one place."

Kristen said, "I think it's about bracing the feet. Danny and I both had to do it. You lose some rhythm, but it's still fun."

Danny turned his gaze to the ceiling and quietly banged the back of his head against the step. "Could you call the dog off?"

"Oh, of course, let me get her."

Out of the corner of his eye, Danny saw Kim dart forward. "No!" he almost shouted. "Just...call her," he finished lamely, because it was too late. Kim had reached the stairs and scooped Peggy up in one hand. She yipped.

Kristen caught the look on his face and said, "Don't worry, my skirt is covering your naughty bits."

"Yeah," Danny said, still looking at the ceiling. "That's my big worry right now."

"You need anything?" Kim asked. "Washcloth?"

"Nope, no, nope," Danny said to the ceiling.

"Thanks," Kristen told him. "We used a condom."

"Then I'll bid you goodnight," Kim said, and retreated back to his apartment.

Once he heard the door close, Danny said, "That was...that's...I..."

"I know," Kristen said. "Really good sex. We are *really good* together."

He shifted his gaze from the ceiling to her face, her wild strawberry curls falling forward as she looked down at him. He wasn't about to mention how incredibly awkward that moment had been. Because she was right. "Yeah," he agreed, risking freeing one hand to push back a stray curl stuck to her neck from the sweat of their exertions. "We are."

She kissed him, slowly, her lips caressing in a sweet, exploratory way. "You're so tasty," she said, then shifted off of him, brushing at her skirt. "I wear pants a lot, but skirts definitely have their benefits."

Danny tucked himself away, and they made their way upstairs and into her apartment, where he disposed of his condom and Kristen brought another one out just in time.

CHAPTER TWENTY-NINE

Danny found it hard to leave Kristen, but he had to be on set early the next day. He was in his apartment when Keesha called.

"Quick update on tomorrow's call sheet," she told him. "The production is currently on hold—don't ask, I don't know why."

"For how long?"

A long pause, unusual for Keesha, who usually went at a brisk pace. "Indefinitely. But keep your phone close for any changes."

A week earlier, this might have been a big blow, but all he could think about now was that he could spend more time with Kristen.

Keesha provided daily updates, and Danny and Kristen started spending all their time together. She took him to a lot of San Francisco's tourist spots, they played with Daisy at the park, and Danny even happily attended many of her yoga classes. He was also texting regularly with his brother, and even though they hadn't said much yet, his heart lifted now that the silence between them was broken. He continued to dismiss the texts from Unknown Caller that told him to *leave the yoga teacher alone*. Cheap threats. He'd known ages ago that he could never leave her. He also knew he'd fallen for her. Hard.

After two weeks of spending almost every moment together, he and Kristen decided to have a picnic dinner at the Headlands, a hilly spot just north of San Francisco that overlooked the Golden Gate Bridge. After the sun set, Daisy pointed at the sparkling lights of the bridge, danced and sang songs without any discernible words, then fell asleep clutching Fuzzy Bunny.

Kristen covered Daisy with a corner of the picnic blanket, then settled in between Danny's legs, her back to his chest. "Can we do this forever?"

He watched the lights of the city and breathed in her scent, tightening his arms around her middle. "I thought that was already happening."

She shifted to peer at his face. "You're serious."

"I love you," he said simply. "Both of you."

She burst into tears.

"Oh, hey." He scrambled around so they could see each other, and took her face in his hands. He brushed at the tears. "I didn't mean to make you cry."

"You didn't think I'd cry when you declared your love not only for me, but for my daughter?"

"I—"

She threw herself at him, practically crawling in his lap. "It's okay. Happy tears. Because I don't have the words to express my joy."

"Well, you could say it back. That'd be a good start."

She did, many times, in between a lot of kisses as they sat under a blanket of stars.

DANNY STARTLED AWAKE when his phone buzzed. He batted at it on the side table, scooped it up and held it to his chest. He looked at Kristen, who lay curled against him, her shoulder rising and falling steadily under the hand he'd wrapped around her. Good, the phone hadn't woken her. He glanced at the display: three forty-seven a.m. A text from Denny.

Wassup bro

Danny typed back with one thumb: *seriously?*

In cali could be there in an hour wanna party

Danny stared at the message. Was his brother saying he wanted to party, or was he asking if Danny wanted to party? And he'd have to chastise him for calling California "Cali." He looked again at Kristen, her curly hair spread out over both of them and tickling his upper arm. Later. He'd chastise much later.

Another text came in while he was thinking of how to respond: *in napa my girl wanted to go to french laundry 10 courses digesting need air.*

You dumbass, Danny thought fondly. Even if he hadn't been lying next to the woman he wanted to spend the rest of his life with, he wouldn't get up to meet Denny.

Busy, he wrote. He thought about adding "sleeping," but what would be the point? He clearly wasn't sleeping, and his brother had boundary issues. He'd ask too many questions and say they could sleep when they were dead, what was he, an old woman or something?

Danny knew the word "busy" wouldn't be enough to stop his brother either, but he was reluctant to put his phone on silent. His twin had finally started talking to him after those rough months of radio silence, and if anyone could get their mother to open up a little, it was Denny. They would have to have a longer conversation in person soon, but in the meantime he wanted to nurture their current dysfunctional relationship in the hope of trading it for a more functional one.

He took a deep breath, the phone still face down on his chest, and Kristen sighed next to him. He almost whispered something naughty to her, thinking she was awake, but her breathing settled into a regular rhythm again.

They'd shared a lot with each other over the last couple of weeks, both of them open and vulnerable, but especially Kristen when she told everyone about Michael. When she described how she'd gone to that jackass's place, so excited to start planning their life together, only to discover that he was a filthy liar, Danny pictured himself in that lobby. He could see the doorman gleefully revealing all to her. He saw himself punch the grin off the guy's face before swooping Kristen into his arms and away from that hellish discovery.

He hadn't been there, of course, but when she told everyone in the Barn about that moment from almost three years ago, he felt her isolation in his own body. He wanted to make up for the pain she'd felt standing in that lobby, absorbing Michael's betrayal.

The doorman might be able to get up a few minutes after Danny decked him, but he wanted Michael in the hospital. He actually wanted worse, but the jackass had other kids out there, and Danny wouldn't take away someone's dad for anything. He'd been there—twice—and no matter the guy's character, his kids just saw him as "Daddy."

He knew Victoria was already researching attorneys and custody law, so that Michael could never come back and destroy the family Kristen had created. The family Danny now wanted to join.

When his phone buzzed again, he smiled and shook his head. Den just couldn't let things go. But when he turned the phone over and looked at the screen, at first he wasn't sure what he was reading.

Last warning.

Danny's skin prickled and heat rushed to his face as he opened the text from "Unknown Caller" to read the rest of it.

Last warning. Leave her or the daddy comes back into the picture and takes his kid from the unfit mommy.

Jenkins. It had to be. But how did he know about Michael? No one in the Barn would have said a word to anyone outside of the group. Kristen had mentioned Liz warning her about Jenkins's power, his incredible reach. Danny could have told her the same. Did Liz know something Danny didn't?

Kristen's life might look unconventional from the outside, but no one could claim she was an unfit mom.

He jumped when the phone buzzed again. Twice. Two images this time from Unknown Caller, both from the picnic. One showing the group of adults sitting in a tight circle; Daisy sat alone a few feet away while a stranger approached, bent low, almost as if to snatch her up. Another of Daisy seemingly walking by herself toward the street. Daisy had never been in danger and someone had always had an eye on her, but the pictures didn't show that. They showed a two-year-old's mother completely ignoring her child while she partied with her friends.

"Son of a…" He held his breath, not wanting to wake Kristen.

When Jenkins first threatened him, Danny assumed if he ignored it, the producer would soon find another distraction. His subsequent texts and these photos proved otherwise. Pictures from that day had made the rounds of all the celebrity gossip sites, so anyone could have copied and texted them. Danny had no way of proving it was actually Jenkins who sent them, which meant Jenkins could deny any involvement while still following through with his threats.

He hadn't admitted it to himself yet, but as soon as he defied PJ by disobeying that first demand, his career had ended. It was one thing when it was just him. He'd have a rough road, but he'd figure it out. But now PJ had threatened Kristen, and Danny wouldn't let anything happen to her or Daisy. He'd do whatever it took to protect them—lie, cheat, or steal—and at that thought, an idea came to him.

Give Jenkins what he wanted—or at least, set it up to look that way.

"Hey," he whispered, brushing Kristen's hair from her face, and tracing his fingers along the soft skin of her shoulder.

Kristen's mouth curved up in a smile. "Hey," she replied in a sleepy-sexy voice.

He didn't want to scare her, so he worked hard to keep his own voice level and calm.

That was his first mistake.

"How would you like to be an actress again?" he whispered.

Her throaty laugh told him how she felt about that. "Terrible at it," she murmured. She burrowed her face in his shoulder. "Not me. I live in truth."

"It wouldn't be for long," he said. When she didn't reply, he wanted to add, "It's important," but his protective instincts suppressed the words. Mistake number two.

"Nooo," she said in a hazy tone, "bad idea," as if she knew what he was thinking. She patted his chest. "Sleep now."

He wanted nothing more than to hold her tight and fall asleep with her, but he needed to let her know about the situation, and get her on board. He ran through—and immediately dismissed—different options on how to get out of this dilemma. There wasn't any other way.

"Just hear me out," he whispered. "Jenkins is making threats, he wants us apart. I'll explain it all in the morning. We just need to act like we split up, that it's over. Then we'll…we'll figure the rest of it out somehow. We can come up with a plan tomorrow."

No response.

"Kristen?"

"Okay," she murmured. Then he heard her breathing grow deeper and steadier.

He looked down at her face in the moonlight. She and Daisy had become so important to him in such a short time. He would do anything for them. They had to make this work.

His insides quivered and jumped. He wanted to rush out and fix everything. Right now. But he forced himself to stay in place, twirling a lock of Kristen's silky hair around a finger that shook with frustration and pent-up anger.

He'd go over it with her again in the morning, he told himself. They had time.

Mistake number three.

HE AND KRISTEN LAY tucked together on her tiny bed. He'd lain awake for another couple hours, Kristen's strawberry blonde curl wrapped around his finger, thinking of—and continuing to abandon—ways they could stay together without PJ interfering. When he finally drifted off into a restless sleep, he still didn't have an answer, and everything had gotten muddled in his mind. He'd been contemplating kissing his way from Kristen's shoulder to her toes when his damn phone buzzed.

Countdown clock has started. Ready to call daddy's number. You have 5 minutes to leave.

Waves of blistering heat and frigid cold crashed through him, and he couldn't distinguish one from the other.

"Son of a—" He shook Kristen's shoulder, calling her name. "We need to—"

Nearby someone squeaked, "Daddy!"

Indica rushed inside the room, shouting, "Sorry, sorry. Oh God, so sorry. She's gotten really fast."

Kristen shot upright just as Indica swooped Daisy up and away. The toddler had been this-close to patting his bare butt, which Kristen adeptly covered before dropping his shirt over her head and stepping into a pair of undies while she went out the door.

Daisy wailed in the hallway, and Indica made shushing noises.

Danny could tell when Kristen reached them, because Daisy cried out as if her world had been torn apart. "Mammaa!"

"You're fine, baby," Kristen murmured to her. It sounded like they stood just outside the door and that Daisy fell into Kristen's arms with a howl.

A glance at his phone: *4 minutes left.*

Danny leapt up to search for his pants. They lay crumpled in the doorway. The memory of him and Kristen tugging and tossing each other's clothes off the night before hit him like a hot wave. Then Indica's whispered words chilled him like ice water because he'd found the answer to Jenkins's threats.

"Did she just call him Daddy?"

Kristen's response was drowned out by a garbage truck rumbling by.

"I'm so sorry," Indica repeated, still whispering. Danny could hear her now that Daisy had quieted. "Do you want me to take her to the kitchen?"

"No, it's fine. We'll have plenty of time together."

"I'd have trouble leaving that fine ass," Indica said.

3.5 minutes left.

Danny lunged for his pants just as Kristen appeared in the doorway, leaning backward to look in the room. She supported Daisy, who cuddled against her with a thumb in her mouth, blinking at Danny. With a saucy smile, Kristen set one foot on his jeans and edged them closer to her while he stood gripping a belt loop.

"What is it?" she asked, her smile dimming.

"Do you remember last night?"

Her face lit up again. "Of course I do. It was magical."

His phone buzzed. "I have to go."

"What?"

He tugged at the jeans and she lifted her foot. He yanked them on and straightened to button them, unable to look at her. He ran a hand through his hair and looked around for his shirt, throwing the sheets aside.

"I'm wearing it." Her voice had lost its warmth.

The sheets smelled like them. Lust rushed up and down his body, combined with doubt, humor, fear for her, anger at PJ, and disgust with himself for what he was going to do. All of it mingled into a complicated ball of confusion.

He couldn't sit here picking through his feelings. He needed to protect Kristen and Daisy. No hesitation. Constant motion had kept him going this far. He grabbed his shoes, and slid his phone in his pocket just as it gave another countdown buzz. Two minutes, he figured.

"Who's texting you?"

From the other side of Kristen, Indica said, "I should just…" but she didn't move.

Kristen and Danny stared at each other for what felt like an eternity; the specter of the countdown clock blared in his head. He couldn't do this. How the hell was he going to do this? Then she took a step toward him, into the room.

He had to go. He couldn't go. But what else could he do? He was on the clock. He had no money, and his own power was diminished. The only way he could help was by leaving—right now—and making it look as real as possible. PJ would back off, having gotten what he wanted.

And Kristen would never forgive Danny.

She must have seen something in his face, because her forward momentum stopped and her own expression turned into a question mark.

"I can't do it," he told her, which was the closest he could come to a confession of how hard this was.

"Then don't." She shook her head at him. "Don't do it, whatever it is."

His throat closed up. "I have to," he rasped. "I don't have a choice."

"You always have a choice."

This time he shook his head. "Just remember last night," he told her, before he dashed around her and Indica and down the stairs.

CHAPTER THIRTY

Kristen ran after Danny, but he'd disappeared. She raced down the inside steps, then the outside, the concrete chilling her bare toes. At the edge of their tiny parking area and the sidewalk, she stopped, hugging herself, and looked up and down the street.

"Danny!" she called into the empty air. "Danny!" She collapsed on the ground, the hard concrete as cold as her insides.

Gone. As if he'd never been there at all. She heard Indica open the door behind her and call her name. "He's gone," she told Indy, although the empty street was silent proof of that.

"Then come inside, honey. It's freezing out here."

But Kristen couldn't move. Even though the cold swept up her bare legs and across her arms and face, it was nothing compared to the ice inside her. He had just left. For no reason. Nothing beyond a few cryptic sentences and that frightened expression on his face. And the buzz of his phone.

"Come inside," Indica repeated, now standing close to her. "Daisy shouldn't be alone."

That was enough to get Kristen moving, and once upstairs she swept her daughter up and hugged her close. Daisy leaned into her, thumb back in her mouth.

"I bet he did think she said 'Daddy,'" Kristen said, as Indica turned the gas on under the kettle. "She said '*Danny*.' She's kind of nasal these days."

"And that was enough to scare him away?" Indica pulled two mugs from their hooks under the cabinet. "That doesn't sound right."

Kristen shook her head. "No. It doesn't. Not after last night."

"What happened last night?" Indica waved a hand around. "You know, besides all the sex."

Kristen couldn't help raising an eyebrow. "All?"

"The rug in the living room was scuffed up and the kitchen island had been moved about three feet." Indica pulled out the buckwheat flour and set it on the counter. "Pancakes with blueberry sauce?"

"I can't eat until I talk to Danny." Kristen stroked Daisy's hair, then set her down with her toys. "But I need to shower and change. I can't think with his shirt on."

"I'm cooking anyway. I need to keep busy. I'll watch Daisy."

Kristen went to her bedroom and straightened the sheets and blankets. She grabbed the bottom of Danny's shirt to tug it over her head, but could only stand there clutching at it until her arms shook. She stumbled onto the bed and fell against the pillows, holding one to her face so the others couldn't hear her cry. But no tears came; she was too much in shock.

She picked up her phone from the side table and checked it. Nothing. She wouldn't expect Danny to text since she'd complained about how long it took to respond on her clunky phone, but she'd hoped for something. A missed call, a message, hey, I was an idiot, *something*.

She called him, fully expecting it to go to voicemail, but he picked up. She drew in a big breath, her lungs expanding. She hadn't realized she'd been holding it.

"I'm sorry," he said in a flat tone, nothing in his voice inviting a discussion. "I shouldn't have left that way, but I couldn't....no time. It's the only way, and you'll be safe now. You and Daisy."

"What? Wait, safer? What do you mean?"

"Nothing. I mean you'll be fine. It's just better, Kristen, trust me on this. I have to go."

And he was gone again. She sat staring at her phone for a long time, noticing her heart pounding in her chest, but not understanding its continued beating when it had just been torn to pieces. Finally, as if watching someone else doing it, she closed the phone, pulled Danny's shirt over her head, and tucked it under her pillow.

When she got out of the shower, she heard voices in the other room. Adult female voices. She pulled on yoga pants and a tank top and went to the living room. Indica, Star, Gail, and Daisy sat around the dining table with plates of pancakes in front of them. They stopped talking when Kristen rounded the corner from the hall.

"I called them," Indica said.

"It's hard for me to believe vegan anything are good, but these pancakes are amazing," Gail said. She set her fork down and added, "But I'd give them up in a heartbeat if you want me to go kick his ass right this second."

"It's all about the blueberry topping," Kristen told her. "I'd like to go with you."

Gail shoved her chair back and stood. "Let's go."

Kristen waved a hand at her. "No, no. I want to eat first." She felt indescribably tired, and far from hungry, but she needed a steadying moment with her people. She pulled out a chair and dropped into it, but could only stare at the plate of stacked pancakes in the middle of the table.

Star picked up Kristen's empty plate, set a few pancakes on it and drizzled warm blueberry sauce over them. "Eat," she commanded. "You need energy to kick someone's tush."

Kristen picked up her fork, but it hung in the air over the plate. "Or go through a breakup."

"Did he really run because he couldn't handle Daisy calling him Daddy?" Gail asked.

"That's what it looked like."

"Dunderhead."

Kristen finally dug into the pancakes. Indica had made them well, the cakes light and fluffy, the topping both sweet and tart, but she couldn't enjoy them. "He's not like that. He was hesitant at first, but then we spent all that time together, and he seemed all in. He told me last night that he loved me. Loved *us*." She noticed the hush that went through the group after that; everyone stopped eating, even Daisy.

"It must be something else. His phone was going crazy. I heard him texting in the middle of the night. I was about to ask him about it when he stopped and pulled me close. He even whispered that he'd take care of me." She took a sip of tea to distract herself from crying again. Had there been something else? Something about acting again? That must have been a dream. "That's not someone who runs because a little girl he adores called him Daddy." She thumped the mug on the table. "And she called him Danny. He ran away from his own *name*, the dunderhead. Let's go kick his ass."

CHAPTER THIRTY-ONE

Danny managed to get a rideshare after he'd run a few blocks to try to escape his own idiocy. It didn't work. He could still see Kristen's hurt expression while the words from Jenkins's last text hung over him like a malevolent thundercloud: *3 seconds to spare.*

He wrote back, knowing it wouldn't make a difference: *where are you, you son of a bitch?*

He opened the text string and re-read it to keep himself from telling the driver to go back to Kristen's. There was still time to save it, he told himself, he could explain and they could come up with a solution together. Then he scrolled up—*ready to call daddy's number*—and reminded himself that putting that on Kristen was more selfish than the hurt he inflicted this morning. He'd heard Kristen coming down the stairs after him, the way she called his name causing him to stumble in his run. If Jenkins or his cronies were watching, they'd have witnessed the dramatic, emotional "breakup."

If Danny went back to Kristen's, and stood up to Jenkins, the producer would find a way to show her as an unfit mother, bring Michael back into the picture, and use his own money for a court battle. And Danny had no funds to fight back. Powerless rage filled him.

If Kristen lost her daughter because of Danny's stupid pride…He shook his head. He couldn't do it. This had to look real to the outside world, and he prayed Kristen would find a way to forgive him.

The car pulled up in front of his building and his phone rang. Liz

Mendenhall. He put a hand out to the driver and said, "Can you hang on a second?" He tapped the screen. "Liz?"

"Danny. You need to come to the warehouse." She always sounded professional over the phone, but her tone was downright brusque this morning. "Right now. Mr. Jenkins wants to see you."

"I'm in a car," he told her. "I'll be right there."

He charged upstairs to get a shirt, put on his shoes, then ran down to give the driver the new address. This was it. Jenkins had a lot of reach. Someone had to be watching Kristen's place for Jenkins to know when he'd left. Once he got to the warehouse, Danny would confirm it was over. Right before he decked Jenkins, goons or no.

It didn't make up for the pain he'd just caused Kristen, but he tripled his tip to the driver and strode up to the warehouse as if he had no cares in the world. He stepped into the crowded office to see Liz off to one side, Jenkins sitting at a desk, and three thugs lined up behind him. He'd never seen Liz in such sedate clothing: a black pantsuit with low heels and a white blouse buttoned to the neck. Her expression matched her outfit and she clutched a clipboard to her chest.

Neither Jenkins's nor his hired thugs' expressions changed when he walked in, but Liz at least attempted a smile. She waved him to a chair in front of the desk, but he said he'd stand. He actually lounged against the wall next to the door, pulling on all of his acting skills to appear nonchalant in front of Jenkins. He'd already taken too much from Danny; if the guy wanted anything else, he'd have to tear it out of him.

Danny sniffed and looked around the room, as if the other men hadn't showered in awhile. "Got your texts." He shrugged, still not looking at Jenkins. "It's done."

Jenkins nodded, a smirk on his face as if he knew.

Danny didn't take the bait. "So what now?"

Jenkins didn't answer, and when Danny looked up, the producer was staring at Liz.

She cleared her throat. "The production is letting you go, Danny. I'm sorry," she added, and she looked about to say something else when Jenkins heaved himself out of the chair.

"Broke your contract, delayed the production—"

Danny straightened, bristling. He'd expected to be fired, but not blamed for breaking his contract. The ironic part was, ever since he'd been with Kristen, his lines had been crystal clear to him. Jenkins had been the one to delay the production. "You have got to be kidding."

"Wouldn't leave your trailer when you were needed on set," Jenkins continued his litany as if he'd memorized it. "Allowed outsiders onto a closed set, late to work, not acting as specified." He leaned forward, his knuckles on the table. "*Bad* acting, but that's not in the contract. Just observation."

Danny pushed away from the wall to stand in front of the desk. "What do you want, you sick bastard? I broke it off. We're done. And that means you and I are done."

Liz rattled some papers. "We can go in the other room," she said, her voice higher than usual. "I just have a few things for you to sign." Danny wanted to reassure her everything would be okay, but he didn't want to take his eyes from the jackal.

"Leave them, Mendenhall and get out of here." Jenkins didn't take his eyes from Danny, either.

"It'll take half a second—" Liz started.

"Get the hell out," Jenkins commanded, glaring at her. "Or Arlo will escort you."

"Leave her alone," Danny said. He edged his body between Liz and Arlo. "Go, Liz. It's fine."

She had her cell gripped in one hand, hidden in the folds of her skirt. She lifted it enough for Danny to see it. Was she recording, or ready to call the police? "Are you sure?" she asked.

He nodded.

She sidled out behind him and through the door. Danny waited for the sound of her car starting up and rolling through the lot before he said, "You had your fun, Jenkins. Are we done now?"

"We're far from done, Linstead."

"Come out from the desk and leave your goons behind so we can finish it like real men."

Jenkins laughed. Actually threw back his head and laughed like a cartoon villain. "You want more added to your list of crimes?"

"Just one," Danny told him.

"Too bad you screwed up, Linstead. I liked you. But I like the girl better. Especially when her kid isn't around."

Danny charged around the table, shoving Jenkins so hard he fell back into his men before they could respond. From the chaos Danny thought he could get a good punch or two in, but something held him back. Kristen saying 'no violence' about Michael. And that hesitation was enough for the goons to recover and grab him. He might hesitate to hit a downed man, as much as he despised that man, but he wouldn't tolerate his own arms pinned back and a stranger's arm around his neck. He struggled, watching the third guy help Jenkins up from the floor and dust off his suit.

While Jenkins pulled out a handkerchief and delicately wiped his mouth, Danny stamped on the insole of one of the guys behind him. The pressure on his neck eased and he was able to take a deep breath in preparation to shake off the other one and charge Jenkins again, this time to take him down. All the anger he'd been suppressing the past year, including Jenkins's threats and mistreatment of Kristen, boiled up and directed itself at the slimy producer.

CHAPTER THIRTY-TWO

Danny trudged up the stairs to his apartment, hoping Glen wasn't home with someone. He'd texted his roommate, but hadn't gotten a response. That didn't mean he was out; he could just be "occupied."

After ducking the goons to give Jenkins a good clip on the chin, the three of them had pinned him to the floor, then tossed him outside. Continuing his cartoon villainy, Jenkins had called after him, "You're finished in this town, Linstead. Finished!" But there was nothing funny about any of this.

Danny reached the top floor, let out a long breath, and unlocked the door.

Olivia sat curled up on one end of the couch, holding a mug in front of her and staring out the window. She turned when he opened the door, but her expression remained pensive.

"Hey," he said. He didn't have the energy to come up with anything more interesting than that, but he did ask, "Where's Glen?"

She shrugged. "Tearing down sets."

"What?" Danny dropped onto the other end of the couch and let his head fall back. He was so tired he barely felt his body anymore.

"Didn't you hear?"

"I've heard a few things this morning, but nothing about sets being torn down."

"The pilot's been canceled."

Blood rushed through Danny's body, and he straightened.

"What?" he repeated, looking at Olivia.

"I haven't gotten the call yet, and I can't get hold of anyone else, so I don't have all the details. Keesha called Glen in and he texted me." She set her mug on the table. "I shouldn't be disappointed or surprised, I've been on plenty of canceled shows, but even with all its problems and delays, I liked this one." She pushed her long hair behind one ear. "And I liked working with you."

Danny eyed her warily.

"It wasn't like that, you doof. I just wanted to be friends, but you were always running from thing to thing, keeping to yourself. And I really wanted to talk to you when Glen and I got together—"

Danny held up a hand. "That's not my department. You know he's—"

"Been with all the girls on set? Yeah, I know."

"I was going to say a good guy, but that's true, too."

"This is all so shitty." Olivia collapsed against the cushions. "All those added hours, but the pay was really good. Oh, that reminds me. That girl showed up here looking for you. With a lot of friends."

"Kristen?"

"Yeah, she said something about kicking your ass."

Danny shot up, patting at his pockets for his keys. "What did she say?"

"Just the ass kicking thing. You know, I didn't like her at first, but she's growing on me."

"So she didn't say anything else?" Danny scanned the room. Where had he put his keys?

"Nope." Olivia pointed across the room. "I think you left them in the door."

He opened the door and heard the keys jangling, but the wall of uniforms stopped him cold.

"Daniel Anthony Linstead?" one officer asked.

Danny nodded. He knew what was coming, but his mind was focused on Kristen. Sure, she'd come here to kick his ass, but at least she'd shown up. She was open to seeing him, and he wanted that, too, even if it meant she yelled at him for the next month. He didn't care, he just wanted to fix his colossal mistake.

But the first officer was reading him his rights, another cuffed his hands behind his back and a third removed his keys. Shades of the goons, only with quiet respect, and this time he didn't resist. It was still quite a show of force and power and he knew Jenkins was behind it. He called back to Olivia that everything was okay, but please don't tell anyone, then let the police take him downstairs and put him in the back of the squad car.

HE DIDN'T WANT ANY PRESS, although Jenkins would probably leak the story. Danny knew it would create a stir to have his twin in the same town, as well as bailing him out from jail, but Denny was the first person he thought to call.

To his credit, Den didn't ask him anything. He just said, "I'm already on my way." And he must have been, because within 45 minutes he stood with two cups of coffee outside the holding cell next to the guard.

He lifted one shoulder toward the guard. "One's for him," he said to Danny, and handed the guy a coffee. He took a sip of the other one. "I've been up all night partying. What have you gotten yourself into, dumbass?"

"It's a long story," Danny said wearily.

"Those are the best kind." Den held the cup through the bars. "Just kidding, little bro. Take this. I gotta take care of the bail."

Danny heaved himself up from the hard bench and took the cup. "Thanks, man."

Den nodded, looking him in the eye. "I got you."

Danny nodded back, blinking. No way he'd cry here.

His brother and the guard disappeared and Danny dropped onto the bench again, staring at the coffee. He was alone in the cell, at least, but his mind was still crowded. He'd gone from lovestruck to fired to jailed in about 24 hours. He knew he should be concerned about losing his income, which meant his repayment plan was gone, and he'd have to add the bail money on top of everything else owed to his brother. But every time he tried to think his way through that, his thoughts wound back to all of the people he'd let down on *City Heat*. And to Kristen. He wouldn't kid himself that the pilot's cancellation was all his fault, no matter what Jenkins said. But if he'd made some different decisions—hadn't kept Jenkins's demands to himself or had taken them more seriously—his job might still be gone, but the production could continue.

But if he'd done anything differently, would the situation have ended up the same with Kristen?

He didn't know, and confinement wasn't helping his thinking process. Or his state of mind. He was pacing, the coffee clutched in his hand gone cold, when Denny returned with the guard.

"Free, my brother," Den declared as the door slid open. "For now, anyway."

Danny didn't know whether to smack him on the shoulder or hug him hard, so he just tossed his cup in a recycling bin and walked out of the huge glass and concrete police headquarters. They stepped out onto the wide entranceway and down three steps, where Den gestured to the left.

"Car's around the corner."

They walked up the block, traffic drifting past them on Third Street, a construction crew working nearby; shoulder to shoulder as always when they were together, but not talking. Usually their conversations flew New York-fast and intense. Danny noticed a few double takes from other pedestrians, but he mostly kept his head down. Den finally reached into his jacket pocket and Danny heard a lighter click and an inhalation followed by a long exhalation.

"Lorelei know you're still smoking?"

Den stuck the cigarette between his lips and brushed a knuckle under his nose. "She knows. She knows everything. She doesn't like a lot of it, but she knows."

Danny shook his head. "Why she puts up with you…"

Cigarette still between his lips, Den shoved Danny's shoulder. "'Cause I'm a sexy son of a gun."

Danny shoved back, shaking his head, but no good retort came to him. He didn't smoke, cheat, or lie, but he'd still screwed up his life, including a relationship with the best woman he'd ever known.

"You gonna tell me about it?" Den asked as they rounded the corner. "Or am I gonna have to read about it on Twitter?"

"Yeah. Let's just get to my place first." Danny stopped dead at sight of the yellow Ferrari F12 Berlinetta. Double parked. "You've got to be kidding me."

"Nope." Den dropped his cigarette and kept walking, crushing it under one boot. "Can't get up to speed for shit on these streets, but how you think I got here so fast?"

Danny directed Den to his small condo complex and was not surprised to see parking right in front.

"I live a charmed life, my brother," he said as he parallel parked into the tiny space.

They got out and Den stood looking up at the six-unit complex, two units on each floor. "Top floor?" he asked.

Danny nodded, pulling out his keys for the front door.

"At least you've got a view. Of the..." Den swiveled around. "Brick building across the way."

"Shut up, dumbass."

"Now that's more like it," Den said, and followed him inside.

Glen was still out and Olivia was gone. After he'd scrubbed his face and hands at the kitchen sink while Den prowled around the small space, Danny opened the refrigerator door. "You want a beer or something?" He didn't even know what time it was. And he didn't care.

"Any bars close by? Strip clubs?" Denny pointed at him. "You need a distraction."

"I need a shower." Danny opened two beers and handed over one of the bottles. "But it looks like I need to entertain my brother first."

Den pressed his fingertips to his chest. "Hey, I'm self entertaining. You do what you need to." He took a long swig, then grinned.

"Well, someone's gotta keep you out of trouble. Lorelei'd take it out on me."

"Says the guy I just bailed out. But yeah, she'd take it out of both of us, bro." Den dropped onto the couch and thunked his boots on the coffee table. "So who'd you beat up?"

"Perry Jenkins." Danny sat, copying his brother's pose.

"Jesus H. Christ, are you serious?" Den crashed his beer on the table. "How are you still walking around alive?"

"Asked myself that a few times this morning. He already fired me, so now I think he wants me to suffer publicly for my insolence."

"So what happened?"

"A woman."

Den grabbed his beer and sat back. "Usually is. She worth it?"

Danny shook his head, not in answer to the question, but because he was unable to find the words. He blinked up at the ceiling, his throat constricted.

"Hell, man, it must be serious. The last time I saw you cry was in fifth grade when Janet Allister kicked you in the nuts. So why isn't this girl here?"

Danny dropped his head back and slung his arm over his eyes. "I was a dumbass."

"Usually are."

Danny couldn't hold back a smile. He'd missed their banter, and his brother's teasing. His shoulders lowered as he told Den about Kristen. When he got to the part about running out that morning, Den thunked his empty bottle on the table.

"Call her," he announced. "Call, apologize your ass off, and get her back. I haven't heard you talk about a girl like this since…never."

Danny almost theatrically thumped himself on the forehead. Kristen had shown up with her friends this morning. He'd been on his way to find her when the cops showed up. He hadn't even talked to her yet.

But the threat was still there, wasn't it? Jenkins may have had his fun and made a point with Danny's arrest, but would that be enough for him to back off? Danny didn't think so and he knew Jenkins would make good on his threats if pushed. Danny would never put Kristen at risk of losing her daughter, but when he thought about a future without her…

He stood up to pace. It was all the same things that had been circling in his head since he got Jenkins's text last night. Stay with Kristen, she might lose Daisy, and that would destroy her world more than his cowardly exit.

"No." He shook his head. "I can't put her at risk. Jenkins would go through with it if he knew I hadn't backed off. He'd pull every dirty trick in the book until she lost her daughter. Just for his own screwed up satisfaction."

Den got up and stepped in front of him to stop his pacing. "So fight back."

"You think I didn't think of that? With what? Jenkins will back up every move with his money."

"The money again." Den veered around Danny and headed for the fridge. "You still stuck on that?" he said, bobbing his head inside.

"Like you weren't stuck on it so much you stopped talking to me for months?"

"How can you only have two beers in your house?" Den straightened, the door still open.

"Denny."

"We need to get drunk."

"That solves nothing and you know it."

"It might loosen my checkbook." He waggled his eyebrows. "Especially if we go to a titty bar."

Danny sighed through his nose. "Remind me how we're identical again?"

Den shrugged. "Got me. But I'm here for you. Even when I was being a dick and not answering your texts, I've been here for you. We'll figure something out." He closed the refrigerator and strode to the coffee table. He scooped up Danny's phone and held it out. "Call her. Tell her you were a dumbass. She doesn't want to talk to you, we go to a bar. Deal?"

Danny took the phone. Ten minutes later, he found himself walking with his brother to the corner bar.

CHAPTER THIRTY-THREE

While Den argued with the bartender about the smoking ban in bars—"It's un-American, dude"—Danny nursed his beer and thought about his conversation with Kristen. She had talked to him, but he couldn't claim it went well.

He'd been surprised she answered the phone at all, but not at the extent of her anger.

"I was an idiot," he told her.

"An ass," she agreed. "A jerk, a n'er-do-well, a loser, an oaf."

He grimaced at the reminder of their conversation in the trailer about Michael. She'd been looking for words to describe her ex, and Danny had supplied the synonyms. "All of those and more," he said. "I know you probably don't want to talk to me right now—"

"Well, I am talking to you right now, obviously. As for want. Yes, I do. Because I want answers. I went to your place earlier—"

"I know, I tried to find you—"

"After running out on me, you do not get to interrupt me."

He waited, in case she wasn't finished.

"You obviously didn't try very hard to find me," she said, "since you know all of the places I live and hang out and I didn't see you in any of them the past few hours."

He deserved her sarcasm, but he cringed at it anyway. She'd never sounded so bitter before. He'd brought this out in her, and he knew, because of Michael's betrayal, she was reacting to both situations. He was ready to take the lashing both for himself and Michael if it meant she'd forgive him.

He opened his mouth to tell her he'd been in a holding cell, but he didn't want to use his arrest for sympathy. Telling her he'd been fired was the same problem; he didn't even want to address the canceled pilot yet. And how could he explain the countdown clock? He finally settled on, "I'm sorry."

"That's a good start. So what happened?"

"Can we talk in person?"

"You deserve that, but I deserve to be treated with respect and not run out on. So give me a good reason to talk in person."

Stumped again. Everything he came up with sounded completely lame: *I did it for you and Daisy. It's better this way. I can't explain it now but someday it will be clear. I just need to get one thing straightened out, and you'll understand why I did what I did.*

She would have every reason to rage at him for any of those options, or just for what he had done that morning. Or for standing there like an idiot and not opening up to her.

Phone still to his ear, he'd sat on the edge of the coffee table and bowed his head. "I don't want to lose you," he finally said. He dropped his forehead to his palm, tugging at his hair.

Silence on the other end. His brother muttered something nearby.

"If I was a normal girl, I'd say you have a funny way of showing you don't want to lose me."

"But you're not normal. You're spectacular. And that's why I love you."

Silence again, but he may have heard a sniffle. Or it could have been wishful thinking on his part. He didn't want to make her cry, but he did want her to feel the weight of his declaration.

"You have a funny way of showing that, too."

"I know. I'm sorry," he repeated.

His brother grabbed the phone, and said, "He's not usually this wishy-washy. It means he really means it."

Through the speaker, Danny heard Kristen say, "Who is this?"

"Can't you tell? Denny Linstead. Danny's twin."

"You don't sound anything alike."

Danny couldn't help snickering at that.

Den socked him in the arm. "He got dropped on his head more as a kid. He made a dumbass mistake. You should give him a second chance."

"I don't usually let twin brothers make my decisions for me."

"Boom!" Den handed the phone back. "I like her."

Danny put the phone to his ear. "Kristen?"

"Call me back when you don't have any distractions."

She hung up.

"Yeah," Denny said. "You need a grand gesture to get that one back. Something big like *Love, Actually*. But let's go to the bar first."

And here they were, with his brother still arguing about Americans' God-given rights to smoke.

How was he going to fix this awful mess?

CHAPTER THIRTY-FOUR

Kristen knew Gail was depressed because she showed up for their sleepover in flannel pajama bottoms, slippers, and a white t-shirt. Everyone else was out of town, or Kristen would have invited them all over; she needed extra support right now. She was so grateful for Gail, grumpy or not.

"No slogan," Kristen said when she answered the door and noticed the plain shirt.

"No statement to make." Gail dropped her overnight bag on a dining room chair, and ran a hand through hair dampened from rain. Then she held out a paper bag. "No rainbows on you."

"Not very sparkly right now." Kristen moved aside the collection of healthy snacks already on the dining table: guacamole and crackers; roasted chickpeas; bananas and peanut butter; soft pretzels; and plain popcorn. "Thanks for bringing this," she said as she pulled items out of Gail's bag and set them on the table. "I never did know how to emotionally eat."

Gail waved a hand over what she'd brought: Oreos; Sour Patch Kids; Cracker Jack; Fritos; Nutter Butter; and unfrosted Pop-Tarts. "You've got the quantity right. Just not the quality. You clearly need me. And I want to reassure you: it's all vegan."

Kristen laugh-sobbed and bumped Gail's hip with hers. "I do need you."

"So are we going to be ugly-crying at any point in the evening?"

"I might if I end up eating all this sugar."

Gail dug in her overnight bag and pulled out a box of tissues. "All set."

Kristen's chin trembled. "I'd hug you if you didn't hate it."

"If you actually eat some Sour Patch Kids, I'll let you hug me all you want."

"How about some Nutter Butter instead?"

Gail nodded. "Deal."

Kristen took the tissue box from her, set it in the middle of the table, then pulled Gail in for a fierce hug.

Her voice muffled against Kristen's shoulder, Gail said, "I didn't think you meant right *now*."

Kristen just held her tighter, and was already reaching for the box before they broke apart. She handed Gail a tissue and dabbed at her own eyes.

"Let's start with chickpeas and pretzels. And maybe some guac, and we can dig into the rest after a certain someone is in bed." She inclined her head toward Daisy, who lay on the floor looking at books.

Gail shoved her tissue in her pocket. "You're still due some Nutter Butters."

They carried the food over to the sheet Kristen had laid on the floor in front of the electric fireplace. Luke & Victoria's cat Frog perched on the back of the couch, watching them. The dogs were always banished to a bedroom if Frog was in the house. Daisy lay on her stomach flipping the pages of *The Thing Lou Couldn't Do* and telling herself the story in enthusiastic murmurs.

"Gail!" she announced, and pushed the book to where Gail had settled herself cross-legged. "*Read.*"

"Child," Kristen said in her firm mom tone. "*Ask* Gail. Say please."

Daisy bumped the book against Gail's thigh. "Gail?" she repeated, more restrained. Then she brightened and said, "Peas!"

"How about we all do some coloring first?" Kristen said after she caught the desperate look on Gail's face. "And have some pretzel bites."

Kristen braced for Daisy's usual rebellion but her daughter had been as subdued as Kristen lately. She seemed to seriously consider the alternate suggestion before responding. She grabbed a box of crayons and waved them in the air. "'Kay!"

Kristen handed her an alphabet coloring book and said, "Would you like to color the D for Daisy?" She flipped the pages to the image of an ornate dragon with long eyelashes and Daisy dumped her crayons on the floor.

Gail took her copy and said, "Can I do E for ennui?"

"You can do whatever you want."

"That could be dangerous."

They settled on their stomachs in a rough circle with the food in the middle and crayons scattered around them. They colored quietly for awhile, the only sounds the scratch of crayons, crunch of pretzels, and patter of rain.

"This is pretty decent," Gail said at one point, "but your neighbor's music is kind of loud."

Kristen raised her head. "Kim and August are out of town again and Margaret next door never plays music. This block is usually really quiet."

She continued coloring, but Gail sat up with a groan. "My body isn't into this kind of position anymore."

Without looking up, Kristen sang, "Yo-ga."

Gail headed to the dining table. "Or-e-os," she sang back. "Maybe I'll see how many I can fit in my mouth at once."

"Maybe you can go for a world record or something."

"Now you're thinking."

Kristen smiled up at her friend as Gail shoved three cookies in her mouth. She shared a chocolate-y grin and started back to their circle. Kristen continued coloring but her head shot up at Gail's muffled, "Holy sh—!" She stopped herself with a hand clapped over her mouth, and stood staring out the window.

"What is it?" Kristen asked.

Gail pointed at her mouth to show she was still chewing, then pointed to the window and made a garbled sound.

Kristen popped up to stand next to Gail. "What?" she asked, looking through the glass. She clapped a hand over her own mouth. "What is he doing?"

Gail swallowed and said, "Making a hell of a statement."

Across the street, Danny stood under the lamp, arms raised in the air as he held a big boombox over his head. The music Gail had noted earlier blared from it. When he saw them watching from the window, he stepped off the curb and walked into the street, arms still raised, rain pouring over him.

Daisy abandoned her book to wrap her arms around Kristen's legs, but Kristen couldn't turn away. "What is he *doing*?" she asked again.

Gail crept closer to the bay window. "You mean you don't know?" She sat sideways on the window seat.

"No." Fascinated by the intense look on Danny's face as he kept it raised to hers, Kristen couldn't look away. He stood in the early evening gloom, the rain darkening his hair, and plastering his t-shirt to his chest. How long had he been standing there, waiting for her to hear him and come to the window?

She lifted Daisy to one hip and sat opposite Gail.

Gail seemed fascinated, too. "That's just too sad," she said, still staring out the window. "He's metaphorical Lloyd Dobler."

Kristen gave her a sideways look. "Who's Lloyd Dobler?"

"*Say Anything*? John Cusack standing in the rain with the boombox over his head playing Peter Gabriel's 'In Your Eyes' because Diane Court broke up with him?"

When Kristen shook her head, Gail said, "We have *got* to get you caught up on some good pop culture. He's recreating that scene in the movie. It's iconic."

"Why did they break up?"

"She's out of his league and they're in high school, so her father convinces her they're not right for each other. But they so are." Gail squinted at Kristen. "Sorry. Thoughtless."

Kristen whispered to Danny's upturned face, "Why do you think I'd know a scene from a movie?"

He stood now at their parking pad by the stairs, directly under the window, his eyes dark in the growing gloom. His arms didn't waver, and the song continued playing. She wanted to yell at him to stop, just stop it. But stop what? Standing there like a lovesick teenager? Declaring his feelings through song? Making her see him even though her heart ached when she looked?

"Funny," Gail added. "I would've pegged him as a *Love, Actually* type."

Kristen shifted Daisy higher, and stepped away from the window. "Movie references. He doesn't know me at all." She reached around Gail to drop the blinds. "I need some Nutter Butters."

CHAPTER THIRTY-FIVE

Stinging from the stupid mistake he'd made with his "grand gesture," Danny told his brother to drive them home. Those closed blinds stuck in his head. For once, Den drove in silence. He didn't even smoke. At the condo, Danny collapsed onto the floor in the small entryway, soaking wet, his arms shaking.

His brother stepped over him, sat on the club chair and said, "Hey, she saw you. You got her attention."

"She closed the blinds." Danny pressed the heels of his hands over his eyes.

"But she's thinking about you. She has to be, after that."

"She's thinking what a complete and utter idiot I am."

"Nah, man, she's mooning over your romantic gesture."

"She doesn't watch TV, Den. Or movies. She closed her blinds. She'll just think I'm a lunatic bench-pressing a boombox in the rain."

"Who doesn't watch TV?"

Danny thought of how Kristen viewed the world. She had no objection to television or film, but she didn't have time for it. Her life was too full of reality to spend it on fiction. He whispered as if to himself, but with a certain reverence, "She doesn't." He pushed himself up and went to stand in the shower until the ache in his muscles subsided.

The next morning, after a long run, another hot shower, some coffee, and return of a little sanity, Danny tried to call Kristen. Straight to voice mail, and he left a message. "I miss you. Please call me."

His brother shook his head. "You need to be aloof, man. You beg, she won't care. You act like you don't care, she'll be all over you."

"Why are you still here?"

"Didn't want you rotting in jail."

Danny did care. And he wanted her to know it. He would keep calling. He still didn't have a solution, but he'd learned fast and hard that the way he'd handled the whole situation was all wrong. He sighed, looking at his phone. Missed calls from his manager, his agent, Keesha, and his mother. He sat up at that, clutching the phone. "Mom called me," he said to the room in general, even though Den stood just a few feet away scrounging up some food in the kitchen.

"I told her what happened." Den held a bag of frozen hash browns in one hand and a box of frozen burritos in the other. "Why do these have OG written on them in magic marker?"

Danny stormed to the kitchen, holding the phone out with its missed calls list as if it directly accused Den of a crime. "What did you say? Why did you tell her?"

"I knew you wouldn't tell her, Mr. Handle It Alone, and she worries about you. Who's OG?"

Danny's shoulders slumped. "Glen calls himself that." He waved the phone at the frozen food. "Those are his. So she only wants to talk to me if you talk to her first?"

"Man, you have got to stop this sad sack shit." Den tossed the food back in the freezer. "She's Ma. She's fine. She loves you."

"She blames me for Vince." Danny collapsed onto a stool at the counter and dropped his head in one hand. "She stopped talking to me."

"Because you're both stubborn idiots."

"Tell *her* that."

"I did."

Danny peered at him.

His brother held up his hands. "From across the room. *I'm* not an idiot."

Danny huffed out a laugh. "I lost all her money. She has every right to be mad at me, to stop talking to me."

"You gotta stop worrying about that, man. I made it back and then some. She's fine," he repeated. "You know how she is. She gets on a tear about something, you can't change her mind for shit." Den gestured toward Danny's phone on the counter. "She wouldn't call you if she didn't want to talk to you."

"Or yell at me."

"That's a possibility." Den pulled out his own phone. "Since I can't eat the OG's food, I'm getting some kind of breakfast thing delivered. You want some?"

"Sure." Danny's phone rang, and he jumped. Keesha. He let out a breath.

"Wanted you to know about this from me before seeing it on the news," she said without preamble. "Perry Jenkins's been arrested for sexual abuse. Multiple victims. The show's still in limbo, but he's dunzo. Kicked out of his own production company. Probably booted from the Academy of Motion Pictures soon."

"Who made the charges?"

"Lots of women, can't name names." She paused, and Danny was ready to ask anyway when she added, "Not your girl."

His chest collapsed with a huge exhale, and he closed his eyes in gratitude, while at the same time his stomach churned at the news of the women Jenkins had hurt. "Thank you. Does she know yet?"

"I figured you'd want to give her the news."

"I do. Thanks, Keesha."

"Sure thing. I'll keep you updated."

As soon as he hung up, he relayed the info to Den, who looked over his shoulder as he scrolled through the news feed on his phone. Not that he doubted Keesha, but it was all true. Arrested. Sexual abuse, rape. Expected to make bail, but in jail for now. Accusations that he tried to stop the charges with blackmail. Women continuing to come forward with claims of his crimes.

He collapsed against the counter. The threat was gone for Kristen. That part was over. He could tell Kristen why he'd run. But was it too late? Had the damage already been done?

He shook his head. That wasn't the most important thing. What mattered most was that Kristen know she was safe, that even if she didn't know the extent of it, she be made aware that Jenkins's harassment was over. He grabbed his keys, hollered at Den that he'd be back, and ordered a rideshare while he loped down the stairs.

At Star's Florals, a woman about his mother's age stood in front of a cooler rearranging flowers; she smiled at him. "They do better with a little attention."

He smiled back. "Just like people. Is Star here?"

"She's not working today. Can I help you with anything?"

He pointed at some flowers in the corner by the register and said he wanted all of them.

At the Victorian, he rang the bell, but no one answered. He called her name as he looked up at the second story bay window, feeling like Tony from *West Side Story*, calling to Maria. He kept it fairly low, though, since he'd already put on a show for their neighbors. He wondered if Kristen had even gotten the reference, or if she just saw him as a demented, thoughtless idiot.

He rang the bell and called again, watching the curtains for any sort of movement, but still no response. None of the cars were in their parking spots and he wondered if her landlords were traveling again. Thinking to walk to her yoga center, he lowered his gaze and there she was, standing in the front doorway dressed in flannel rainbow pajamas.

"Gail told me what you did was supposed to be romantic. Are those supposed to be romantic, too?"

She lifted a chin toward the rainbow hued roses and he practically felt them wilt under her glare.

He nodded. "I got them at Star's. She wasn't there."

"She's in Nashville with Cort and the band. They're recording."

That explained why he hadn't yet got an ass kicking from that contingent. He'd take that kind over this one any day, especially as Kristen just stood there without saying a word, her lack of expression more upsetting to him than her direct anger.

"They remind me of you," he said, and immediately wanted to shove the roses in his mouth. Lame, and more lame. Nothing like he'd practiced on his way over. She didn't move, or tell him he was an idiot, so he kept talking. At the very least, she needed to know about Jenkins. "There's a reason I left the way I did. The other day. When Daisy..."

"Called you by your name."

"Right. Perry Jenkins had his eye on you and he didn't like us being together. Or he just didn't want me to have you. He never said. He threatened to bring Daisy's father here, to show you as a bad mother and pay for a child custody case, if I stayed with you."

She swayed, and grabbed the door jamb. He took a step toward her, but she held up one hand. "Did he do it? Did he find Michael?"

"No." Danny hoped it sounded reassuring; Jenkins had claimed to have found his number, but not called him. "He was arrested last night. Jenkins. For sexual abuse. He's in jail."

Her knuckles went white. "You didn't tell me. You ran away and didn't tell me."

"I couldn't. I believed him. I believed he'd make good on his threat. So I removed myself. He—"

"And left me vulnerable."

"What?"

Instead of answering she stomped outside and stood one step above him. When she raised her eyes, his gut clenched at her expression. Blank. If asked, he wouldn't have been able to describe Kristen without some animation to her face, usually an expression of joy or wonder. But now, smooth features. At least until she started talking again. Then he saw the tightness in her eyes. The pain. "You left without explanation, but you withheld information. What if he considered you were protecting me but once you were gone—by his demand—I was alone, easy prey. "

"I—"

"I *wasn't*." She shook her head and her wild hair flew around her face before settling around her shoulders. "I already knew he was dangerous, but I didn't know he was after me. If I knew that, I could have done something. Keesha, Liz, and Olivia all told me things were in the works to stop him. Did you know that?"

He shook his head, misery flooding him.

"Did you even consider that I might have resources, that my family has resources, that *we*—" She started inhaling, but didn't get a full breath in. "No, you didn't. You're such a lone wolf, you just did as he demanded, without talking to me. You didn't trust me. You didn't trust *us* enough to figure out how to deal with him."

He dropped his head and stared down at the roses that had seemed like such a good idea at the time. Just like he'd had it all figured out, how he'd be the big man and step aside to protect her. Her lone wolf reference echoed what his brother had said about dealing with things on his own. Had he been doing that? He set the roses on the wide steps next to her feet and stood facing her. "You're right. I was an idiot."

"Us, Danny," she said as if she hadn't heard him. "We could have figured it out together, but you didn't trust me. Which means you didn't trust *us*." She turned. "You should just go."

"No. I'm not leaving you again. I made that mistake once, but I won't do it again."

She faced him. "You had your moment. You can't fix that huge mistake by being persistent now. Just go."

Instead of moving away, he leaned closer. "I'll take my chances. No more leaving you. Please don't push me away. We need to talk about this. There's so much to talk about."

"I'm not pushing you, I'm shoving."

"It's not the time to do either. You were right. About us. We were strong enough to figure it out together, and I didn't trust that. I won't make that mistake again, and I'd hate myself if I just walked away right now."

She crossed her arms over her breasts, holding herself rigid. "I'm kind of hating you right now."

He went up one step to stand next to her, holding his hands out from his sides and speaking in soothing tones. "Then you're going to hate me a lot, because I'm not leaving. You've only said I made a mistake. You haven't said anything about us being over, or that your feelings for me have changed. I'm not leaving," he repeated.

Her face crumpled for just a second before it hardened again; but that glimpse lasted long enough for him to see the pain peeking through and no way in hell he'd abandon her right now.

"You *have* to," she said, but some of the strength had gone out of her voice; he couldn't stand the pleading tone that had snuck into it and hated that he'd done this to her.

"Why?" he asked, his voice still soft. "Why do I have to leave?"

"Because," she whimpered, "I'm about ten seconds from falling apart and I can't do that in front of another person anymore." She hitched in a breath. "I have to be strong."

"You are strong," he told her. "No one would ever doubt that. But I'm here and I can take some of the heat and be strong for you."

She shook her head, then bowed it, but not before he saw tears tracking down her cheeks. She pressed both palms to her face, and that did him in. No more discussion and no more trying to talk her out of making him leave. He held his arms out in a wide circle, then slowly enfolded her. As soon as they touched her sides, she went rigid, then fell into him with a sob, hands still over her face, and he pulled her to him.

She cried hard, gasping and sobbing, her face warm against his neck, and he just held tighter, murmuring soothingly at her. She had let go, fallen into his arms, but he could still feel tension throughout her body, as if she'd fragment into tiny pieces if she let go completely.

She gave herself so generously in life, he hadn't fully appreciated how hard it might be for her to give in and let go. She took care of everyone around her, and he'd completely screwed up as the person who should have been her support. Her crying hadn't slowed down, but when he tried to ease her to a sitting position, so he could pull her on his lap and hold her even closer, she resisted, that iron core keeping them in place.

So he rubbed her back, and rocked with her, eventually humming low in her ear, nothing specific at first, just something to soothe her. She slowed down a little, but when her sobs turned to hiccups, he started singing, Little Big Town's "Girl Crush," quietly to her, almost monotone, just to give her something else to focus on.

When her breath turned to longer hitches, she sagged a little against him, but still wouldn't move.

"Hell with it." He swept an arm under her knees and carried her to the inside stairs. He settled at one end with her in his lap and she pressed her nose to the base of his jaw just under his ear. Her damp lashes brushed his cheek, painting it with her tears.

"Oh, baby," he said, moved more by that than he had been by her crying.

She scrambled off his lap to stand a few feet away from him in the small entry space. "No. No babies. I'm not your baby. Not any more."

"Kristen—"

"Stop." She held a palm out. "Thank you for the flowers," she said in a polite tone. "Daisy will love them."

Danny let out a strangled noise and slapped his thighs. "I screwed up again, didn't I? Roses aren't your favorites."

"They're not."

He stood up slowly. "It's daisies."

"Of course it is. Thank you," she repeated in that formal tone. "And for letting me know...about everything."

She stood rigid, everything held close to her body and treating him as if they were co-workers who only passed each other at the water cooler. She glanced up the stairs and he followed her look.

"Where's Gail?"

"Watching Daisy and ready to kick your ass if necessary. I should go."

"Don't."

She shook her head. "I have to."

"Why?"

"I can't do this again. I can't fall in love and be hurt again. I can't trust someone and have him not trust me. I can't know someone who doesn't know me at all. And I can't be abandoned again. I won't, Danny."

She pushed past him up the steps and through the inner the door. He let her go. For now.

Despite her words, she'd given him hope. And an idea.

CHAPTER THIRTY-SIX

The first daisy showed up the next afternoon while her daughter was napping. The delivery girl gave Kristen a small rectangular package. When she tried to hand over a tip, the girl waved her off. "Taken care of," she said, and bounded down the stairs.

Kristen walked inside and into her own flat and stared at the package. It was a little bigger than a postcard, wrapped in plain white paper. It looked benign, but her hands shook when she removed the paper. It was a framed watercolor of a bunch of daisies. A yellow envelope had been taped to the back.

Now her chest shook when she breathed in. "This is way too dramatic," she told herself, and pulled out the card.

Danny's blocky handwriting: *Counting down...See tomorrow's daisy for more...*

Tomorrow. She propped the framed picture on the faux fireplace mantel, looking forward to the next daisy despite what she'd said to him. She'd meant it—she couldn't go through another betrayal or abandonment—but that didn't mean she'd stopped loving him.

She called Victoria in Nashville and told her everything practically in one breath.

"I can be on a plane in an hour."

"No, don't do that. I just need your patented brand of practicality. What do you see in all this?"

"Kristen, you have never listened to me. Why would you start now?"

"I've listened to everything you've ever said. I just don't always act on it."

"Oh. Well, there's always a 'pros' and 'cons' list…"

Kristen groaned, and fell against the side of the couch, her head dangling off the edge. "That's *you*, not—"

"Kidding! Wow, I hardly ever get one in. It's usually you."

Kristen straightened, pulling her hair out of her face. "That was a good one. But seriously…"

"Right. Seriously. I've had to hold Luke back from jumping on a plane to, I believe he said, 'make mincemeat out of the guy,' but to me he seems like a good man with good intentions. He made a mistake. Make your decision once you've heard him out. Or gotten all of his daisies or whatever. Be clear with him that you need time to make the right decision for *you*."

Kristen decided to see it through. She wanted to hear what he had to say. Should one well-intentioned mistake negate everything else he'd done? She didn't think so, but he'd triggered all of her issues and fears. He'd come back and explained and apologized—where Michael hadn't—but if he ran once, would he do it again?

The next package showed up during her break between yoga classes and Daisy's nap time, as if Danny knew their schedule. She glanced around the flat and said to Frog, "Better not be bugged or anything."

Frog flicked an ear at her. No help there.

The manila envelope flexed in her hands, again seeming very benign. But her heart beat hard as she pulled out the coloring book, all daisies. Today's note in the yellow envelope had her calling Indica, who was attending a marketing conference in Sacramento.

"It says 'at the end of the week, put the daisies together for the first clue.'"

"Well, that's intriguing."

"Why don't you sound surprised?"

"Don't I?"

"*Indy.*"

"I'm not supposed to say," she cried. "Please don't make me."

"What's going on?"

As if to herself, Indica said, "I don't know how he thought we could keep anything from you."

We? Kristen asked herself. How many people were in on this?

"Because you don't," she told Indica. "He knows that." Kristen stopped. That rang a bell in her mind somewhere. "*You* don't." She emphasized the first word. The bell in her mind rang louder. Danny knew that, because he knew her and Indica. She sat down. "We don't keep things from each other, and he knows that," she repeated. "So you should tell me what he said."

"Do you think he really meant for me to tell you?"

"I told him once that you and I don't have any secrets. If someone tells me one, they might as well tell you, too."

Kristen heard Indica take a deep breath. "Okay. He called and asked me to hear him out because you are more important to him than breathing."

"Well, that's impractical."

Indica laughed a little. "But romantic. He said he wanted to prove to you that he's not Michael—"

"Wait, what? Of course he's not."

"He's afraid you see him that way because you said you refused to be abandoned again."

"He told you about that, huh?"

"You want to tell me your side?"

Kristen recounted their conversation when he showed up with the rainbow roses.

"He made some dumbass moves," Indica said. "But all in the name of caring about you. And maybe that's not enough, but he is trying to make it up to you."

"What else did he say?"

"Pretty much that. He said he didn't want me to try to convince you, he knows that's between the two of you, but he did ask for my help with the daily daisies."

"Danny's Daily Daisies," Kristen murmured to herself. "I don't know what to do, Indy."

"I know, honey. Do you need me to come home early?"

Kristen told her to stay at the conference. She wanted her friend with her, but this was important to Indica, and Kristen knew her situation wasn't life and death. Her family would be right there if she asked, but she appreciated the quiet time she was spending with Daisy, even if part of it was contemplating this dilemma.

The third day was her day off, and the package arrived mid-morning, when Daisy was still awake. Kristen looked down at the box. When she shook it, the contents made a sliding sound and Daisy's eyes got big.

"Open, Mama."

"Let's do it together."

She set the box on the floor and they kneeled in front of it. She let Daisy tear most of the wrapping away and pull off the lid. It was filled with painted white and yellow wooden daisies that hooked together to make a chain. Some were blank, but a few had words printed on them—"we met," "bring Daisy," "the first place," "go to"—along with a date and time.

Kristen gave the blank ones to Daisy to play with, and lined up the others, rearranging them into a sentence.

On Friday at noon go to the first place we met. Bring Daisy.

"Well, that's the yoga studio," she said out loud. He wanted to meet her at the yoga studio? Should she go? Yes. She had to.

During the few block walk to the studio, Kristen focused on keeping Daisy from running to every interesting thing she saw—which mostly seemed to be across the street. She didn't want to concentrate too much on what would happen next. She could speculate all she wanted, but she didn't know Danny's plan. Her heart beat hard and felt lighter all at the same time.

In Room B at Priya Yoga Center, Indica sat cross legged at the far end of the empty space, Kristen's boombox at her side playing Sade's "Your Love is King."

When Daisy ran to her, Indica scooped her up and all three of them hugged.

"I'm so glad you're here." Indica turned off the music. "I really didn't want to listen to Sade for hours." She shifted Daisy higher on her hip and reached for a yellow envelope on the bench. It matched the ones that had come with the other daisies. "The next clue."

Kristen, written in Danny's handwriting. He'd handwritten this note, too.

"Go to the place I bought those mistake roses," Kristen read aloud. "Bring Daisy and Indica." She looked at her friend, who snuggled her daughter close. "He really thought this through."

"You ain't seen nothin' yet." Indica clapped a hand to her mouth and Daisy put her hand over Indy's.

"Nothin' yet," Daisy repeated and bounced up and down.

When her mouth was free, Indica said, "I wasn't supposed to say anything." She tucked the boombox in its cubby near the floor, tilting Daisy sideways until she laughed. "But let's go. This is *so fun*."

Kristen wanted to ask a million questions about Danny and the treasure hunt, but instead asked Indica about the conference, so grateful her friend had come back for the day. She tried to keep focused on Indica's responses, but when they reached the front of Star's shop, her mind went blank.

She stopped at the door. "I'm scared," she said, staring up at the awning

"Of what?"

"Too good to be true."

"You need to do what's right for you, but at least hear him out."

Kristen clutched Indica's sleeve. "He's in there?"

"Let's find out."

Inside, Daisy wriggled down from Indica's arms. "Sar!" She ran across the small space and Kristen held her breath, hoping she wouldn't knock anything over, and wondering if Danny would step out from the back. The rest of the shop was too small to hide him and she didn't see him anywhere.

This time, all four of them hugged before Star handed over an envelope while holding Daisy close.

"You're supposed to be in Nashville with Cort," Kristen said to Star.

"Some things are more important," Star told her. She pointed at the envelope. "Read it."

Kristen's name again, Danny's handwriting. That alone caused her heart to beat faster. "Go to the place where you convinced me vegan might be tasty."

Kristen laughed, remembering their fun with ice cream the night after the picnic. "That could be more than one place, but I think I know what he means."

They walked the block to *Dessert Delights, Ice Cream & More*, now a team of four, to find Gail standing outside eating a waffle cone with rainbow sprinkles. The t-shirt under her leather jacket showed a picture of Ruth Bader Ginsburg. "Hey, peeps."

Daisy reached out a hand and said, "Gail," in her flirty voice before ducking her head into Kristen's neck.

"The rest of us have been doing group hugs at each stop," Kristen told her.

Gail rolled her eyes, but beckoned them forward with her free hand. "All right, bring it in."

She held her cone up high while they piled into each other. When they parted, she took another lick and said, "Vegan ice cream is an abomination."

"Then why are you eating it?" Indica asked.

"I'm not. I got the real stuff, birthday cake with sprinkles." She bit into the cone. "My point is, he must really love you to say he likes it." She dug into her back pocket and held out a yellow envelope.

Kristen took it and stared down at her name in blocky letters. "You guys," she began, drawing out the words. "He's not going to propose, is he?" She looked at all of their wide eyes, but couldn't tell if they were surprised she guessed his plan, or trying to hide that he wasn't planning to propose.

Actually, only Star and Indica had those expressions. Gail kept calmly crunching her cone.

"Would that be a bad thing?" Star asked.

"Maybe you should read the note," Indica added.

"We still have a lot to talk about," Kristen said. "It's too soon for marriage, but..."

"But?" Star prompted.

Kristen shook her head. Instead of finishing the thought, she pulled out the next note. "Go to the realm of NRUF. Bring Daisy, Indica, Star, and Gail."

"Dolores Park," Kristen said. They all nodded. "You knew that, didn't you?"

"We had to be in on it," Gail told her. "Actually, we insisted."

"We were pretty mad at him," Star added. She twirled a length of hair around her finger.

"On your behalf." Indica patted Kristen's arm.

"We weren't going to go along with some half-assed egocentric plan of his just to impress you and get in your pants so he could up and leave again without talking to you if things got weird." Gail crunched the rest of her cone and tossed the napkin in the garbage.

Kristen hoisted Daisy higher on her hip and blinked back tears. "No matter what happens, you all are the most important people in my life."

Gail shrugged. "We know. I think everyone should get ice cream before we go."

Star got a cup with honey lavender, Indica couldn't decide between coffee toffee and cookies-and-cream, so she got both, and Kristen shared her chocolate coconut with Daisy as they sauntered down the sidewalk. It helped distract her from what she would find at the park.

When they reached the grass, she saw them right away. A large group of people standing almost in a line at the spot where they'd had their picnic. She tossed her cup in a recycling bin and set Daisy down. The little girl ran straight to uncle Luke, who picked her up and put her on his shoulders before slinging an arm around Victoria. Next to them, Gabe & Teresa stood close, Teresa's engagement ring sparkling in the sun as she pressed a hand to her chest. On the other side of Luke, Cort held out an arm and Star ducked under it, snuggled up to his side. Indica's parents stood next to Kim and August, who had the puppies on their leashes. Indica and Gail put their arms around each other's shoulders and joined the group.

All of her favorite people together, here from various locations and important life events. With one missing. She scanned the line of people again. No Danny, but she did notice the edges of a picnic blanket on the ground behind everyone, and when the clump of people split in the middle like curtains, they revealed a very handsome man sitting on the blanket. Black hair, ice blue eyes, sharp cheekbones, and a big smile.

Kristen cocked her head, confused. "You're not Danny."

"Nope." The guy stood up and held out a hand for her to shake. "Twin. I thought it was time we met in person." He held an envelope in his other hand. "Last clue."

She showed him her shaking fingers. "I'm too nervous. Will you read it?"

He looked doubtful, but pulled the card out and started to read. "You are the treasure in this quest." Another voice joined his, layered together in stereo. "And I want to spend the rest of my life showing you that."

Kristen whirled around. Danny stood there. His twin stopped reading, but Danny spoke as if there were one more line on the card. "If you'll let me."

"Oh."

He took a few steps closer until they were a foot apart. "Hey."

"Hi," she breathed.

"I was a dumbass."

"Yes."

"I would do this every day if it showed you how much you mean to me."

"I can't eat that much ice cream."

He laughed and ducked his head. He had one more envelope.

"Go to the place where I knew I was in love with you," she read. "I don't…"

"It's right here." He pointed between the two of them and then at his heart. "It was when we first stood in front of each other and every time we've been together since. I just didn't realize it at the time." He held out his hands, and she automatically took them in hers. "I'm really sorry," he continued. "What you didn't know is that I tried to talk to you that night, but you fell asleep. When we woke up, Jenkins had sent me a text. He was going to call Michael if I didn't get out of your place in five minutes."

Kristen shuddered. "That's…"

"I believed him. But I still should have told you. I should have woken you up, been clear about it all, told you about the deadline."

"Yes," she agreed. "You should. But…it sounds like you didn't have a choice."

His head dropped as if he'd been holding up the weight of the world. "If you will have me back," he said slowly as he raised his head, "I'll never leave you again. No one will separate us. There isn't anything anyone can do or say to make me leave."

"Nothing?"

He shook his head, his blue eyes dull. She wanted to ease his pain, to smooth away the wretchedness on his face, and in his soul. What he'd done for her—and Daisy—tore her apart. She wished she'd known. She threw her arms around his neck and clung to him. His body tensed under hers, then he squeezed her so hard she couldn't breathe. She didn't care.

"No secrets between us *ever*," she whispered in his ear. "And no leaving."

"Never again, even if it means waking you up to talk." He let out a shaky breath. "Nothing can keep me away."

"Be careful what you put out there. I just signed a contract for a yoga video, and I'd like you to be in it."

"Absolutely." They pulled away enough to smile at each other.

"Congratulations."

She stroked the side of his face. "I want to meet everyone important in your life." She tilted her head at his brother. "Lorelei. Your mom."

He nodded. "We had a really long talk the other day. Well, she yelled a lot, but we cleared the air on a lot of things."

"I'm so glad you connected again. I want to know everything about you, inside and out."

He seemed to be getting his equilibrium back. "I got offered the *Warhawk* sequel."

"That's amazing." She twined her fingers in his hair. "I want a big wedding."

He didn't even blink. "Done."

"With the puppies as ring bearers." When he still didn't flinch, Kristen threw out, "On a cliff edge overlooking the ocean. And everyone in tie dye and bare feet. And a sugarless, vegan cake."

"As long as Daisy is our flower girl," he replied.

She released a breath, as if she'd been holding it for days. Weeks. Years. "You really meant everything you just said."

"I meant it. I'm not going anywhere, and nothing will keep me away from you. *Nothing*."

She pulled him closer, and when his arms went around her, she breathed in his ear, "And I want more babies. Soon."

He pulled back again to look in her face. Those sharp blue eyes softened. "Yesterday."

Her throat tightened so much, she couldn't speak for a second. "When do we start?"

He pressed his palms to her cheeks. Then he let out a giddy laugh, grabbed her around the waist, and twirled her once before setting her down. "Yesterday," he said, his voice husky.

Then he kissed her. And kept kissing her.

Star said, "Should we give them some privacy?"

"We're in a public park," Gail said. "And no way, this is giving me ideas for my next book."

Kristen broke the kiss with a laugh. She turned to her family and waved them closer. "Don't you dare leave. We need a group hug."